By the Book

A NOVEL

JULIA SONNEBORN

CENTER POINT LARGE PRINT
THORNDIKE, MAINE

This Center Point Large Print edition
is published in the year 2018 by arrangement with
Gallery Books, a division of Simon & Schuster, Inc.

The text of this Large Print edition is unabridged.
In other aspects, this book may vary
from the original edition.
Printed in the United States of America
on permanent paper.
Set in 16-point Times New Roman type.

ISBN: 978-1-68324-775-3

Library of Congress Cataloging-in-Publication Data

Names: Sonneborn, Julia, author.
Title: By the book / Julia Sonneborn.
Description: Center Point Large Print edition. | Thorndike, Maine :
    Center Point Large Print, 2018.
Identifiers: LCCN 2018003806 | ISBN 9781683247753
    (hardcover : alk. paper)
Subjects: LCSH: Women college teachers—Fiction. | First loves—
    Fiction. | Large type books. | BISAC: FICTION / Contemporary
    Women. | FICTION / Romance / Contemporary. | FICTION /
    General. | GSAFD: Love stories.
Classification: LCC PS3619.O535 B9 2018b | DDC 813/.6—dc23
LC record available at https://lccn.loc.gov/2018003806

To Lisa Sternlieb

By the Book

chapter one

W HAT TIME'S YOUR CLASS, Anne?" my best friend and fellow English professor Larry asked. He was standing at the door to my office in his pressed shirt and tortoiseshell glasses, his balding head shaved close and his hand clutching an interoffice mail envelope.

"In fifteen minutes," I said, scrolling through my backlog of student e-mails. "Ugh, listen to this one." I read aloud: " 'Hey, Prof! It's Mike. I'm going to miss class today because I'm stuck at Burning Man and can't get a ride back until tomorrow. See you Wednesday!' I mean, can you believe it? *Burning Man*? Why not just say you're sick?"

"At least he's being honest," Larry said. "I mean, I wish *I* were at Burning Man."

"DELETE," I said. "God, why don't they make kids take a class on e-mail etiquette during freshman orientation? You know, like address your professors by their full title, not 'Prof' or 'Yo.' "

"I once got an e-mail from a student that began with 'What up, Lar?' I have to admit, I was a bit charmed."

"Hmph," I said. "I'd kill my students if they tried to call me Anne."

Larry was a Henry James scholar. He wore cashmere sweaters and tweed jackets and shoes custom-made by John Lobb. You know how people start to look a lot like their dogs? Well, professors start to look a lot like their subjects.

"Your office is looking . . . disheveled," Larry said, eyeing my piles of library books, the empty Starbucks cups littering my desk, the academic journals I subscribed to but never read, instead using them as a doorstop. He walked over to my desk and picked up my broken wall clock, which was lying facedown on a stack of papers.

"What happened here?" he asked.

"It needs a new battery," I said without looking away from my computer screen. "I just haven't gotten around to it."

"This clock has been lying here for at least six months," Larry said. "No wonder you're always running late! How do you know what time it is?"

"I have my phone," I said. "Clocks are obsolete."

"Preposterous!" Larry said. He always wore an elegant watch with an alligator-skin band, passed down from his grandfather. He disappeared from my office, carrying the clock. A few minutes later, he reappeared, fiddling with the clock hands.

"I'm setting your clock five minutes ahead," he announced. "By my calculation, you should be in class right now."

"Wait, what? Really?" I yelled, jumping up from my chair and spilling my coffee onto the keyboard. "Where are my lesson plans? Where's my book?" I rifled through my desk, looking for napkins and cursing.

Larry picked up my dog-eared copy of *Middlemarch*, its cover stapled on, its pages bristling with Post-it notes. "Is this what you're looking for?" he said drily.

"That's it!" I said, snatching it from him. I threw it into my book bag, scrambling around the outside pouch to make sure I had dry-erase markers, my lipstick, a pen.

"I don't know how you make your students read that book," Larry said. "It's one thousand pages of pedantic moralizing."

"I don't know how you can read Henry James," I retorted. "What was it that Twain said? 'Once you've put down a James novel, you can't pick it back up again'?"

"Twain was a philistine," Larry said, unperturbed. He handed me a lint brush. "You have cat hair all over your skirt."

"Ugh, I need to take Jellyby to the groomer. She's shedding like crazy."

"Another lion cut? Don't you think that's a little undignified? She's a house cat, not a beast in the jungle."

"Har-har," I said. I dove under my desk to find my heels, which I'd kicked off as soon as

11

I'd arrived in my office that morning. "Will I see you after class?"

"I have my shrink appointment now, but yes, I'll see you later—you'll be at the reception for our new president, yes?"

"We have a new president?" I asked, shoving my feet into my heels. Our previous president, a Civil War historian, had retired only a few months earlier due to health issues.

"He was hired over the summer! Didn't you see the e-mail? Or did you delete it, like Mr. Burning Man's missive?"

"I don't check my school e-mail over the summer," I said. "Who is it? Oh, wait—let me guess. I bet it's an MBA who wants to raise money for a new stadium."

"No, this guy actually sounds interesting," Larry said, hanging my clock on the wall. He stood back for a minute, making sure it was straight. "He majored in English as an undergrad, you know. In fact, you might have known him—he went to Princeton, too."

"Really? I'm sure he must have been years ahead of me." I slung my book bag around my shoulder and headed to the door.

"Actually, he's around our age," Larry said. "Fortyish."

"I'm thirty-two," I snapped. "What's his name?"

"Adam," Larry said. "Adam Martinez."

"Wait, are you sure that's his name?"

"Yes, why? You recognize it?"

"Maybe," I said. "But it can't be the same guy. It's a common name, right?"

"I'm late for my appointment, and you, my dear, are late for your class," Larry said, pushing me down the hall. "Oscar Wilde may have always been late on principle, but you don't have tenure yet!"

I RACED ACROSS CAMPUS, my heels punching holes in the lawn. I hated wearing heels, but since I was barely five foot two, I needed all the help I could get. As I walked, I applied my lipstick and tried to smooth down my hair. I breathed into my palm and sniffed. Not great, but not rancid.

The campus smelled like freshly mown grass. All around the quad, students were sunbathing or playing Frisbee or making out. It was September at Fairfax, a small liberal arts college tucked into the San Bernardino foothills. The town reminded me of an East Coast college town, just transplanted to Southern California. A two-block Main Street held a constantly changing array of frozen yogurt shops, pizza places, and clothing boutiques. There were picturesque Craftsman-style bungalows on streets named after Ivy League and Seven Sisters colleges—Harvard Street, Cornell Place, Wellesley Road. There was even collegiate Gothic architecture. One of the college's early benefactors, a railroad tycoon,

had donated his fortune to the school under the stipulation that all campus buildings be modeled after his alma mater, Yale. If it weren't for the palm trees on the edge of campus, you would think you were in the middle of Connecticut.

Adam Martinez. It couldn't be him, I thought as I cut across the quad. I pulled out my phone and tried to search through my inbox for the invitation to the candidate reception. I had 14,335 messages in my account. Apparently, I hadn't deleted quite *enough* e-mail. I searched for "Adam Martinez" and came up empty. Maybe it had gone into my spam folder. Or maybe Larry had just gotten the name wrong.

I reached my classroom just as the campus clock tower struck ten. There were maybe twenty-five students in the class, minus one or two or five who were stuck at Burning Man or "sick" or hungover. As I'd expected, most of my students were women. The class was "Introduction to the Nineteenth-Century British Novel," and it was full of wide-eyed English majors who had read too much Austen and Brontë when they were in middle and high school. I could spot them a mile away because I used to be one of them—young, mousy, and naive enough to believe Darcys and Rochesters existed. My job, I often told myself, was to force my students to look at the novels critically, analytically. These novels weren't about love. They were about money, and power,

and imperialism, and real estate. At least that's what I said to them, even though, deep down, I was as big of a sucker for the romance as they were.

I'd assigned the first few chapters of *Middlemarch* to kick off the class, but it was pretty clear that many of the students hadn't finished the reading. I knew what they were thinking: Casaubon was a loser, and Dorothea was an idiot, and God, how annoying was it that the Victorians were paid by the word? I could just imagine my students furtively texting each other beneath their desks:

Student 1: "u read the book?"

Student 2: "TL; DR."

Besides that, school had just started, so we were still in "shopping week," that period of free choice and zero commitment that students loved and professors resented. Most of my students were still in vacation mode, relaxed and giddy at reuniting with their friends after the summer.

I briefly lectured, then broke the class up in smaller groups and had them analyze passages.

"Don't just give me a plot summary of the passage," I told them. "Trust me—I've read the book." The class snickered. "Slow down and look more closely at the language. Why does Eliot make certain word choices? What metaphors does she use and why?"

As I walked around the classroom, dipping in

and out of group discussions, I scolded myself for being so distracted. I was as bad as my students, counting down the minutes until class was over, desperate to check my phone to see if Larry had texted or e-mailed me. A student raised her hand and I hurried over, grateful for the interruption.

ON MY WAY TO my next class, I checked my phone again. Larry had forwarded me the message with the reception info. I scrolled through the event details, and there he was. The new president was named Adam Martinez, and he had previously been provost at the University of Houston.

It can't be, I thought, stopping dead in the middle of the quad. Hands shaking, I clicked on the attachment. Slowly, Adam Martinez's CV downloaded onto my phone. I frantically scanned his work history. He'd been provost at the University of Houston for three years. Before that, he'd served as dean of their law school. Before that, he'd worked in something called "private equity." And before that, he'd worked as an in-house counsel for a Wall Street bank. I searched for his degrees. JD/MBA from Columbia University. Bachelor's in English from Princeton.

I suddenly felt faint. My former fiancé was my new boss.

chapter two

ADAM MARTINEZ, *THE* ADAM Martinez, was my college boyfriend. My first boyfriend, my first (and only, really) love. I hadn't spoken to him in more than ten years, ever since we broke up in spectacular fashion the night before our college graduation.

I looked around the quad in a daze. There were dozens of young couples sprawled out in the sun, oblivious to the world around them, oblivious to me standing frozen beside them. It was September, they were eighteen, nothing else was important except the warm body next to them. In class, I'd assume they were paying attention to my lectures and taking notes, but then I would notice the wandering glances and dreamy eyes and realize that the real drama was right there in front of me. Crushes, jealousies, misunderstandings, heartbreak—it was like an endless soap opera, with new cast members introduced every semester.

Most of the time, I found it entertaining. The romantic travails of undergrads were as predictable as the academic calendar. This was

the day school started. This was the day finals began. And this was the day you ended up in the infirmary because your boyfriend cheated on you with your best friend and you drowned your sorrows in a handle of tequila.

Every once in a while, though, I'd be reminded that what I found amusing was, for my students, practically a matter of life or death. Once, a young woman dressed in ROTC fatigues had tearfully approached me before class, asking if she could please go home. She was usually impeccably made up, crisp in her uniform and with her hair pulled back in a neat bun, but now her face looked raw, her eyes red and swollen and her cheeks wet with tears. "Of course," I'd said, assuming someone had died. "I'm so sorry—are you OK?"

The girl glanced despairingly over her shoulder, toward a handsome classmate with a crew cut. Crying so hard I could hardly understand her, she wept, "My fiancé just broke up with me."

I felt a sudden pang of recognition and sympathy. I'd been like her once, convinced that my life was over after Adam and I broke up. "You're so young," I wanted to tell her. "You're about to deploy to Afghanistan. You should be worried about coming back home safely, not about some stupid boy. You'll find someone better, and one day, you'll think back to how dumb you were for shedding a tear over this guy."

But I didn't say that to her. Instead, I gave her a hug and told her to go home.

That was years ago, but I thought of her now, her face so full of anguish. I felt my own face tighten and fiercely told myself to get a grip. I had another class to get to.

By the time I arrived at my next class, I'd successfully composed myself and put on my game face. Inside fifteen students were seated in three rows, waiting for me expectantly.

"Pop quiz!" I announced.

The room erupted into groans.

"Already?"

"But it's shopping week!"

"I haven't even bought my books yet!"

"Try your best," I said, pulling a stack of papers from my bag. "I'll drop your lowest quiz grade at the end of the semester."

One of my students, a premed with sandy hair and glasses who had taken my class the previous spring, groaned theatrically and pretended to face-plant on his desk. His girlfriend, a no-nonsense senior, patted him on the head and said, "I told him he shouldn't play *League of Legends* all night."

"Is there extra credit?" another student asked, vibrating nervously at her desk.

"Yes, as a matter of fact, there is." I walked to the board and wrote down a question: "What is EKPHRASIS?"

The premed whimpered quietly in his corner.

"Can I write in pencil?" someone else asked.

"Pencil, pen, your own blood, I don't care," I said. "Just make it legible."

I passed out the quizzes, stepping carefully over students' legs, backpacks, and the occasional skateboard. At the last row, I got to Chad Vickers, good old Chad, who always started the semester off strong but then imploded halfway through, showing up erratically and then not at all. This was the third time he was taking my class, and he'd vowed to me he'd actually complete it this time. Last year, he'd disappeared for two weeks. Turns out he'd gotten drunk, punched out a cop ("I didn't realize he was a cop until later!"), and spent those two weeks in jail. It was a new school year now, though, and Chad was riding the optimism of new beginnings and fresh starts. He pulled out his earbuds and grinned at me, giving me a thumbs-up.

After passing out the quizzes, I sat at the front of the room and watched the students with their heads studiously bent over their papers, periodically giving updates on how much time was left. For the next twenty minutes, they'd be focused on Victorian poetry while I waited to answer any of their questions. I let my eyes drift across the classroom and toward the large windows facing the quad. They were closed, but the sounds of laughter and distant music still

filtered in from the outside. Distracted, I began leafing through my poetry anthology, pausing when I got to Alfred, Lord Tennyson's "The Lady of Shalott." In spite of myself, I began to read.

ADAM AND I HAD met in English class. I was a freshman, a shy, bookish girl from Florida who had never been away from home before and who found the Northeast practically a foreign country. In high school, I'd been editor of the lit magazine, a member of the swim team, and concertmaster of the local community orchestra. At Princeton, I was a nobody. I tried out for the school lit society and was rejected. I was too slow to be on the swim team. And while I successfully auditioned for the college orchestra, the conductor asked if I might be willing to switch from violin to viola since they were a little thin in that section.

About the only thing I looked forward to was English class. I'd already read half the books on the syllabus and worshipped the professor, an eminent Victorianist named Dr. Ellen Russell whose first book, a massive study of nineteenth-century women writers, was considered a landmark work of feminist literary criticism. "That's Dr. Russell," people whispered when they saw her walking across campus. She was a heavyset woman in her sixties, prone to wearing the same outfit day after day (she was fond of one eggplant-

colored suit), her gray hair in a nondescript bob. People said she'd once been married and even had a grown son living somewhere in Texas, but no one knew much else about her personal life. "General Russell," her graduate students called her.

We were covering "The Lady of Shalott" the day Dr. Russell called on a dark-haired guy sitting in the corner.

"Adam, could you read the poem for us?" she asked.

I'd never paid much attention to Adam before because he rarely spoke in class and kept to himself, arriving just as class started and leaving immediately afterwards. But that day, I could hear Adam's deep voice clearly, drifting across the room toward me. As Adam read the lines— "And sometimes thro' the mirror blue / The knights come riding two and two: / She hath no loyal knight and true, / The Lady of Shalott"—he seemed to cast a spell on the class. I looked at him—really looked at him—for the first time. His hair was so dark it was almost black, and it curled over his temples. He had dark eyes, a strong nose that looked like it had once been broken, and the beginnings of a five o'clock shadow. His body was lean and sinewy, his shoulders powerful, his arms tan and muscular. I could see a tattoo on his right arm, peeking out from his T-shirt. *He must be a senior,* I thought.

I felt a tightness in my throat as Adam finished the poem and looked up. I was staring right at him, my mouth agape, and he caught my eye and smiled. I blushed clear to my ears and looked quickly away.

"Thank you for that, Adam," Dr. Russell said and began to lecture on the poem, talking about Arthurian legend and the ballad form and how the poem could be read as an allegory of female desire and blah blah blah. At least that's what I wrote in my notebook. I hardly heard what she said. I was too busy trying not to look in Adam's direction.

Just as class was finally coming to an end, Dr. Russell announced that she was returning our most recent papers. There was a general murmur of anticipation and trepidation in the classroom—Dr. Russell was a notoriously tough grader. "Your prose hobbles along like a lame show pony," she'd once written on someone's paper. As Dr. Russell walked over to me, I felt my hands grow cold.

"Come speak to me during office hours," she said, handing me the paper.

I blanched, flipping through the pages to the back, preparing myself for annihilation. She had written just one sentence in pencil.

"A pleasure to read. A."

I felt myself flooded with a mix of joy and gratitude. Hugging the paper to my chest, I

turned around to leave and walked straight into Adam, who'd been standing behind me.

"Oof," I said, finding myself up against Adam's chest. He was tall, much taller than me, six feet, at least. "I'm sorry," I squeaked, blushing again, hardly daring to look up and catch his eye.

"You're Anne, right?" he asked, smiling at me.

"Yes," I said, wondering how he knew my name.

"I'm Adam," he said. "Listen, I have to run to work, but I wanted to know if you were free for coffee later this afternoon, maybe around four? I get off my shift then."

"Today? Four? Sure, I'm free. That sounds great!" I babbled.

"Great, I'll meet you at the student center. See you later."

I watched him walk out of the classroom, his backpack slung across his shoulder. I was stunned. What did he want to have coffee with me for? I wondered. It couldn't possibly be because he was interested in me. I was the smart girl, the one boys wanted to hang out with because I was a great study partner. *That must be it,* I told myself. *Adam probably just wanted to borrow my notes.*

BACK IN MY CURRENT classroom, I heard the university carillon clock chime the top of the hour and loudly cleared my throat. "Time's up," I announced. I gathered the quizzes, glancing

at them quickly before I filed them away.

Chad had taken a stab at the extra credit: "EKPHRASIS: a popular club drug." I stifled a laugh.

When I got out of class, there was a text message waiting for me from Larry.

"Meet you at reception. Heading there now."

I texted back, "Not feeling well. Might just go home." My stomach did feel a little queasy.

"No excuses," he texted back. "Steve will be there. I'll save you 🍷."

I groaned. Steve was our department chair, a rotund medievalist with a Vandyke beard who liked members of the department to be "visible" at campus events. I was eager to prove my devotion to the college, especially if it improved my prospects for continued gainful employment. If I could just show them what a great teacher and scholar I was, how collegial and hardworking and responsible, maybe they'd keep me around a little longer. *I'll just stop by briefly,* I told myself—mingle a little so my colleagues saw I was there, then duck out without having to see Adam. The reception was bound to be packed, so no one would notice my quick exit.

Still, I spent a few extra minutes in front of the bathroom mirror, fixing my makeup, adjusting my hair, making sure I wasn't covered in cat dander. I was thirty-two, and while I tried to take care of myself, walking to and from

campus, drinking plenty of water, and always wearing sunscreen, no one would mistake me for the eighteen-year-old Adam had fallen for. I'd gotten my hair cut recently—a few layers, nothing too dramatic—but I thought it made me look more stylish. My hair, once a dark brown, had lightened in the California sun, and I now regularly wore mascara and a little bit of blush. The round cheeks I'd so hated as a teenager were gone, and I'd finally grown into my looks—or so I hoped.

I thought back to when I first started teaching nearly ten years earlier. Back then, I'd had trouble establishing authority with my students because I was so short and looked so young. I took to wearing my hair pulled back, dressing in business suits, and never cracking a smile. No giggling, no bringing in cookies, no ending my statements with a girlish uptick. As I got a little older, I loosened up, partly because I became more confident in my teaching but partly, too, because I no longer looked like such a child. My students now saw me as vaguely "older"— someone whose inner life they couldn't really imagine or identify with, a stranger. I still walked into the classroom wearing my armor, but now I occasionally offered peeks into my personal life, carefully calibrated to offer just a hint of intimacy.

I looked at myself now and thought I looked

professional—maybe not beautiful or young, but capable, tasteful, even attractive. *You can do this,* I told myself. *You're a smart, accomplished woman.* I tucked a loose strand of hair behind my ear and smiled bravely at myself in the mirror. Before I could change my mind, I walked briskly out of the bathroom and crossed the campus toward the faculty club.

chapter three

THE ROOM WAS PACKED. A buffet table had been set up with trays of crudités and cut fruit, a platter of cheese and crackers, and a pyramid of tea sandwiches. A red Fairfax banner hung on the wall, fringed in gold. I grabbed some grapes and one of the sandwiches as I walked in, less because I was hungry than to have something to do with my hands. I scanned the room as casually as I could. Where the hell was Larry?

Standing there awkwardly, I remembered how anxious I'd felt before meeting Adam for coffee that first time. I'd practically run back to my dorm room, located in an ancient Gothic tower all the way across campus. There, I spent an hour agonizing over what to wear, changing my clothes five times before settling on a black skirt and a cardigan. I even briefly contemplated blow-drying my hair straight, decided that was too obvious and try-hard, and ended up pulling it back in its usual ponytail. Once I got to the student center, I'd spent several minutes strategizing how best to situate myself, choosing a table in the corner of the coffee shop, a little out

of the way but not so hidden that Adam wouldn't see me. I'd even brought my Norton anthology with me so if Adam just wanted my notes or to be study partners for the midterm, I could act like of course I knew that was why he wanted to meet, no big deal, happy to help out anytime.

Now, though, I was armed with nothing but finger food. Slowly, I walked the periphery of the room, glancing at the various people sitting at the tables or standing in small groups conversing, plastic name badges pinned crookedly to their lapels. Larry wasn't at the bar, which was jammed with people waiting for a beer or plastic cup of wine. I did, however, catch sight of Steve, who was already flushed from drinking and who waved excitedly when he saw me.

"Delightful to see you here!" he said, raising his plastic cup of red wine. "I always like seeing my junior colleagues at these events. Shows a commendable esprit de corps."

"I wouldn't miss it," I said, smiling brightly.

"We should schedule a meeting next week to talk about your, er, your future here. I believe your employment contract expires in the spring?"

"It does—but as you know, I'd love to stay at Fairfax." My voice sounded strained and overeager.

"Oh, and we'd love to have you," Steve said. "But as you know, it all depends on your getting your book published. How's that going,

incidentally? You haven't secured a book contract yet, have you?"

"Not yet," I said, feeling my stomach sink. "But I've sent out some proposals, so I should hear something soon."

"Well, my dear, *bonam fortunam*!" Steve said. "I'm glad you're working on it. You should be just fine so long as you have a book contract by the new year. Any later than that, though, and I'm afraid my hands are tied." He spied an opening at the bar. "Now please excuse me as I go refresh my libation."

As I watched him amble away, I wondered what I'd do if I lost my job. Adjunct? Tutor the SATs? Go to law school, like my father had always wanted? Each option was more dispiriting than the last. For the millionth time, I wondered if I'd made a complete mess of my life. Here I was with zero job security and so much student debt that by my calculation I'd be sixty-two by the time my loans were paid off.

I finally caught sight of Larry in a knot of people, talking animatedly, a cup of white wine in each hand. He'd saved me a drink like he'd promised, thank God. I was heading over to him, calling out his name, when the crowd shifted slightly and I realized with a shock who Larry was talking to.

It was Adam, listening thoughtfully to Larry and nodding in agreement. I could feel myself

go cold with excitement and anticipation. He was still lean and athletic, with a restless energy that kept him constantly in motion, his hands gesturing, then folded across his chest, then released again. His dark hair was cut shorter than I remembered, and it was turning silver at the temples, but his face—his face was the same. The dark brows, the brown eyes, the sharp profile. In his dark suit and silk tie, Adam looked like the lawyer he once was, someone who took clients out to lunch at the Four Seasons and had an office in a sleek skyscraper. He was someone I'd see in the airport and assume was off to broker a big deal or pass legislation or counsel governments. I couldn't believe it. He looked presidential.

It was too late to hide. Larry had heard me calling his name and was motioning me over with a big smile. I could see him leaning toward Adam as if to say, "Here's someone you must meet!" and Adam turning slightly to see who it was. I felt myself flush. I wasn't ready yet. I stood there paralyzed as Adam half met my eye and gave me an imperceptible nod. Then he turned away.

Did he not recognize me? I thought. Was he ignoring me? Was he *mad* at me?

Larry was still motioning to me wildly, tipping his head toward the cup of wine in his hand. I had no choice. I had to say hello to Adam. My

stomach clenched, and my throat felt tight. *Go,* I ordered myself. *Go and get it over with. At least it'll be quick.*

"Anne!" Larry cried, handing me the glass of wine and giving me a quick peck on the cheek. "Are your ears burning? I was just talking about you. This is President Adam Martinez. But the two of you already know each other, from what I gather."

"Yes," Adam said, shaking my hand. His palm was warm, his grip strong. As he let go, I could still feel the imprint of his hand in mine. "We went to undergraduate together."

He was being so formal. As if we were just passing acquaintances.

"Welcome to Fairfax," I said. "I hope you've settled in well."

"It's beautiful here," Adam said.

Polite. He was being too polite. We weren't friends or former lovers. We were professional associates. Even on our first date so many years ago, he'd been open and warm from the start, our casual coffee date quickly turning into dinner and so much more.

Now, though, Adam was tight-lipped, offering nothing, barely even making eye contact with me. Ten years was a long time, both of us had changed, and apparently he wanted to make that clear to me.

"It's really a nice little college town," I

33

ventured lamely. "I mean, it must feel like a huge difference from Houston."

"It does," Adam said. He took a sip from his glass of water.

"You must be exhausted, meeting all these new people," I tried again.

"It *is* busy," he said, nodding.

"Adam! Here you are!" Tiffany Allen interrupted. The director of the Office of Development, Tiffany was a tall, bubbly blonde who grew up in Newport Beach and used to play volleyball at USC. She was a fund-raising machine, always throwing mixers for young alums and charming large donations out of the old. I sometimes saw her driving around campus in her white convertible, with its USC and Fairfax decals and her sorority letters on her license plate frame.

A group of women hovered behind Tiffany, waiting for an introduction. Adam turned to them and shook their hands, expressing his pleasure at meeting Danielle from the VP's office, Rhonda from the registrar, Celia from student affairs. They'd worked at the college for years, these older women in their sensible separates and pumps, quietly keeping the campus running from behind the scenes. I saw how they looked at Adam with delighted eyes, seeing in him someone who could bring excitement to this sleepy college town, someone who was

easy on the eyes, someone who they wouldn't mind attending meetings with. I stepped back as Tiffany took Adam's arm and elbowed me aside, guiding Adam across the room.

"Looks like he needs to make the rounds," Larry said.

"Yeah," I said, taking a big gulp of my wine.

Larry was happily tipsy, taking me by the arm and whispering excitedly in my ear.

"He's divine," Larry said. "You know these admin types, they're usually so stiff and bureaucratic, but this guy—you can tell he's got principles. He really seems to *get* this place. He believes in the humanities! He believes in the life of the mind! I mean, after our last president, that *moron,* Adam's just a breath of fresh air! So you have to fill me in. What was he like in college? Give me the dirt!"

"Um, he was great," I said. "I really don't have any dirt. He was a nice guy, really good student." I couldn't bring myself to tell Larry the truth— not yet, at least. I was still reeling from Adam's frosty reaction to me.

"He's certainly popular with the ladies," Larry said, glancing over at the knot of women surrounding Adam.

I nodded. Adam had always had that effect on people. When we'd first started dating, I could tell people were looking at us, wondering how someone as charismatic and good-looking as

Adam could be with someone as regular as me. Adam had laughed when I told him this, told me I was beautiful and that, if anything, the situation was reversed. In his eyes, I had the perfect heart-shaped face, the clearest brown eyes, the softest skin and hair. When we were alone, he would cup my face in his hands and brush his lips across my face, and in those moments, I believed him, believed that he found me attractive and desirable. But when we were around others or when I was alone, I only saw my stubborn, curly hair, the smattering of freckles on my nose and cheeks, the zit on my forehead that refused to go away.

"Yeah," I said to Larry, keeping my voice unemotional. "He was like that in college, too."

"Boo. That's too bad. I don't like it when people are too perfect. What is it with this guy? He's got the fancy degrees, the high-powered CV, and he's good-looking, too! I mean, why do some people get all the cookies? I want some cookies, too!"

"Larry, you've got plenty of cookies on your own," I said, rolling my eyes. "I mean, give me a break, you're a tenured professor with a PhD from Harvard. What more could you want?"

"Oh, a *personal* life, maybe. Or some more hair would be nice," Larry said, pretending to pout. *"I just want more cookies."*

I started laughing, and Larry joined in. When

we finally caught our breath, Larry paused to take off his glasses and clean them with his handkerchief.

"But seriously, Anne," he said, putting his glasses back on. "Why is he still single? There must be a reason."

"He's single?" I gulped. "How did you find out?"

"I just asked him."

"Larry!" I yelled, whacking his arm. "That's so tacky!"

"Anne, honey, calm down. I don't like being physically assaulted," Larry said, rubbing his arm ruefully. "I did it *discreetly*. And *obliquely*."

"How?"

"I told him that our local public schools were excellent and that if he had kids, they would thrive here. Clever, yes?"

"And what did he say?"

"He said, 'Oh, I don't have kids. I'm not married.'"

So he was single. I felt a prick of hope inside. Maybe we could rekindle things? Maybe he could forgive me and we could start over? If we could just spend some time together and I could explain myself, explain how stupid I'd been, how sorry—

Larry yawned. "It's really too bad you two didn't know each other better," he said. "I was hoping that seeing you might help jog his

memory, but when I first waved you over, he had no idea who you were. 'That's Anne?' he said. 'I wouldn't have known her.' "

I wouldn't have known her. My heart sickened. Of course. How dumb I was to think there might be something still there. He might not be married, but for all I knew, he probably had a serious girlfriend, maybe even a fiancée. It had been more than ten years, after all. Of course he'd moved on.

And I'd moved on, too. After our breakup, I'd dated plenty of other guys—a fellow grad student in my program, a musician in a terrible rock band, even Larry's brother, Curtis. None of the relationships had worked out, but it wasn't as if I'd been sitting around, waiting for Adam. I'd grown up, become a different person. I wasn't that girl anymore—he'd said so himself. If Larry hadn't pointed me out to him, he would've had no idea who I was. I was just another face in an endless sea of academics and administrators.

The only problem was that Adam still looked exactly the same—better, even. The years had made him more attractive. He looked worldly and sophisticated, secure in himself, accomplished. Even the traces of gray in his hair just made him look more distinguished. I felt a tug of longing and shame. Adam might not have recognized me, but I—I definitely recognized him.

"Hey, Larry, I think I'm going to head home," I

heard myself say. "I have a ton of grading to do."

"Good luck," Larry said, giving me a sympathetic look. "Set an egg timer. And have a double scotch. It will fortify you." He kissed me on the cheek and headed back to the bar.

I walked home in the late-afternoon sun, down the tree-lined streets of Fairfax with its rows of charming cottages and meticulous hedges and lawns, past the president's mansion, a turn-of-the-century Craftsman covered with red cedar shingles, and around the corner to my apartment, the top floor of a three-story Victorian. "The Garret," Larry called it whenever he visited.

The place reminded me of my undergraduate dorm room, a tiny single on the top floor of a Gothic dormitory, with diamond-shaped window panes oxidized green around the edges and tendrils of ivy that crawled in through the gaps in the stone. I remembered how Adam could always pinpoint my window from across the quad. "See?" Adam had said. "That's your room over there, to the right. The window that's dark." Sure enough, there was a row of windows lit up like a string of Christmas lights, with one light missing. My room. "That's how I know you're not there," Adam said. "That you're here, with me."

I sighed. My apartment now was dark, but no one was around to notice if I was home or not. No one except Jellyby, who was waiting for me

by the front door, mewling for her dinner. I ran my hand over her back and down her plume-like tail, then walked to the kitchen, where I scooped out some dry food and watched her eat. I poured myself a glass of wine from a half-empty bottle and sat on my couch, watching the sun go down.

On a whim, I stood up and walked to my bookcases, packed floor to ceiling with novels and reference books and journals, the tools of my trade. I cast my eyes on a far corner of one bookcase, running my fingers along the dusty spines until I found what I was looking for, a slim, well-worn Penguin Classic with its distinctive black binding.

THE BOOK HAD BEEN a gift from Adam my senior year.

Our relationship had begun slowly at first, over coffees and dinners, talking about class and about the books we were reading and the papers we were writing. Over the summer, between my freshman and sophomore years, Adam returned to Los Angeles to work construction, and I returned to Florida to help my father run credit checks and field tenant complaints. Out of boredom and loneliness, we wrote each other long letters, mine filled with gripes about my father and sister, his filled with descriptions of his coworkers and high school friends. He usually signed his

letter "*abrazos*," but sometime that summer, it changed to "*besos*." When we returned to school in the fall, he came straight to my dorm room from the airport, his luggage in hand. When I answered the door, he was standing there trying to catch his breath, unshaven, his hair longer than I remembered. I reached out to give him a hug, but he grabbed my hands and pulled me closer. I felt myself stop breathing. Adam was looking at me so intensely that I nervously dropped my eyes. "Anne," he said, and I looked up, my whole face aflame. The next minute, he was kissing me full on the lips, softly at first, then with growing passion. I felt the scratchiness of his stubble and the warmth of his lips and I went limp with joy.

Over the next few years, we became serious about charting our future together. Back then, both of us were planning to go to graduate school, me in English, him in education. While studying together in the campus library one evening, Adam asked me to find a reference book for him while he put more money on his copy card. I took the stairs down two flights and wandered into the deserted stacks, breathing in the cool basement smell of old books. The motion-sensor lights switched on row by row as I scanned the catalogue numbers. At the correct row, I skimmed the book spines for the number Adam had jotted down for me on a slip of paper, my eye eventually

coming to rest on a paperback book that looked curiously out of place among all the drab green and brown library-bound hardcovers. The book had no identification number, but it was in the spot where the book Adam wanted should have been. Pulling it out, I saw that it was a pristine copy of Jane Austen's *Persuasion*, my favorite novel, which I'd recently lost on the train to New York. I looked up, and Adam stepped out from behind a neighboring stack, smiling broadly.

"You replaced my book!" I said, holding it to my chest.

"Open it," he said.

I did and found a slim silk bag tucked between the pages.

"What's this?" I asked, tugging at its strings. A delicate pink-and-gold cameo ring fell into my palm.

Adam came over to me and closed his hands over mine.

"Annie," he said, "will you marry me?"

I looked at him, my heart painfully thumping in my chest.

"Aren't we too young?" I asked.

"I'm twenty-six, Annie. I'm ready to get my life started. And I want it to be with you. I know it's not a diamond—I can replace it with something nicer, once I pay off my student loans—"

"No! Don't you dare! It's—it's perfect."

Adam took the ring from my hand and dropped

to one knee on the linoleum floor of the library, surrounded by a thousand silent books.

"I love you, Annie," he said, looking up at me. "Will you marry me?"

I felt myself overwhelmed with emotion. He loved me as much as I loved him—more, even, if that were possible.

"Yes," I said, my eyes filling as Adam slipped the ring on my finger. He stood and swept me up against the book stacks, knocking a few books onto the ground. A little while later, we crept out of the library, guiltily glancing at each other and stifling our laughter as a reference librarian looked at us, eyebrows raised, as we scurried past the circulation desk and into the cool autumn night.

THE BOOK WAS NOW yellowed with age and soft from use. I flipped to the title page. *Persuasion*, by Jane Austen. Written underneath in pen was the note:

For Annie,
I have loved none but you.
Besos,
A

Staring at the familiar handwriting, the slanted capital letters scrawled across the page, I felt a surge of bleak certainty. Adam had once cared

for me. He had loved me enough to write dozens of letters, to give me books, to want to marry me one day. And it was my fault that I'd turned him away. I'd listened to others instead of trusting myself, and in the process, I'd hurt him badly. So badly that it was no wonder he wanted nothing more to do with me. I was a traitor, weak-willed, and so, so naive. I didn't deserve him.

I threw the book to the ground, where it landed facedown, pages ruffled, prostrate. I stared at it for a few seconds. Then, feeling guilty—it wasn't the book's fault, after all—I picked it up, dusted it off, and mutely shoved it back into my bookcase.

From: Stephen Culpepper <S.Culpepper@Fairfax.edu>
To: <English Department Faculty>
Subject: Presidential Inauguration
Date: September 10

Dear Esteemed Colleagues,

As you are well aware, the inauguration of President Martinez will take place *this Saturday,* September 15, and will serve as an official convocation for the beginning of the school year. As such, the entire department is expected to attend in *full regalia* (gown, hood, and cap).

Faculty members are expected to arrive no later than 2:00 p.m. Many of you have not yet RSVP'd to the reception afterwards at the President's House. Please do so *magna cum celeritate.*

I am, yours faithfully,
Steve

———

Editor, *"Piers Plowman" Reader*
(Cambridge UP, 2011)
Coeditor (with Ron Holbrook),
Early Medieval Grammar (CLIO Press, 2006)
Editor, *Journal of Anglo-Norman Studies*
(2005–present)
Member, Medium Aevum, the Society for the Study of Medieval Languages and Literature

From: President Adam Martinez
<A.Martinez@Fairfax.edu>
To: <Students and Faculty>
Subject: A Message from the President
Date: September 10

Dear Members of the Fairfax Community:

Many thanks for your warm welcome to campus. I have only been here for a couple weeks, but I have already been struck by the passion and commitment

of Fairfax students, faculty members, and staff. I very much look forward to the year ahead.

The coming months will see the launch of several ambitious projects essential to Fairfax's future. Tiffany Allen, Director of the Office of Development, is in the midst of planning a major fund-raising campaign, with a public launch in October of this year. As college costs continue to rise across the country, this campaign will focus on defraying the cost of tuition through scholarships, grants-in-aid, and an expansion of the college endowment. As well, we will begin a major multiyear program to renovate Chandler Library, update student dormitories, and transform the plaza outside the Student Center into a central meeting place that will host outdoor activities, student groups, and other community events.

I will be in touch in the months ahead with more news and other announcements. In the meantime, please stop by my office with any questions, thoughts, or concerns you might have. My door is always open.

Sincerely,
Adam Martinez

From: Sallie Mae <CustomerService@salliemae.com>
To: Anne Corey <A.Corey@Fairfax.edu>
Subject: Your Sallie Mae Statement is Available
Date: September 7

Dear ANNE COREY:

Your monthly statement is now available. Please log in to your account at SallieMae.com to view and pay your bill.

Total Payment Due: $498.04
Current Amount Due Date: October 13
Balance: $96,194.25

As the nation's No. 1 financial services company specializing in education, we appreciate the opportunity to serve you.

Sincerely,
Sallie Mae Customer Service

From: Linda Hacker-James
<hackerjames@bloomsburypress.com>
To: Anne Corey <A.Corey@Fairfax.edu>
Subject: book proposal and query
Date: September 7

Dear Dr. Corey,

I've read your proposal and am afraid we will have to pass on your manuscript. While *Ivory Tower: Nineteenth-Century Women Writers and the Literary Imagination* has an interesting premise, we do not believe there is a market for such an esoteric topic. I wish you the best of luck in your future endeavors.

Sincerely,
LHJ

chapter four

MY PHONE RANG AS I pulled into the parking lot of the Huntington Library in San Marino. It was my sister, Lauren.

"Hello?" I said, meanwhile trying to angle my car into a spot near a bank of eucalyptus trees.

"Anne! Where are you?"

"At the library. I have to work on my book."

"You're not done with that damn thing already?"

"It takes time, Lauren. It's a slow process—"

"I just got a call from the Y. It's about Dad."

"Oh no. What happened?"

My dad went to his local YMCA in South Florida every morning to swim laps in their pool. He was constantly complaining about the temperature of the pool and the lack of towel service, and he'd recently been reprimanded for fighting over a locker with a fellow member.

"Did he get into another fight with someone?" I asked.

"No, worse. They had to pull him from the pool this morning because, well, he wasn't wearing a suit."

"He wasn't wearing a suit? You mean, he was *naked?*"

"Yup. He'd apparently forgotten to put it on. He had his cap and goggles on, but no swimsuit."

"That's awful! He must have been so embarrassed!"

"Nope. He just went back into the locker room, put on his swimsuit, and then hopped back into the pool as if nothing had happened. The director at the Y called because he's worried it might be a symptom of dementia and wants us to get him checked out ASAP. I'm flying out to Florida the day after tomorrow—can you come?" Lauren asked.

"I can't," I stammered. "I have to teach."

"Can't you get someone to cover your classes?"

"I could. It's just, um"—and here I lowered my voice, filled with shame—"I'm kind of broke right now, and I'm not sure I can afford the plane ticket."

My money situation was a particularly sore spot with Lauren. Like my father, she had always thought my choice of career a foolish one. While I'd gotten a PhD, racked up debt, and hopped from one temporary position to another, she'd gotten her MBA, landed a high-paying job in marketing, and married a hedge fund manager named Brett. She was now a stay-at-home mom to three young boys and lived in a huge house in Los Angeles. Not once had she ever offered to

cover a plane ticket or spot me some cash, seeing my poverty as a character flaw that should not be condoned.

"Oh," Lauren said, her voice snippy. "Fine. I'll just deal with it myself."

"Thanks," I said. "I'm sorry."

I hauled myself out of the car and made my way to the reading room. The previous day, Steve had reiterated to me, yet again, the importance of my landing a book contract.

"Publish or perish, as they say," he'd chuckled, and I'd stifled the impulse to throttle him.

"Easy for you to say," I wanted to cry. "*You* didn't have to write a book to get tenure. Back when *you* were coming up, your adviser just had to pick up the phone and recommend you for a position and bam! You had a job!"

But I smiled at him pleasantly, left his office, and managed to get home before having a nervous breakdown. I'd since roused myself from my pool of self-pity to drag myself to the Huntington, where I was finishing up some research on my book. My personal life was a mess, I told myself, but maybe my professional life was still salvageable.

I flashed my reader badge to a security guard in a blue blazer and then stashed my belongings in a locker, taking only my laptop and phone with me to the reading room, a glass-enclosed space where readers were hunched over manu-

scripts and other documents, some of them using magnifying glasses. The reading room had a long and intimidating list of rules. No food or drink, no pens, no cameras. Always use gloves and a cradle, use special weights to keep the pages open, don't bend the pages, don't put things out of order, don't even breathe.

I submitted a request slip to the archivist and, as I waited, scrolled through my manuscript on my laptop. My book was about nineteenth-century women writers, but it might as well have been about spinsterhood and romantic rejection. Jane Austen never married, though she did once receive a marriage proposal from an unattractive, oafish guy with the unfortunate name of Harris Bigg-Wither. Charlotte Brontë was plain, tubercular, and always falling in love with married men. She eventually settled for a nice guy she didn't really love, but then she died of pneumonia while pregnant with her first child. And George Eliot, according to good old Henry James, was horse-faced and "deliciously hideous." Thumbing her nose at polite society, she had a long-term relationship with a married man, but when he died, she ended up marrying a much younger guy who jumped out of a window during their honeymoon—maybe because he was depressed, or maybe, people joked, because he was fleeing her carnal embrace.

For the umpteenth time, I wondered why I couldn't have written a book on, oh, sanitation reform in Charles Dickens's novels. "Book topics are always autobiographical," Larry used to tell me. "Thanks a lot," I'd snapped at him.

The archivist approached me with my requested item—the library's first edition copy of *Jane Eyre*. It was a triple-decker, meaning it had originally been published in three volumes. The books arrived enclosed in a green folding case, their faded brown-and-gilt spines lined up like an encyclopedia. I slid on a pair of gloves, pulled the volumes out one by one, placed them gently on the foam cradle, and opened the dry old pages, using weighted velvet cords to hold the corners down.

JANE EYRE
An Autobiography

Edited by
CURRER BELL

In Three Volumes
VOL. 1

LONDON:
Smith, Elder & Co., Cornhill
1847

It was strange to be treating a book so delicately. I knew that first editions were rare, fragile, and very, very expensive, and I was careful to touch it with the utmost delicacy. My own copy of *Jane Eyre* received no such treatment. It was crosshatched with pencil markings, bound together with tape, dog-eared and brimming with Post-it notes. All my thoughts, from when I was a teenager to today, were in those pages. "Gross," I'd written in the margins when Rochester was first introduced (what had I been thinking?). On other pages, I'd doodled hearts and question marks, notes to my friends ("so bored. luv ya!"), and some half-hearted lecture notes: "St. John— pronounced SINJIN" and "bildungsroman: novel of development."

In college, when I reread the novel for Dr. Russell's class, I tried to blot out the hearts and the dumbest comments ("JTT is so hot"), and I aggressively annotated the novel to compensate. "Governess Novels: genre that includes Anne Brontë's *Agnes Grey* and W. H. Thackeray's *Vanity Fair*" and "Gayatri Spivak: Bertha Mason and 'the axiomatics of imperialism.'" The notes were helpful when I later used the novel in my dissertation and then taught it to my students. Meanwhile, the book became rattier, every page marked with something, whether a note to read a passage aloud in class, a student comment I'd found interesting, or a reference I'd

looked up. It was a history of my reading life.

The book in front of me, in contrast, was pristine. Of its original owner, I knew nothing other than that he or she was probably wealthy. Triple-deckers weren't cheap, costing about $100 for the whole set when they were first produced. Part of me wondered if anyone had ever read it, or if it had simply been forgotten in someone's wood-paneled library until a book dealer spied it in an estate sale. I began typing up some notes on my computer, carefully flipping the pages of the original to double-check quotations.

At lunchtime, the reading room emptied out. I returned my materials to the archivist's desk and joined the flow of people heading to the café at the adjoining museum, where our reader's badge got us a 10 percent discount on food and beverages. As I crossed the courtyard, I saw a large placard standing outside the museum's main lecture hall. It read:

The Huntington Library presents
The Susan Bartholomew / Dickens Club
Lecture in Literature and Society

"THE WORLD OF THE NOVEL"
Richard Forbes Chasen
Author of *The Nation State*, *War's Citadel*,
and *Subterranean City*

OPEN TO THE PUBLIC

"Hurry! The lecture's about to start," an elderly museum volunteer said, nudging me inside before I could protest. I squeezed into a chair in the front row, one of the only empty seats remaining. The audience was packed with old people, academics, curious visitors, and even a reporter from the *Los Angeles Times*. Wearing a white shirt that was open at the collar, a black blazer, and jeans, the author Richard Chasen was at the podium, flipping through his notes and adjusting his microphone, sending crackling sounds over the speakers. I'd heard Chasen interviewed on the radio before, but I was unprepared for how good-looking he was in real life. He was in his thirties, with wavy blond hair and hazel-green eyes, black glasses, and a few days' worth of stubble.

The director of the Huntington, a white-haired man with glasses, a little mustache, and a bow tie, gave a brief introduction, covering Chasen's illustrious career. Born in the United States but educated in England, Chasen had burst onto the literary scene at the age of twenty-one and had immediately been hailed as "the voice of a generation" and "a once-in-a-lifetime talent." His first book had won several prestigious literary awards. His second book, a war novel, was picked up by Oprah and sold in the millions. And his third book, a historical thriller set in Dickensian England, had recently been awarded the Booker Prize. The audience broke into loud applause and

cheers. A professional photographer stepped in front of me to shoot pictures of Chasen, forcing me to lean over to one side. I glimpsed Chasen placing his hand to his chest and giving a slight bow to the audience before vigorously shaking the director's hand and thanking him for the wonderful introduction.

Chasen cleared his throat and the room quickly hushed. He spoke with an elegant British accent, leaning over with his arms resting casually on the podium.

"I'm so glad to be here among such great scholars and lovers of literature," he said. "Every time I visit the Huntington, I feel like I've entered a wormhole into the past. This place is a real hidden treasure." He paused to acknowledge another round of applause. "Much of the research for my last book, *Subterranean City*, took place here, and I look forward to spending more time in the archives as I've just accepted a writer-in-residence position at Fairfax College."

I straightened up. I hadn't known Chasen would be teaching at Fairfax.

"My lecture today is from an article I'm working on for the *New Yorker*," he said. "I was asked to contribute my thoughts on contemporary fiction." He paused. "I guess Jonathan Franzen was unavailable." The audience laughed at his self-deprecating humor, and Chasen gave a wry half smile.

Chasen straightened up, adjusted his glasses, took a quick drink of water. "The world of the novel," he began, his voice suddenly booming and authoritative, "is a world that is, by its very nature, mimetic, appropriative, and voraciously imperialistic." He was confident, even brash, as he described his literary technique. I pretended to be listening attentively, but I was really just staring at his face. He didn't look like a writer. He looked like a mountain climber, or an Australian movie star, or a Nautica model. I glanced at his hand. He wasn't wearing a wedding ring.

Beside me was an old man wearing a Dickens Club T-shirt with a picture of Tiny Tim waving his crutch. He turned to his wife and loudly asked, "What the hell is he talking about?"

"I don't know, honey," she whispered back, patting his hand. "I thought he was going to lecture on *The Old Curiosity Shop*."

Chasen must have heard them because he glanced in our direction. Before I could look away, he had locked eyes with me and given me a coy wink. *My God,* I thought. *Is he* flirting *with me?* I looked down at my lap, but every time I looked up again, Chasen seemed to be seeking out my gaze, his eyes holding mine for a second before moving away again. He spoke for perhaps twenty minutes and then took questions before being besieged by a crowd of fans clamoring for him to sign their books.

I lingered afterwards, debating whether to introduce myself. I wasn't usually one to speak to authors after readings or lectures. Most writers, especially the ones whose books I most admired, were awful to meet in person. A lot of them didn't even seem to *like* their readers. I'd once met a famous author in graduate school who was on a visiting fellowship and would occasionally sit in on our graduate seminars. She was young—just around my age—and gorgeous, with an angular face that demanded she be a fashion model if the writing thing didn't work out. While the rest of us watched in cowed silence, she would get into fierce arguments with our professor, challenging his readings, asking for citations, ignoring the rest of us in the room. Later that semester, she gave a reading at the local bookstore, and I approached her afterwards, book in hand.

"I—I loved your book," I said, knowing how trite I sounded but not knowing what else to say because it was the truth. She was a beautiful writer.

She looked at me disdainfully. "Name?" she asked.

"Oh! Of course. Anne with an *e*," I said.

"You're in that seminar with me, aren't you?" she asked.

"Yes!" I said, incredulous and flattered that she recognized me. "It's a great class, isn't it?"

"It's a fucking waste of time," she said, slamming the book shut and handing it to me.

I'd learned my lesson after that. It was a rookie mistake, imagining that I could be *friends* with my favorite writers. Now I knew that I preferred my authors to keep at a safe distance—and they preferred the same of me.

Richard Chasen was different, though. I'd never read any of his novels, for one. And we *were* going to be colleagues, after all. Besides, he seemed to be encouraging me to come over. From behind the scrum of fans, he glanced in my direction, his green eyes pleading, "Please come introduce yourself. I'm waiting." I stayed in my seat for a few minutes, watching as he finished being interviewed by the *Times* reporter and started signing books. A small cluster of die-hard fans clustered around him, asking for selfies and tittering as he made some dry jokes.

He's busy, I thought and got up to leave. But Chasen saw me and hastily excused himself from his fans.

"Forgive me," he said, catching up to me. "Have we met before?"

"I don't think so," I said, suddenly embarrassed. "I'm Anne Corey."

"I'm terribly sorry," he said. "I could have sworn— Well, never mind now. Please, let me introduce myself. I'm Rick. It was very kind of you to come to my lecture."

I shook his hand. His attention was flattering but also strangely disconcerting.

"I was meaning to introduce myself to you," I said. "It looks like we're going to be colleagues at Fairfax. I teach in the English department there."

"You do!" Rick said. "How serendipitous!" He glanced behind him at the group of fans who were staring at us curiously. "Are you free for lunch?" he asked. "I've got a few hours before I head back to the airport, and it'd be lovely if you could join me." Leaning over, he whispered into my ear, "Please rescue me, I'm begging you." He smelled wonderful, like soap and some kind of cologne.

"Sure," I said, tentatively.

"Let's try the tearoom," he said. "I hear it's quite good."

After wrapping up his signing, Rick opened the door for me with a chivalric flourish and we headed onto the grounds of the garden, strolling down stone pathways surrounded by large green lawns. To our right was the original library, festooned with banners advertising the exhibits inside; to our left, the special gardens, like the cactus collection, the tropical gardens, and the orchid greenhouse. We followed the signs to the tearoom, situated next to the rose garden. The roses were in full bloom, climbing up the latticed terraces and creating a white cloud around a

temple that housed a sculpture of Cupid and a young maiden.

We didn't have a reservation at the tearoom, but the hostess made an exception for us, leading us to a small table tucked in a corner. A server brought us a pot of tea and a basket of scones. The rest of the food was in a central buffet that looked unappealingly like a pig trough, with people loading up on finger sandwiches, strawberries, and pastries.

"So tell me about Fairfax," Rick said. "Do you enjoy it there?"

"Oh, it's a great place to teach," I said, taking a bite out of a strawberry and hoping none of the seeds would lodge themselves in my teeth. "The class sizes are small, and the students are generally smart and motivated."

"And the town?"

"It's charming and quiet," I said. I laughed nervously. "I mean, don't get me wrong. It's not LA or New York. There's not a ton going on."

"That sounds quite nice, actually," Rick said, looking pensive. "You know, I was embedded with coalition forces in Fallujah for almost a year, and that was rather *too* much excitement."

"You were in Iraq?" I asked. Most of the writers I knew never strayed beyond a five-mile radius of Brooklyn.

"Yes, doing some reporting. Nearly lost my

life when our convoy was struck by an IED." He paused, his voice suddenly quiet. "One of my mates didn't make it. Bled out on the side of the road."

"Wow," I breathed. "I'm so sorry." I thought about my own research, which rarely required more than a library card and some trips to dusty archives. What I did wasn't dangerous or even particularly exciting most of the time. But Rick was out there *doing* things, risking his life, witnessing real tragedy.

Rick shook his head as if to clear it of painful memories. "Fairfax sounds positively heavenly. You must be so glad to be there."

"I am," I said. "Though honestly, I may not be there for much longer if I don't get my book out soon." I felt a wave of despondency come over me.

"You haven't found a publisher yet?"

"No. In fact, I got a rejection from Bloomsbury just the other day. It was pretty depressing."

"Oh, it's terrible, isn't it?" Rick agreed, his eyes on mine. "Like a punch in the gut, really. But you must carry on. If I could tell you how many times my work has been rejected . . ."

"Really? But you're so . . . successful."

"We all have to start somewhere," he said, smiling. He looked at me thoughtfully. "Now that I think about it, I actually know a few people at some academic presses. I could call them up

for you. Would you consider going with a place like Cambridge? Or Oxford?"

"*Would* I?" I said, gaping at him. "That would be a dream!"

"Let me see what I can do," Rick said, his finger pressed to his lips.

"I'm speechless—thank you." I couldn't believe it. Rick was a Booker Prize–winning author, and he wanted to help *me?* He'd barely met me! He'd never even read my work! Yet here he was, being unbelievably generous.

"I enjoy helping other writers," Rick said, as if reading my mind. "It's a solitary profession, and we have to support one another."

He reached across the table and took my hand in his. I suddenly imagined what it would be like to kiss him and felt my heart flutter.

He squeezed my hand. "I know that things will work out."

chapter five

"D R. COREY," I HEARD Larry boom from in front of the chapel. "You're late for convocation!"

"It's only five past two!" I protested, jogging up to him. "The ceremony's not starting for another half hour!" I was wearing my black polyester doctoral robe, rented from the bookstore, with my dark blue hood slung sloppily around my neck and my mortarboard tucked under my arm. It was eighty degrees out, and I was sweating under my robe.

"How do I look?" Larry asked.

Larry was dressed in his full Harvard doctoral regalia. The robes were supposed to be crimson-colored, but in the sun they looked more like a hot pink. His sleeves were edged in black velvet stripes, and he was wearing a dapper black velvet tam with a large gold tassel. Around his neck was a collection of medals, some on chains and some on pieces of ribbon.

"What's all that metal around your neck?" I asked.

"Oh, these?" Larry said. He picked up a gold

medallion on a red ribbon. "This one is for a teaching prize I got at Fairfax." He picked up a silver medallion on a blue ribbon. "This one I got for distinguished scholarship." He fiddled around and found a third medal shaped like a book. "This one is from the English Honor Society."

"What about the others?" I asked.

"Oh, *these?*" Larry pulled another three or four medals from the tangle around his neck. "This one I got for running a 5K in Santa Barbara last year. And this one's my niece's gymnastics all-around medal. Oh! And this one's my favorite. I got this at Mardi Gras when I was in college. Isn't it nice?" He admired the purple-and-green fleur-de-lis medal on its plastic beaded chain.

"You look like Mr. T," I said.

"Thank you!" Larry said. He carefully arranged his medals in a neat fan across his chest.

A faculty marshal was yelling at all of us to get into some semblance of a line so we could process into the chapel. Everyone ignored him. No one was worse at listening to instructions than a bunch of professors—we were used to telling people what to do, not being told what to do.

"So how's your father doing?" Larry asked, talking over the marshal's pleas.

"Not good," I sighed. "Lauren called me from Florida the other day and said it looked like an episode of *Hoarders* in my dad's condo. She found six months' worth of unpaid bills under a

pile of garbage—it was a miracle the electricity was still on."

"Uh-oh. What did the doctor say?"

"She was seriously concerned. Lauren tried to get my dad to take some cognitive tests, but he flat-out refused. I don't know what we're going to do—we can't leave him the way he is. The doctor thinks we should consider moving him to an assisted-living facility."

Larry whistled. "That's a huge decision. When my grandma was first diagnosed with dementia, she wouldn't even let us take away the keys to her car."

"Yeah—my dad's *not* going to be happy. There's a place here in Fairfax we're hoping he'll like—it's more like a retirement community than a nursing home. I'm crossing my fingers it works out."

A bagpiper appeared and started droning away. After several more pleas, each more heated than the one before, the marshal started physically herding us into line. I got in line beside Larry, just behind a group of economics professors who were clearly whispering about all the medals around Larry's neck. "Is he the provost?" I heard someone ask. Larry smiled smugly at me and tossed his gold tassel like a ponytail.

The line began to move, following the bagpiper as he entered the chapel and led us past rows of gaping students. Larry hummed "Here Comes the

Bride" under his breath as we walked, tipping his head graciously to each side. There were faculty members in purple robes with gold details, gray robes with red details, orange robes with navy blue details, powder-blue robes with black details. And the hats! There were plain, boring mortarboards like mine, but then there were also black velvet tams like Larry's, Tudor bonnets with feathers, eight-cornered hats that looked like muffins. One professor, who got his doctorate in Finland, wore a silken top hat and a sword.

The first few pews of the chapel had been cordoned off for us with velvet rope. I squeezed next to Larry, a few seats away from the center aisle, watching my colleagues file in and waving at the ones I knew. Beside me, Larry fished two pink cans of champagne from his sleeve.

"What's this?" I asked.

"A toast to the new school year," he said, cracking a can open, sticking in a pink straw, and handing it to me. "Cheers."

The orchestra struck up a coronation anthem, led by trumpets and backed by a full chorus. By some unspoken cue, everyone abruptly stood up and craned their heads toward the back of the chapel, where the board of trustees was making its entrance, led by a wizened old professor, the longest-serving faculty member at the college, carrying an oversized ceremonial mace that looked like it weighed more than he did. Adam

was the final member of the procession, and a great hush fell over the crowd as he walked in, alone, backed by the triumphant orchestral music. He was also dressed in black academic regalia with a scarlet stole embroidered in gold and an enormous university medallion draped around his neck. I heard Larry gasp beside me. "Now where do I get one of *those?*" he asked.

Adam was tall, and his gown didn't pool around his feet like mine did but hung several inches above the ground. His robes made him look even more distinguished, emphasizing his broad shoulders and upright posture. The silence gave way to a great wave of applause. Around me, even my curmudgeonly colleagues began to clap. It was the beginning of a new era—the Martinez era. Fairfax was giddy with the possibility.

I joined the applause, feeling increasingly self-conscious as Adam walked closer to my pew. I tried to stare at his shoes, then let my gaze drift up, pausing at the big gold medal before I glanced at his face. He was smiling slightly and acknowledging the applause with a slight nod of his head. As he passed by, he caught my eye. I saw him register the slightest bit of surprise—his left eyebrow raised and his smile stiffened—and felt myself wanting to hide in my ceremonial hood.

Around us, people began flipping through their programs as the college chaplain recited a

blessing and the president of the board of trustees began the investiture ceremony. I slumped a little farther in my seat. This was going to be a long, long year.

THE RECEPTION AFTERWARDS WAS held at the President's House. Larry and I changed out of our regalia and headed over, crossing through the campus in the mellow afternoon sunlight. The lampposts lining the quad had been hung with festive red banners to celebrate the convocation, and even the streets of Fairfax looked more charming than usual. All the houses looked freshly painted, all the gardens replanted, all the hedges trimmed. The mansion was strung with lights and red bunting, with the sound of a string quartet drifting from the garden, where cocktails and hors d'oeuvres were being served by waiters in black vests. Larry grabbed two flutes of champagne as we walked in. "Round two! And check it out—they sprang for real glassware, not plastic!" he said approvingly.

From the corner of my eye, I saw Adam surrounded by a thick knot of college benefactors, all dressed in suits, some wearing bow ties in the Fairfax College colors. A lavish spread of cheese, fruit, and crudités had been arranged on two long banquet tables, along with a dessert display of miniature tarts, brownies, and cheesecake bites. In the center was a huge three-tiered cake with

the college seal piped in red and gold on the top. "Congratulations, President Martinez," it said in cursive script.

"This feels like a wedding," I said.

"The union of President Martinez and the college," Larry said. He grabbed a Thai-chicken skewer from a passing waiter and nibbled on it tentatively. "Not bad," he said. "I can't wait for the cake."

We walked up the back porch stairs and into the house, where servers were walking back and forth from the kitchen with trays of hors d'oeuvres and empty glasses.

"Let's take a look around!" Larry said, conspiratorially. "Just for a quick sec."

The mansion's public rooms were large and gracious and were often used for campus holiday parties or receptions. I'd been in them a few times before, drinking warm punch while staring at the large paintings of past presidents that hung on the wall. The rooms were empty now and bathed in a warm light. Larry and I stood for a moment on the thick Persian rugs, surveying the intricately carved wooden fireplace, the antique furniture that lined the walls, the stained glass windows, and the elegant flower arrangements scattered around like in a magazine spread. It was hard to believe that this was now Adam's house. How different it was from his college dorm room, with its cinder block walls and threadbare carpet!

"He had the furniture reupholstered," Larry said approvingly. "I like it."

We drifted into an adjoining room where the previous president, a military buff, had once displayed his large collection of antique muskets and swords. The room had felt like a museum exhibit, with its glass cases of weaponry and mounted deer heads on the wall.

"Oh, wow," Larry said, peeking in. "He totally redid it!"

I peered inside and gasped. Adam had turned the room into a library and reading alcove. The guns and taxidermy specimens were gone, replaced by floor-to-ceiling bookshelves packed with books, books, and more books. A rolling ladder leaned against the shelves. A comfortable leather couch and club chairs were arranged against one wall, and a window seat had been built under the stained glass windows, large enough and deep enough to read comfortably for hours or even stretch out and take a nap.

"I die," Larry whimpered. "It's his own home library."

I watched as Larry inspected the books on the shelves. "Oh my God," he cried, pulling one out and opening it. "They're *real!*" He started pulling book after book off the shelves. "He's got good taste, too!" he called out over his shoulder. "Lots of literature and history, the complete Shakespeare, the complete Austen. And they've

been *read.* There are even notes inside! I think I might be in love."

I leaned against the doorsill, feeling sick to my stomach.

Back in college, Adam and I had fantasized about living in a small college town, in a home filled with books and comfortable places to read and maybe a pet or two. We liked to wander around Princeton, into the gracious neighborhoods abutting the campus, gawking at the grand old houses with their stone and brick facades, painted shutters, and autumn wreaths hanging on the front door, imagining our lives in twenty years.

"That one's my favorite," I remember telling Adam, pointing to a gray stone house with white-trimmed gables and a bright red door, a child's wagon resting on the front porch. "I like that one better," he said, pointing to a red brick house that looked like Monticello, with its white columns and dark green shutters. "Or that one," he said, pointing to a white clapboard house with a widow's walk that stretched across the entire roof.

"Could you imagine living in one of them?" I remember asking dreamily. "I mean, look at that!" I pointed to a house with a large dormer window. We could see a whole wall of books through the glass. "That's my dream library," I sighed.

"I'll buy it for you one day," Adam laughed. "Once I make my fortune."

"What fortune?" I joked.

"I might not be able to get you the house, but I promise you can have your dream library," he said.

Seeing Adam's library now made me feel ill with want. I felt like he'd stolen part of my dreams, like he was living the life *I'd* wanted. "This was supposed to be *my* library," I wanted to scream. Was he taunting me? Showing me the life I could have had if we hadn't broken up?

"Let's go," I snapped. "I need another drink." I hurried out of the library in a cloud of self-pity and fury, not waiting to make sure Larry was following.

"Anne!" I heard. I spun around, my face a thundercloud.

"What?" I snapped.

Adam was standing in front of me, a glass of wine in one hand.

"Whoa," he said. "Are you all right?" He instinctively reached his hand out to touch my shoulder but then pulled back self-consciously.

"Oh, yeah, sorry," I said. "It's nothing." I forced myself to smile. I couldn't think straight. His eyes were the same dark brown color I remembered, with the same thick lashes and heavy lids that gave him such a pensive look. I could see the clean line where the barber had

shaved his sideburns. He'd gotten a haircut recently—maybe even that morning. I could swear I smelled the lingering scent of aftershave.

We stood there a moment, Adam fiddling with his wineglass.

"I've been meaning to talk to you," he said. "I saw you in the chapel earlier. How are you doing?"

"Me? I'm fine. You know, busy, um, with stuff."

"It's been a long time . . ." Adam trailed off.

I nodded. We stood there awkwardly for a second. "So, um, how about you?" I asked, trying to sound nonchalant. "How does it feel to be President Martinez?"

"It's a little surreal," Adam said, looking around the room. "Just trying to process it all." He looked at me, not unkindly. "How's your family doing?"

"They're OK. Lauren's in LA now. She's married and has three kids."

"And your father?"

"Oh. Well, actually, he's not doing so well. He, um, he's been having some health issues recently, and we think it's better if he moves out here, closer to us."

"I'm so sorry," Adam said, looking genuinely concerned. "I hope he's OK."

"He'll be fine," I said. "He's a tough guy. Always has been."

"That's true," Adam said. "He *is* tough."

I reddened. Adam had met my father once, when I'd brought him to Florida for Thanksgiving break. My father had spent the whole time ignoring Adam, instead complaining about his tenants and yelling at the television. When I tried to broach the subject of our engagement, my father had cut me off. Switching the subject, he'd asked if I'd given more thought to law school, and when I said no, he'd started on Adam, informing him that his "Latin background" meant he'd get into any law school he wanted. Years later, I still cringed at the memory.

"What are you teaching in your classes?" Adam was now asking.

"Oh, the standard," I babbled. "Austen, the Brontës, Gaskell, Eliot, plus some other, lesser-known writers."

Adam was nodding at the names in recognition. He suddenly grinned, looking like the boy I remembered from college. "Remember when you took that class with Dr. Russell junior year—the one where she assigned a novel a week and you had to keep pulling all-nighters to keep up?" he asked.

"Don't remind me," I laughed, surprised at how natural and pleasant it all seemed. "I promise I'm not so cruel to my own students, though they still like to complain about the reading load."

"I bet," Adam said. "Well, it sounds like a great

syllabus. I kind of wish I were taking the class myself."

"You're more than welcome to drop by anytime," I said, surprising myself with my boldness.

"Maybe so. You'll have to send me the reading list. Which Austen are you reading again?"

"Oh!" I said. "Well, um, actually, this semester I'm teaching *Persuasion*." I felt my face grow warm. Adam, too, seemed suddenly embarrassed.

"Your favorite novel," he murmured.

"Ha-ha, yes. I'm surprised you still remember."

"Of course I still remember," Adam said, his eyebrow cocked. "How could I forget? Is it still your favorite novel?"

"I guess so," I said, feeling almost ashamed. He must be wondering how anyone could still be so foolishly loyal to a two-hundred-year-old book.

"That's great," he said softly. "It must be wonderful to be teaching books you love. I'm happy for you—you seem like you're doing really well." He paused, as if uncertain whether to go on.

"I've done a lot of thinking," he began again, "about what happened—"

"Anne! Where'd you go? Look who I found!"

Larry was lurching toward us, dragging with him a faintly bemused-looking Rick Chasen.

"Rick!" I said, startled. "I didn't realize you'd gotten into town!"

"Just arrived this evening," he said, giving me

a kiss on the cheek. "Wonderful to see you again, Anne."

"I recognized him from his author photo!" Larry was saying. "President Martinez—this is Rick Chasen. He's our new writer-in-residence. It's quite the coup for us."

"Nice to meet you," Adam said, reaching out to shake Rick's hand.

"We've met before," Rick said pointedly. "At Houston."

"That's right," Adam said.

"Rick just won the Booker Prize," I said. "He gave a lecture at the Huntington the other day. It was absolutely packed."

"Congratulations," Adam said, but his voice was muted. He glanced across the courtyard, where Tiffany was waving her arms. "I'm sorry—it looks like I'm being summoned. Please excuse me."

As he walked away, Larry leaned over to Rick. "So you knew President Martinez at Houston? When he was provost?"

"Yes, we knew each other," Rick said, choosing his words carefully. "Or rather, we knew *of* each other. He's a complicated fellow."

"What do you mean?" I asked. He sounded like he knew something about Adam but didn't want to say.

"You know how it is. He's an administrator— rather humorless and rigid. The faculty didn't

get on with him. I was one of the leaders of the union, and I can tell you, we did *not* see eye to eye. He was a bureaucrat. Wanted to limit academic freedom, plus cut our benefits."

"Reeeeaallllllly," Larry said. "Very interesting. I have to admit I'm a little surprised. From what I've seen so far, he seems like a real intellectual. We just got a look at his library, and let me tell you, it's *to die for.*"

"Don't let that fool you," Rick laughed. "Just because someone owns a lot of books doesn't mean they actually care about reading and writing. Sometimes they just want people to *think* they care. He's all about the bottom line. He doesn't care about 'humanistic values' or what-ever he says. Believe me—he wants to corporatize the university, make it more profitable and less accessible."

"I don't know," I said hesitantly. "I knew him back in college, and he definitely cared a lot about books back then. In fact, he even wanted to be a teacher at one point."

"No kidding!" Rick said, his eyes widening. "You knew him?"

"Sort of," I said, feeling sheepish. "Actually, we dated for a little while."

"You *did?*" Larry exclaimed. "Why didn't you tell me earlier?"

"It was so long ago," I said, shrugging. "We'd totally lost touch since. It really wasn't a big

deal. I mean, he didn't even recognize me when he first saw me."

"Did he always have that hard-to-read demeanor?" Rick asked, winking at me. "You know, where you can't tell if he likes you or really hates your guts?"

I found myself laughing out loud. "I guess he's always been a little hard to read," I admitted.

There was a murmur behind us, and the three of us turned. The head of the board of trustees was standing at a podium, raising a glass to toast Adam, who was standing quietly beside him. A professional photographer stood to one side, snapping a barrage of pictures.

As the trustee gave his toast, I saw Adam's eyes drift over the crowd. I saw his gaze stop short when he saw Rick still standing with Larry and me. Something passed between the two of them—a kind of cold détente. I knew Adam well enough to know the look. He didn't like Rick.

"See?" Rick leaned over and whispered to me. "He thinks I'm an asshole. I'm not scared of him, though. Someone needs to stand up to the Man."

I nodded. What did I really know about Adam now? He had an important job title, a big house, and a fancy library. He was kind enough, but it was clear there was no feeling left on his side. From where I stood, I felt like I was staring across a huge abyss. I stepped closer to Rick.

From: Rufus Chang <rufuslchang@hup.edu>
To: Anne Corey <A.Corey@Fairfax.edu>
Subject: book query
Date: September 18

Dear Anne Corey,

HUP is moving away from literary criticism. Good luck in placing your manuscript.

Rufus Chang

From: Lauren Corey Winston <lauren@toteally.com>
To: Anne Corey <A.Corey@Fairfax.edu>
Subject: book club info
Date: September 18

Here are the details re: book club. Don't be late.
I told the ladies you'd lecture a little on the novel, give historical context, etc. Keep it short and sweet.
   Jack Lindsey might stop by for a little while. It's ok for Larry to come, but tell him NOT to harass Jack for a selfie.

---------- Forwarded message ----------
From: Elizabeth.B.Lindsey@gmail.com
To: <undisclosed recipients>
Subject: Book club
Date: September 1

Hi Ladies!

Let's plan to meet at my place on Sunday, September 23 at 2 p.m. Just a reminder, we're reading *Jane Vampire* by Sylvia Celeste. Should be a fun read! Lauren's also going to see if her sister can join us to talk a little about the novel's link to *Jane Eyre*. Thanks, Lauren!

> 800 Stone Canyon Road
> Los Angeles, CA 90077

(Buzz the intercom when you get to our driveway and someone will let you in.)

xo bex

From: Tiffany Allen <T.Allen@Fairfax.edu>
To: Anne Corey <A.Corey@Fairfax.edu>
Subject: Thrive! Fairfax Capital Campaign
Date: September 18

Hi Anne,

Hope you're as excited about the new school year as I am! We have so many wonderful things planned around the launch of our capital campaign! As you know, Fairfax is trying to raise $500 million over the next few years to help fund scholarships, renovate the library, and replenish our endowment. Our official gala and launch is scheduled for October 28. Save the date!

I was hoping you'd agree to be one of the faculty captains in our capital campaign. You'd be tasked with reaching out to alums who majored in the humanities, many of whom have gone on to great success in film, television, technology, and finance. I know you're busy, but this would be a wonderful service to the school and would, I'm sure, look absolutely terrific in your tenure file. I've already spoken to your chair, and he wholeheartedly agrees that you'd be perfect for this job!

Our first training session is on October 5. I know I can count on you being there!

Go Wolverines!!!!!!!
Tiff

From: Lawrence Ettinger <L.Ettinger@Fairfax.edu>
To: Anne Corey <A.Corey@Fairfax.edu>

AHAHAHAHAHAHAHAHAHAH SUCKA!!!!!!!

Go Wolverines!!!!!!!
Larry

On Sept. 18, Anne Corey <A.Corey@Fairfax.edu>
wrote:

WTF

---------- Forwarded message ----------
From: Tiffany Allen <T.Allen@Fairfax.edu>
To: Anne Corey <A.Corey@Fairfax.edu>
Subject: Thrive! Fairfax Capital Campaign
Date: September 18

(. . .)

From: Jerome Corey <jerrycorey1944@aol.com>
To: Anne Corey <A.Corey@Fairfax.edu>
Subject: TESTING TESTING THIS IS YOUR FATHER PLEASE REPLY
Date: September 19

ARE YOU GETTING THIS? PLEASE REPLY SO I KNOW IT'S WORKING
   THIS PLACE HAS ABSOLUTELY TERRIBLE FOOD I'M BORED AND THE PEOPLE HERE ARE DINGBATS.
ALSO I CAN'T GET ANY SLEEP AS THE BED HERE IS VERY UNCOMFORTABLE
   PLEASE BRING TUMS THE NEXT TIME YOU VISIT

From: Info@ucpress.com
To: Anne Corey <A.Corey@Fairfax.edu>
Subject: [automatic reply]
Date: September 20

We do not accept unsolicited submissions.
   Please do not reply to this message. This e-mail was sent from a notification-only address that cannot accept incoming mail.

chapter six

"I CANNOT BELIEVE YOU KNOW Jack Lindsey," Larry said, clapping his hands excitedly. We were on our way to Lauren's book club, and I was trying hard not to miss the Sunset exit off the 405. "I used to watch him on *Days of Our Lives* religiously. *Such* a hottie."

"Yeah, well, I doubt he remembers me," I said. "We only took a couple classes together. I'm warning you, though—he's not the sharpest tool in the shed."

"Who cares how sharp you are if you look like *that?*"

I'd known Jack Lindsey since college, back when he was just another pretty-boy baseball player from the Midwest. All the girls had a crush on him. He was handsome in a corn-fed, conventional way, with thick brown hair, tan skin, dimples, a strong jaw. The fact that he was dumb as a rock didn't seem to detract from his appeal. He was like a golden retriever or a Lab—easygoing, friendly, impossible to hate.

"What's his wife like?" Larry asked.

"Bex? Well, she's really pretty. And she's *super* smart."

Jack and Bex had dated all the way through college. Bex was tall and willowy, with the kind of blond hair that looked like it was spun from gold. One of the campus buildings was named after her great-grandfather, who was a trustee back when Woodrow Wilson was president of the college. In class, it felt like she'd read everything and been everywhere, and sometimes it felt like she and the professor were having their own private conversation while the rest of us listened in. I wanted to hate her, but I couldn't. I wanted to *be* her.

"How long have they been married?" Larry asked.

"Forever," I said. "I remember seeing their wedding pictures in the alumni magazine. I think they got married in Nantucket. It seriously looked like something out of *Martha Stewart Weddings*."

I sighed. It was hard not to be envious of Jack and Bex. I knew that after graduating, Jack had headed to Hollywood to be an actor—even though he'd never taken an acting lesson in his life, never appeared in a play or done anything besides play baseball. Within two weeks of arriving in Los Angeles, he'd landed a recurring role on a soap and quickly moved into a series of playboy and heartbreaker roles on various

television shows. Every so often, I would flip through channels and stop when I saw Jack's face on the screen, now playing a jock on a CW show, now a hot resident on *Grey's Anatomy*, now a young JFK in a History Channel mini-series.

I drove past the campus of UCLA on one side, then made a left through the distinctive white gates of Bel-Air. With Larry navigating, we climbed up the hills, passing mansions on enormous lots hidden by fortresses of trees and hedges.

"Did you finish the book?" I asked Larry.

"Oh, goodness no," he said. "You know I don't read anything published after 1920. I'll just wait for the movie. I can't *wait* to see Jack as Rochester!"

High in the hills, I pulled into a driveway with a slablike gate. I buzzed the intercom, announced myself, and waited as the gate slowly swung open. The car faced a steep incline that curved around a hill thick with bougainvillea and olive trees. I stepped on the gas, and Larry and I slid back in our seats as my car strained its way up the hill. The driveway wound around like a party ribbon and then leveled out as we pulled into a circular motor court with a stone fountain burbling in the center.

"This place looks like a hotel," I whispered to Larry as we drove up to the front of the house.

"No, it looks like the Playboy Mansion," Larry whispered back.

We made our way into the house, down a long, cool corridor lined with hand-painted clay tiles and looking onto a beautifully landscaped garden thick with purple lilies of the Nile. The drawing room had soaring ceilings and an enormous stained glass dome that glowed orange and yellow in the light. There were soft rugs on the floor, comfortable chairs, and some modern furniture mixed in with the antiques so the place didn't look like a museum. Larry peered at a full-length painted portrait of a woman in an opalescent silken gown with enormous puff sleeves and a strand of pearls crossing her bodice.

"Christ, is that a *real* John Singer Sargent?" he wondered.

"Come into the kitchen!" someone called out. We followed the voice through a formal dining room, another sitting room, and into a large, bright kitchen that opened onto a stone-paved patio. Bex was at the kitchen counter, cutting heirloom tomatoes and talking animatedly to Lauren and an assortment of friends. They were all drinking glasses of white wine and looking impossibly relaxed.

"Anne! Larry!" Lauren said, her voice pitched higher than normal as she quickly introduced us to the group. I recognized Lauren's friends

Marni and Celeste, friends of hers from the beach club and PTA who'd first invited her to join the book club. The two other women I didn't recognize. One was a very tall brunette with hair slicked back into a low ponytail who Lauren introduced as Quincy, a PR rep for one of the studios. The other woman, a pale redhead wearing lots of bangles and rings, was named Schuyler and was a jewelry designer married to a movie producer.

And then there was Bex. I wish I could say she'd aged badly, but she looked just as naturally beautiful as she had in college. If anything, she'd loosened up a little, become less prim and preppy. She was wearing a white tank top that showed off her tanned arms and silky pants that made her legs look even longer than I'd remembered. Her hair was loose and wavy and streaked with gold, and her face was fresh and youthful, unblemished by any makeup.

"I'm so glad the two of you could come," Bex said, wiping her hands on a dish towel and giving the two of us a kiss on the cheek. I could smell her perfume or shampoo, a mix of white flowers and grapefruit.

"How's work going?" Marni asked. "I heard you're writing a book! When are we going to be able to read it?"

"It's not that kind of book," I said. "It's academic."

"Oh! So it's not a novel?"

"No—it's about novels, but it isn't a novel." I felt myself getting tongue-tied. "It's a scholarly study of several nineteenth-century novelists, like Austen, and Brontë, and Eliot."

"Eliot? I *love* him! What's that poem? Where the women are talking about Michelangelo?"

"That's T. S. Eliot," I said. "I'm working on George Eliot."

Marni looked disappointed. I wasn't writing a novel she could buy at the bookstore, and I wasn't even writing about an author she liked. She was still smiling at me fixedly, but she'd clearly run out of things to say.

Suddenly Jack peeked his head around the corner. "Hi, ladies!" he said, his dimples showing. "Just wanted to say a quick hello."

"Jack!" Bex said. "I wanted to introduce you to some people."

Jack walked into the kitchen, barefoot, wearing a tight T-shirt that showed off his gym physique and a pair of designer jeans. His time in Hollywood had smoothed away any of the fratty, country quality he once had. He wore gel in his hair, a giant watch on his wrist, and his face looked like it had been airbrushed. He went around the room, getting air-kisses from all of Bex's friends and then giving Bex an affectionate kiss on the cheek. I glanced at Larry, who looked absolutely starstruck.

"I'm Jack Lindsey," he said, holding out his hand to me. "It's a pleasure to meet you."

"Anne went to Princeton with us, honey," Bex said.

"You did? What year were you?" Jack asked.

"2003," I said.

"So was I!" Jack said, as if he couldn't believe the coincidence.

"This is my colleague, Larry," I said. "He teaches with me at Fairfax."

"You're a professor?" Jack asked, shaking Larry's hand.

"Uh, yes," Larry stammered. "Henry James, mostly."

"Do you teach any Twain? He's my guy. I've read all of his stuff."

"I *love* Twain," Larry said. I looked at him incredulously, but he ignored me.

"Did you know his real name was Samuel Clemens?" Jack asked.

"You don't say," Larry breathed.

"And he was a riverboat pilot on the Mississippi?"

"Nooooo, really?"

"And he was born with Halley's Comet, and he died with Halley's Comet?"

"I did *not* know that!"

"Yeah! I got a book I want to show you." Jack turned to Bex. "Is it OK if I steal Larry away for a minute? While you ladies get settled?"

"Of course!" Bex said. "We'll be out on the patio."

Larry practically sprinted out of the room with Jack. Bex led the rest of us through the French doors onto her shaded patio. It looked like an extension of her house, with plush outdoor furniture, a large dining table with small wildflower arrangements, and more rugs covering the stone walkway. The patio had a stunning view of the city below, spreading outward in all directions, with the bristling outcroppings that marked Century City and downtown Los Angeles in the distance. From where I stood, I could even make out the misty blue haze of the ocean. I walked to the edge of the patio and saw an infinity pool built into the lawn below us, a modern brushed-steel sculpture on one end. To the right was the bright green rectangle of a tennis court.

Holy crap, I thought. *My entire apartment could fit on Bex's patio.* Everything was meticulously designed and maintained, from the lighting fixtures to the velvety moss that grew in the crevices of the flagstone path. My own apartment had ancient plumbing and so many layers of thick, gloppy Navajo White paint on its walls that when it rained, you could peel the layers off like bark from a tree.

"Have you been getting Dad's e-mails?" I whispered to Lauren as we seated ourselves on the couch.

We'd moved my father into Fairfax Retirement Home, a small assisted-living facility near my apartment and the only place, in the end, that could take him on such short notice. Lauren had instructed me that since she was taking care of the bills, I'd be responsible for keeping an eye on my father and checking in on him regularly.

"Yeah. They're full of sunshine, aren't they?" Lauren said, making a face.

"Maybe you could come down next weekend? It might cheer him up. There's a Fall Fest on campus we could take him to. The kids would really like it—there'll be rides and games and live performances."

"Ugh, do you have any idea how bad the traffic is from LA?" Lauren sighed. She thought anything east of La Brea wasn't worth the trip from the Westside. "I'll have to check with Brett first."

She heard Bex clinking her wineglass with a fork, calling the book club to order. Leaning over to me, she whispered, "Make sure not to go on and on for too long. This is book club, not Lit 101. And *please* don't embarrass me."

Schuyler was the first to jump in.

"When Jason bought the movie rights for *Jane Vampire* a million years ago, we had *no idea* it was going to be such a huge deal! I assumed it was just some tween thing, but then it was like *Twilight*—all the mothers started reading the

book and recommending it to their book clubs, and now it's a *phenomenon*."

"I can't wait to see it," someone said. "Who's playing Jane again?"

"That British actress, Rachel . . . Rachel . . ."

"Rachel Evans," Bex said. "Jack told me she broke up with her boyfriend and wouldn't leave her trailer for two days. It threw off the whole shooting schedule."

There were a few sympathetic clucks followed by a smattering of gossip about Rachel Evans—who she was dating now, what her type was, and why she couldn't seem to date anyone for longer than three months.

"How's Jack feeling, now that he's in post?" Quincy asked.

"What's 'post'?" I whispered to Lauren. "Is that like rehab?"

"Shhhhhh!" Lauren hissed. "She means post-production, dummy."

"Great!" Bex was saying. "We took a quick trip to France after filming wrapped. It was so lovely—we got a chance to visit Musée Marcel Proust in Illiers-Combray." The words "Musée Marcel Proust" and "Illiers-Combray" floated off Bex's tongue like champagne bubbles. I remembered that on top of being perfectly beautiful and perfectly smart, Bex was also perfectly fluent in French, the result of a gap year spent in Paris working at an art gallery.

"I love Proust," I said. "Though my French isn't good enough to read him in the original."

"I wrote my senior thesis on *À La Recherche du Temps Perdu*," Bex said. She hesitated, her eyes growing distant, then murmured, " '*Autrefois on rêvait de posséder le cœur de la femme dont on était amoureux; plus tard sentir qu'on possède le cœur d'une femme peut suffire à vous en rendre amoureux.*' "

While everyone stared at her, transfixed ("I have no idea what you just said, but that sounded *amazing*," Marni blurted), I clumsily tried to translate the quotation in my head. *In the past, a man dreamt of possessing the heart of the woman he loved,* I managed before getting irretrievably stuck. I marveled at how easily Bex quoted the passage. She would have made a great professor, I thought.

"So what's *Jane Eyre* about?" Lauren asked, suddenly turning to me. "That's the book *Jane Vampire*'s based on, right?"

"Um, well," I stammered. Where could I even begin? "Jane Eyre's a governess."

"What's a governess?" someone asked.

"It's kind of like a teacher but also a nanny," I said. "Brontë worked as a governess, and so did her sisters. She hated it."

"Why?" Schuyler asked, looking mystified. "I'm kind of jealous of my nanny. She gets to

go to the park with the kids and take them on playdates, and she gets paid for it!"

"Did governesses clean the house, cook healthy meals, and do light laundry, too?" someone else asked. "If so, maybe *I* need to hire a governess."

"It's so hard to find a good nanny," Quincy said. "They're so unreliable. And they can be *so* moody."

"We make ours sign a confidentiality agreement," Marni said. "You can never be too careful."

"So true," agreed Schuyler. "I mean, I told the agency I only wanted them to send over 'mature' ladies—i.e., over the age of fifty."

The women were getting progressively more and more tipsy, and soon any discussion of the book had been abandoned and everyone was simply gossiping and refilling their glasses of wine and milling around the patio. I took a deep breath, relieved that my part, at least, was over. As I stood up to refill my glass of wine, Bex came over to me, a copy of the *Princeton Alumni Weekly* in her hand.

"Did you get this week's *PAW*?" she asked.

"Oh, I haven't updated my address in a while," I said. I'd stopped reading the *PAW* years earlier, when the giddy updates about weddings and babies and promotions became too much for me to stomach.

"I'd been meaning to ask if you knew anything

about the new president of Fairfax. He sounds great."

She handed me the magazine. On the cover was a huge photograph of Adam, dressed in a suit and tie, his arms crossed. "Adam Martinez '03, President of Fairfax College, Blazes New Path," it read.

"Wow," I said, flipping through the magazine. "I didn't realize he'd made the cover."

Inside was another photograph of Adam, this one his senior class photo. Adam was in quarter profile, grinning broadly, wearing a collared shirt and a tie I'd bought him for the occasion. I'd gotten it at Jos. A. Bank on Nassau Street, using money I'd saved from my work-study job. *God,* I thought, *we were such babies.* Quickly, I skimmed the article.

Adam Martinez '03, President of Fairfax College, Blazes New Path

Adam Martinez '03 remembers the first time he stepped foot on Princeton's campus. "I'd just taken my very first plane flight, and it felt like I was walking into a whole new world," he says. Born in Guatemala City and raised in Los Angeles by a single mother who had fled the country's civil war, Martinez and his mother settled in a predominantly Latino

community east of downtown. Adam was a precocious child and talented athlete, and he soon caught the attention of his mother's employer, who offered to help pay his tuition at a local all-boys Catholic school. Adam flourished there, lettering in soccer, volunteering as a court translator, and being elected president of his high school class.

When it came time to apply for college, Martinez assumed he'd stay near home. "My mother didn't want me to go far away," he said. "I'm her only son, and if it were up to her, I'd probably still be living with her!" A chance encounter with an attorney while volunteering at the courts introduced him to Princeton. "This young guy, an assistant DA, asked me where I was thinking of going to school. I said I hadn't really thought about it, and he encouraged me to apply to Princeton, his alma mater. He thought it was important that I experience the world outside LA, and he made Princeton sound like a real possibility for someone like me."

Martinez applied and was accepted on a full scholarship. He arrived on campus excited and full of plans.

"In retrospect, I had no idea what I was getting myself into," he said. "In

my mind, Princeton was wrapped up in so much mythology. I'd read *The Great Gatsby* in high school and knew F. Scott Fitzgerald had gone to Princeton, so I went to the library and checked out every book written by him. I read *This Side of Paradise* at least three times and thought I was prepared. Boy, was I wrong."

Martinez describes a lonely freshman year, full of homesickness and self-doubt. At the end of the year, he decided to take a leave of absence, unsure if he would return. "I thought Princeton had made a mistake in admitting me," he said. "I knew people assumed I was an affirmative action admit, and I felt incredible pressure to prove them wrong. I was doing well in my classes, but in the end, I gave up."

Time away helped Martinez gain perspective. "I needed to grow up a little. I worked a series of odd jobs while I was away from school, but I kept reading in my free time—anything I could find in the library, history, economics, literature, the newspaper. I realized I missed school." After a hiatus of almost five years, Martinez returned to Princeton, joining the class of 2003 as a sophomore. His experience was very different the second time around. "I was more open," he said.

"I made a decision to reach out more, to take more risks."

I felt like I was reading about a stranger. None of the information was new to me—I'd *been* there, for God's sake—but it felt strangely bloodless and incomplete. It was as if I'd never existed in Adam's life, that I'd been edited out of his biography because I hadn't, ultimately, mattered that much. Numbly, I paged through the accompanying pictures—a photo of Adam posing with his law school mentor, another of him receiving an honorary citation from the city of Houston, a candid shot of him lecturing in a classroom. His life after me. I quickly skipped to the end of the article.

Some have expressed surprise at Martinez's relative youth. At just thirty-eight, he is one of the youngest college presidents in the United States, and one of only a handful of Latino college presidents. When asked about this, Martinez laughs. "Woodrow Wilson was forty-five when he became president of Princeton," he says. "I know I'm considered young by some standards, but I'm not new to university administration." Board member Ahmanson concurs, "Martinez has a wealth of experience, and we hope he

will also bring youthful energy to the campus." In fact, for the board of trustees, Martinez's age was part of his draw. "We wanted someone who was early in his career and wasn't just coasting to retirement," says Annette Fowler, a longtime donor and board member.

Martinez has only recently arrived on campus, but so far, he has earned high marks from faculty members and administrators for his visible presence on campus. An avid runner, Martinez can often be seen running on local trails early in the morning with his rescue dog, Charlie. For years, he has also been active in Big Brothers Big Sisters of America, mentoring at-risk youth who, like he did, are growing up without a father figure. His other hobbies include reading and travel. Evidence of this can be seen in his office, in the bookcases full of classics like *Great Expectations* and *Moby-Dick* and in the framed photographs of distant locales.

"In some ways, I feel like I'm starting college again," he says. "I'm new, I don't know many people, and I'm excited and nervous." He sits back in his office chair, gesturing at the walls of books, the imposing executive desk, the

decorative fireplace, an old painted portrait of Fairfax's first president, Theodore Hubbard. He shakes his head wonderingly. "I still can't believe I'm really here."

I closed the magazine and handed it back to Bex. Reading the profile had made me feel dizzy. On the one hand, I felt like I knew way too much about Adam. On the other hand, I felt like I knew nothing at all. That was him, all right, but it was a slick, prepackaged version of him.

"I read that the school's launching a capital campaign in the fall," Bex said to me. "I'd like to get involved. My cousin went to Fairfax, and she always talked about how much she loved it there."

"I can give you the name of someone in the development office," I said, thinking of Tiffany.

"What are you guys talking about?" Lauren asked, wandering over.

"The new president of Fairfax," Bex said.

"Let me look at that," Lauren said, snatching the magazine from my hand. "Is that who I think it is?"

"His name is Adam Martinez," Bex said. "He graduated our year, but I don't think we ever crossed paths. I was asking Anne if she knew him."

"Knew him?" Lauren snorted. "Anne *dated*

him. He even visited us over Thanksgiving one year."

"Really!" Bex said.

"It was a long time ago," I said, giving Lauren a dirty look. She'd treated Adam with disdain and even hostility during his visit, alternately peppering him with questions and then ignoring him. Now, though, Lauren was skimming the *PAW* article and nodding approvingly. "Whoa," she said. "He's done well for himself. It says he's one of the youngest college presidents in the country. Who would've thought?"

She turned to me. "So how long have you known about this? And when were you planning to tell me, anyway?"

"Oh, it all happened pretty recently," I said, shrugging. "I only just found out about it myself."

"Does he know you're at Fairfax?" Lauren asked, narrowing her eyes.

"Yeah," I said. "It's no big deal. We bump into each other every once in a while."

"And you've been in touch with him all this time?"

"No!" I snapped. "It's been over ten years, Lauren. It's ancient history."

"How funny," Bex interrupted, her voice so soft I could hardly hear her. "I married my college sweetheart." There was an uncomfortable silence, and Bex laughed a little self-consciously. "But you're right. It feels like ancient history."

"Does anyone know where Larry is?" I asked, looking around. "I should probably get going."

"Oh, Anne," Lauren groaned. "Did you really leave Larry with Jack this whole time? How could you? I *told* you not to let him harass Jack!" She indignantly turned around and marched into the house to rescue Jack.

"I bet Jack's talking Larry's ear off," Bex said apologetically. "I'll go help your sister find them." She leaned over to give me a kiss. "It was wonderful to see you. Thanks for coming to talk to us about the book." She paused for a moment, then almost shyly admitted, "You know, I'm a little envious. I always wanted to be a professor—I took the GREs and everything."

"Really!" I exclaimed. "I was just thinking that you would have made an amazing professor."

"Oh, no," Bex said, waving me off modestly. "That's very kind of you, but it just wouldn't have been possible. All that course work, all that writing—"

"It would have been easy for you. You were always such a great student. And you're so good with languages—I mean, look at the way you just tossed off that Proust quotation!"

Bex shook her head. "No. I couldn't. I—I had to make a choice. When Jack and I got married and moved to LA, and then his career really took off, and then of course I got pregnant and, well, you know how it is—"

Bex was avoiding my eyes, and it suddenly hit me. She was embarrassed. She thought I was judging her.

"It's not too late—" I said, but Bex had already moved away.

From: info <info@ashgate.com>
To: Anne Corey <A.Corey@Fairfax.edu>
Subject: query
Date: September 26

Ashgate Publishing has been acquired by the Taylor & Francis Group, a subsidiary of Routledge. We have closed our academic books division.

Please go to http://www.routledge.com for further information on Publishing with Us, Getting Your Project Started, Current Authors, and Promoting Your Work.

From: Emily Young <E.Young@Fairfax.edu>
To: Anne Corey <A.Corey@Fairfax.edu>
Subject: rec letter
Date: September 27

Dear Dr. Corey,

I was wondering if I could stop by during your office hours to ask your advice about grad school. My

parents want me to go to med school (of course) but I'm not into it. I'm going to take the MCAT to get them off my back, but I also wanted to take the GRE and apply to PhD programs in English, too. If you'd be willing to write me a letter of recommendation, I'd be very grateful.

Love, Emily

From: Tiffany Allen <T.Allen@Fairfax.edu>
To: Anne Corey <A.Corey@Fairfax.edu>
Subject: Elizabeth Beckington Lindsey
Date: September 28

Dear Anne,

Thank you for your e-mail regarding Elizabeth Beckington Lindsey and her interest in building a relationship with Fairfax College. This is great news, and I've reached out to Mrs. Lindsey's assistant to set up a meeting with President Martinez and myself. I will keep you posted on any developments.
See you at our first training session next week!

Go Wolverines!
Tiff

From: Rick Chasen <rfc@richardforbeschasen.com>
To: Anne Corey <A.Corey@Fairfax.edu>
Subject: [none]
Date: September 28

I've left a little something for you in your department
mailbox.
//Rick

Richard Forbes Chasen

_____

Curator, Storyteller, Critic
richardforbeschasen.com

From: Isaac Jones <isaacjones@palgrave.com>
To: Anne Corey <A.Corey@Fairfax.edu>
Subject: book proposal
Date: September 29

Dear Anne Corey,

Many thanks for your book proposal. Before I request
a complete manuscript, I wanted to ask about
reframing the project in a few ways.
    —Why focus on just women writers? Male writers
have private lives, too, yes?
    Could you expand the focus of your book to include
novelists like Dickens, Thackeray, and Trollope?

It currently reads as rather old-fashioned feminist criticism.

—Why is Margaret Fuller included in the proposal? You have five British novelists and one American novelist. Perhaps take Fuller out, or add a few more Americans, like Emerson and Thoreau?

—You talk about all three Brontë sisters. Isn't this redundant? Could you perhaps limit yourself to discussion of just Emily? Or perhaps cut them out completely? In my opinion, the Brontës are rather overdone.

—The book chapters are currently organized by author. Could you reorganize the chapters to follow thematic lines, instead?

If you can make these changes, I would be happy to look at a revised book proposal.

Isaac Jones

_____

Senior Editor
Palgrave Macmillan

chapter seven

I ARRIVED ON CAMPUS EARLY Monday morning, hoping to fit in some writing before my scheduled office hours. The office was quiet, and I was relieved to see that Pam, our department secretary, hadn't yet arrived for the day.

Pam was in her forties, but she'd been working for the college since she was eighteen and was planning to retire the day she hit thirty years of service and her pension kicked in. I got the sense that her marriage, like her job, had become routine and unexciting, and she seemed to get a kick out of following the dating lives of the single women on campus, of which there were many. When she saw me, she'd shake me down for information: Was I dating anyone new? Was I on Match.com again? How about eHarmony or OkCupid? Did I know that Sarah from psychology was close to getting engaged?

I tried to be as vague as possible about my own life, because I always had the disconcerting feeling that the minute I left, she'd call one of the other secretaries and share the latest bit of gossip.

111

Part of me suspected there was a campus-wide betting pool, with each single woman carrying certain odds of getting married, getting laid, or getting dumped. As I passed her empty desk now, I grimaced at her collection of Beanie Babies, the baskets of fake roses, the Anne Geddes calendar of babies dressed up like fairies and sunflowers.

I stopped by the mailroom to run off some Xerox copies and check my box. Along with some advertisements and journals, I found a package from a distinguished literary publisher, and I opened it curiously, wondering if they were desk copies I'd ordered and forgotten about. Inside was a cream-colored card, with the publisher's distinctive imprint at the top. It read:

With the compliments of the Author

I pulled out three thick hard-covered volumes with moody black-and-white dust jackets portraying urban landscapes. Richard Chasen's three novels.

I gazed at the books reverentially. *Three books!* I thought. I couldn't even get *one* published. I opened up *Subterranean City*, now graced with a gold badge that read, "WINNER *of the* BOOKER PRIZE." On the back flap was an author photo of Rick, his head resting pensively on his hand, his hair rakishly swept back. The bio read, "Richard Forbes Chasen is an internationally acclaimed,

best-selling journalist and author. He has covered major news stories in Iraq, Afghanistan, Bosnia, and Sierra Leone, reporting on human rights abuses, war crimes, and genocide. He lives in New York City." I closed the book, thrilled to think I actually *knew* Rick—that he considered me, in fact, a friend.

My phone buzzed. A message from Larry.

"😩🔫" *Kill me now.*

The phone buzzed again.

"🙏" *Please.*

Uh-oh, I thought. Before I could text back, a third message came through.

"🔪✂️"

Oh shit, I thought. Larry was about to Lorena Bobbitt someone.

I headed down the hall to his office. The door was open, and I could see Steve parked in a chair, droning to Larry about something or other. From where I stood, the back of his neck looked like a piece of rare prime rib. I cleared my throat and gave the prearranged signal.

"Excuse me," I said. "I'm so sorry to interrupt!"

Steve slowly craned his head around.

"I need to talk to Larry," I said. "It's about a student."

Steve didn't move. Clearly he wasn't getting the hint.

"Uh, it's a FERPA issue," I said, lowering my voice meaningfully. FERPA was the Family

Educational Rights and Privacy Act, and the administration was always warning us not to violate it. Steve had no idea what FERPA was, but the acronym was scary-sounding enough to get him out of the chair.

"Oh," Steve said. "I should leave you two, then." He lumbered to the door, and I let him pass.

"Any news about your book?" he asked on his way out.

"Not yet," I said, smiling tightly.

Larry frantically motioned to me to close the door behind Steve.

"What took you so long to get here?" he groaned the minute the door latched shut.

"I came as fast as I could!"

"He. Would. Not. Stop. Talking." Larry collapsed into his chair beneath a row of framed posters he'd hung on the wall behind him: a photograph of Oscar Wilde with a green carnation in his lapel, a John Singer Sargent painting of Henry James, a poster of Keanu Reeves in *Speed*. Larry's gallery of gods.

"I got more bad news about my book this weekend," I said. "Ashgate went bankrupt, and Palgrave says they *might* look at my manuscript if I just, you know, rewrite the whole thing so it's a different book."

"Oh, honey," Larry said. "I'm sorry."

"It's almost October. If I don't land a contract

soon, I'm out on my ass." I felt myself getting choked up.

The only reason I even had a job at Fairfax was because of Larry. We'd become friends in graduate school, when I'd briefly dated Larry's younger brother, a lawyer and aspiring politician named Curtis. While things with Curtis hadn't worked out—I'd dumped him after he started talking about how I had all the attributes of a perfect political wife—my friendship with Larry had flourished. Larry kept me sane as I hopped from one temporary teaching position to another, despairing at ever finding a permanent job. When he'd called to tell me there was an opening at Fairfax, where he'd just been tenured, I remember screaming out loud. He'd been confident I'd get the job, even though I was sure the search committee would think I was stale goods after so many years on the job market. But in the end, he was right. The first-choice candidate turned down the offer to stay at his home institution. The second-choice candidate withdrew. I was the third choice.

That July, I remember, I packed up my U-Haul and left the East Coast, taking two weeks to cross the country before arriving in Southern California. Pulling off the 10 and driving down the quiet streets of Fairfax, I couldn't believe my good fortune. I was here for at least three years—longer, if I could manage to get my book

out—and the prospect of settling down filled me with something like joy. I pulled up in front of Larry's house, a gray-shingled cottage covered in overgrown honeysuckle and blowsy rose bushes. Larry was sitting on the porch, drinking a gin and tonic, an overweight tabby on his lap.

"Annie!" he shouted out. He took a look at my dusty trailer and sunburnt face and grimaced. "God, you look like an Okie."

"Shut up, Larry," I said. "You look like Little Edie."

"I've missed you," he laughed. "Welcome home."

"I don't want to leave," I told Larry now, trying not to cry. "I really like it here."

Larry stood up to give me a hug. "Sweetie," he said. "We were meant to be together. I have faith." He straightened me up and took me by the shoulders.

"Now for some tough love," he said. "YOU ARE NOT ALLOWED TO GIVE UP. Did I tell you that I was rejected by *twenty* publishers for my last book? I'm a *glutton* for rejection. I spent half my thirties in a state of despair. But as my wise old fourth grade teacher once said to me, 'Larry, winners never quit, and quitters never win.' You can have a pity party for exactly twenty-four hours, but then you have to pick yourself up and try again."

"But Larry," I wailed. "I can't take all the

rejection! I want to crawl into a hole and die."

"You gotta stick to your guns," Larry said. "No excuses! Remember: CLEAR EYES, FULL HEARTS, CAN'T LOSE!" Larry spun me around and pushed me out the door. "Now go send out some more proposals!" he yelled after me.

I TOOK MY LAPTOP to the patio outside the student center, sitting in a quiet corner underneath some trees. I contemplated doing some online retail therapy—didn't I deserve a new pair of shoes?—but just then my phone buzzed with a message from Larry.

"RU WRITING???" it read.

I sighed, put in my earbuds, and started editing my book proposal, pausing only to refill my coffee at the cafe. After working for an hour or so, I noticed a skirmish across the courtyard. I looked up and saw Rick walking across the quad in the distance, a television reporter beside him and a bevy of cameras and boom mikes bobbing around them. A crowd of students had gathered to watch, as if he were some visiting dignitary or movie star. I watched as some goofballs tried to bob into the frame with peace signs and others pulled out their phones to snap pictures. The interview continued for a minute longer, at which point Rick shook hands with the reporter and I saw him trying to escape into the student center, waving sheepishly as he left. Once inside, he

headed toward the patio, stopping to say hello to a few of our colleagues at another table before catching my eye and making his way over to me.

"Mind if I join you?" he asked, sounding slightly breathless.

"Not at all—please sit!" I said, smiling. Across the patio, I could see my colleagues glancing over at us and whispering.

"Thank you so much for your books," I said. "I just got them this morning—I'm really touched."

"Oh—don't mention it," Rick said, shrugging. "I'm sorry I didn't get a chance to sign them for you."

"That's OK. You look like you've been busy."

"Let's just say it's been interesting. I've been getting a lot of interview requests from the local media. It's like they've never met a writer before."

"You're a celebrity!" I said. "Usually no one pays attention to what we do here." It was true. The last time a television crew had appeared on campus, it was to cover a norovirus outbreak in one of the dormitories.

"You'll get a kick out of this—President Martinez sent me a welcome note along with a huge gift basket," Rick said. "I'm sure it killed him to do it."

"He's probably hoping you'll stay at Fairfax. It's great publicity for the school to have you here."

"If he wants to offer me a permanent job, I'll take it!"

Two pretty undergrads approached Rick, giggling and blushing. "Oh my God! It's Professor Chasen!" they tittered. "Can we get a selfie with you?"

"Of course," he said. "But please—call me Rick." The girls hopped around him like little sparrows as he stood up.

"I can take the picture," I said, taking the phone and waiting for them to arrange themselves, one on either side of Rick. He patiently humored them, even agreeing to sign a copy of his book for one of the girl's mothers.

After they left, I said, "You were so nice about that. How do you do it?"

"It's no big deal," he said, laughing easily. "Besides, I doubt either of them has actually read my damn book." From time to time, another student or colleague passed by to wish him welcome and congratulations, and Rick responded in his warm and easygoing way each time. It was hard not to be charmed.

"I'm so sorry about all the interruptions," he said after the latest well-wisher had left. He pulled a large stack of paper from his leather bag and, with a sigh, placed it on the bench beside him.

"What's all that?" I asked.

"I've got to read through almost a hundred

writing samples to pick the fifteen students who will be in my fiction workshop," he groaned. "It's daft! I've never had so many students apply to get into my class!"

"I told you—you're famous!"

I'd heard my students gossiping about Rick. All of them wanted to get into his workshop. He was a distinguished writer, sure, but more importantly, he was considered incredibly sexy and cool. He dressed in vintage jeans and rode a motorcycle, and he asked the students to call him Rick, not Professor Chasen. Already, he seemed to have a constant trail of female admirers following him across campus.

"I wish I were a little less famous," Rick said. "*You* try reading bloody awful student writing for hours on end."

"I already do," I laughed. "I read badly written essays all the time!"

"This is worse," Rick grumbled. "It's student fiction. I would much rather read a crap essay on Wordsworth than a crap short story."

"What's the difference?" I asked. "Bad writing is bad writing."

"No, it's not," Rick said. "Not when the bad writing is about dorm sex or getting high or being anorexic."

"But aren't you supposed to write what you know?" I asked. "Isn't that the first thing you learn in Creative Writing 101?"

"If that's the case, the students need to get more interesting lives," Rick said, sighing. "Or maybe I'm being an old sod. I guess I forget what it's like to be eighteen."

He jammed the stack of papers back into his bag. "Pop over for a drink tonight?"

"Sure," I said, trying not to sound too eager. He leaned over to give me a kiss on the cheek, his lips brushing tantalizingly close to mine. I watched him stride off, his bag slung casually over his shoulder. And I wasn't the only one watching. I saw several pairs of eyes follow him as he crossed the patio and duck out a side entrance. A few minutes later, a motorcycle started up and roared away.

THEY SAY TEACHERS SHOULDN'T play favorites with their students, just like parents shouldn't play favorites with their kids, but every teacher I knew had a pet, and Emily Young was definitely mine. She was tall, athletic, and long-limbed, and cocaptain of the tennis team. How she went to practice and traveled to matches while still doing all her homework and getting straight As, I had no idea. She never asked for an extension, never asked for special accommodations. Since switching her major to English in her sophomore year, she'd taken every class I offered.

I found her waiting for me outside of my

office, dressed in her tennis whites, a huge bag of rackets beside her.

"How are you doing?" I asked, giving her a hug and letting her into my office.

"I'm good," she said, smiling shyly. "I just submitted my application for Richard Chasen's fiction workshop this morning."

"How funny—I just bumped into him at the student center. You never told me you wrote fiction!"

"Oh, it's just something I do for fun," she said, looking embarrassed. "I probably won't get in, anyway, but I figured it's the opportunity of a lifetime and I might as well try."

"Don't say that! You shouldn't sell yourself short."

"I know," Emily laughed, "but there are people who are practically camped out in front of his office begging to be let in. I heard one girl sub-mitted an entire novel as her writing sample!"

Poor Rick, I thought.

"How's tennis going?" I asked as Emily set down her tennis bag in the corner. "Didn't you just have a big tournament?"

"Yeah—we were in San Diego last week and we leave tonight for Ojai." She lowered her voice slightly. "Did you know President Martinez sometimes practices with us?"

"Really?" I said. I had no idea Adam even played tennis.

"He's pretty good. He practices with this blond woman—she's an administrator, I think. It's sort of crazy, though, to see the *president* on the court serving and stuff."

"Yeah, that's crazy," I said, smiling weakly.

Pulling a folder out of her bag, Emily said, "So I was thinking of applying to grad school . . ."

"Don't do it," I said, cutting her off. "Don't ruin your life."

"What do you mean?" she asked, her mouth open in surprise. I could see her glancing at the framed diplomas on my office wall and the bookcases filled with books.

"You don't want this. Trust me." Even I was surprised at how vehement I sounded.

"But this is exactly what I want to do!" Emily protested. "I'd love to read and write about books for the rest of my life. I can't imagine anything better, honestly."

I softened in spite of myself. I couldn't help it—Emily reminded me so much of myself at that age.

"Grad school's a slog," I said to Emily, trying my best to temper her optimism. "You'll spend all your time in the library."

"I love the library."

"And there's zero job security. Take me, for example—I'm not even sure if I'll be employed next year."

"I'm willing to take my chances."

"And I don't know if you have a significant other, but you'll have to think of the future. Do you want to settle down? Do you want to have kids?"

"I'm not dating anyone, thank *God.*"

I paused, flummoxed. How could I explain to her that this—this office filled with books, this job at Fairfax, this life of the mind—had cost me more than I'd ever expected? I hadn't dated anyone in years, my student debt was the size of a mortgage, and my job could easily be eliminated at a moment's notice.

I thought back to my own adviser, Dr. Russell, and how she'd tried to warn me of the rigors of the profession. She'd never displayed any interest in where I was from, what extracurriculars I pursued, whether I was going home for the holidays or working retail over the summer. Our relationship was strictly academic. What was my contribution to the existing critical literature? When was I submitting my next draft? How was I refining my bibliography? My senior thesis was about women and courtship in nineteenth-century novels, and we'd never actually talked about women or courtship as they pertained to *me.* Instead, it was all abstract analysis about virtue and modesty and regulating women's desire.

So it was with something akin to shame that I finally admitted to her that I had a boyfriend and was considering my graduate school options

based on their geographic proximity to San Francisco, where Adam had decided to take a job in consulting to help pay off his student loans. Even now, I could remember the disgust that settled in the corners of her mouth.

"How old are you, Anne?" Dr. Russell asked me.

"Twenty-one."

"Ah. Twenty-one." She looked at me appraisingly. "When I was twenty-one, I was married and pregnant. By twenty-three, I was divorced with a toddler. Still, I managed to finish my undergraduate degree at a local college and then to enter graduate school at Yale, where all my classmates were single men who had maids clean their rooms and cook their meals so they could focus on their studies. Meanwhile, I was working two jobs and taking care of my son while still managing to graduate at the top of my class."

"That must have been hard," I said lamely.

"You have no idea. When I think of the advantages women of your generation have had—the opportunities, the privileges—I don't understand why you would throw all of it away. What do you want, Anne? Do you want to be married and have babies?"

"Ye-e-s, I think so?"

"You think so? With this boyfriend of yours?"

"Yes. We're planning to get married. It's serious."

"Serious? I see. Are you serious about your graduate studies? Are you serious about attaining your doctorate? Are you serious about the level of sacrifice it entails, the long hours in the library, the trips to archives and conferences, the job insecurity, the total personal investment you must make if this is your vocation?"

"Yes, I do know. My boyfriend—Adam, that's his name—he's very supportive."

"How supportive will he be if your job takes you to various remote college towns? Or if you must meet a deadline and can't have dinner ready on the table? Or what if you have a child? Will you drop out of your program and be content to be a housewife or a kindergarten teacher?" The way Professor Russell said "housewife" and "kindergarten teacher" made it clear how dimly she considered these positions.

"But you made it work," I said.

"I didn't have a husband to accommodate. I had a son, who had no choice but to go along with what I deemed best. Your boyfriend wants you to move wherever he ends up. Not because it's the best decision for *you* but because it's the best decision for *him.* What will you do if, heaven forbid, he breaks up with you? You'll be stuck in a graduate program that isn't a good fit, you will have wasted your time and your talents, you will have wasted *my* time and my investment in you."

"That's not— He wouldn't— You misunder-stand—"

"This boyfriend, you believe he loves you?" Professor Russell asked bluntly.

"Yes, absolutely."

"Then he should want what is best for you. I firmly believe you should go to Yale—it's where I was trained, and it's an excellent program, and you've been accepted, which is no small feat. This boyfriend, if he loves you, should allow you to fulfill your intellectual potential. If he doesn't want that for you, he is not the right man. California is not Mars. There are planes, you know. You can still visit one another."

Why *was* I following Adam around? I remember asking myself. Was I worried he'd cheat on me? Was I too weak to take care of myself? The thought of being separated from him by several thousand miles filled me with dread—but why?

Afterwards, when I'd told Adam about my conversation with Professor Russell, he quietly asked me, "*Do* you want to go to Yale?"

"It's a great program," I remember mumbling. "And the funding package is super generous, and Professor Russell thinks it would be a perfect fit. I don't want to disappoint her. But then again, who cares, right? It's my life, and I want to be with you."

"You *will* be with me. Don't worry about

that. But I don't want you to turn down a great opportunity just because we'd be long-distance. You're too smart—you can't waste your talents. I agree with Professor Russell. You should go to Yale, and we will make it work."

At the time, I'd nearly wept with relief. I wouldn't have to go against Professor Russell's wishes, and I wouldn't have to lose Adam. I could have a fulfilling professional life *and* a fulfilling personal life. I could have it all.

Looking at Emily now, I couldn't bear to tell her how thoroughly I'd been deceived. Dr. Russell had known, deep down, that I'd eventually have to choose. That a life of the mind required the denial of other desires.

"Don't end up like me," I wanted to tell Emily. Not because I didn't want her to be a professor, but because I didn't want her to end up alone.

THAT EVENING, I HEADED to Rick's house. He lived on the other side of campus, on a shaded eucalyptus-lined street where a lot of longtime professors lived. The home owner, a member of the philosophy department, was on sabbatical for the year and had been so delighted by the prospect of having a prize-winning writer as a tenant that he gave Rick a discount on the rent and even threw in the use of his car, a maroon Subaru Outback.

Rick had left the side gate unlocked for me,

and I pushed it open, stepping over some mossy bricks and a big hydrangea bush.

"I'm back here!" I heard him yell. The path led to a detached guesthouse with French doors open to let in the breeze. Rick was sitting on a lawn chair outside, smoking a cigarette and drinking a beer.

"Hey—thanks for coming," he said, looking me up and down appreciatively. I'd changed into a summery wrap dress and sandals and pulled my hair out of its usual ponytail.

"You look nice with your hair down," he said.

"Thanks," I said, blushing at the unexpected compliment.

He left to grab me a drink from inside the house. I looked around his backyard. It was lush and green, planted thickly with flowering bushes, a large jacaranda tree dropping its purple blossoms on the grass. A small wooden fountain burbled in one corner, surrounded by a couple of stone frogs and a bunny rabbit.

"Like the wishing well?" Rick asked when he reappeared, catching me looking at the fountain. "There's a gnome around here somewhere." He handed me a bottle of beer. "Here," he said. "Hope this is OK with you."

"This is great," I said. It felt good to drink a cold beer on the warm autumn evening.

Rick stretched out in his chair and ran his hand through his thick hair. He was wearing faded

jeans and an old T-shirt. "Hope you don't mind if I smoke," he said.

I shook my head.

"I'm trying to quit," Rick confessed. "I hadn't had a cigarette all summer, but then I saw the local bodega carried my favorite brand"—he pointed to a nearly empty box of Export As next to his ashtray—"and I caved. I figured after the week I had . . ." He trailed off and then ruefully laughed. "Listen to me trying to rationalize it. I don't even sound convincing to myself."

"How's it going with the student submissions?" I asked. "Have you figured out who you're letting in?"

"Christ, no," he groaned. "Each one's worse than the one before. I think I've gotten through half, maybe."

"My student Emily Young is trying to get into your workshop. Did you get to her application yet?"

"Emily Young, Emily Young—honestly, I don't remember. You like her, though? She's a good student?"

"The very best. She's a great kid."

"Then she's in!" Rick said, snapping his fingers. "Easiest decision ever. Thanks for helping me out."

"Wait, wait, wait," I laughed. "You aren't just going to let her in without reading her material, are you?"

"Why not? I trust your judgment. If you like her, she must be great. Case closed."

"Promise me you'll at least read her sample," I begged.

"If you insist," Rick sighed. "You really want to punish me, don't you? Making me read all these bloody awful stories."

"Come on," I teased him. "They can't be that bad. Give me an example."

"Well, there was the creative writing exercise some guy submitted, written from the point of view of a teenage girl. Except he couldn't stop describing his own breasts. He actually called them 'fun bags.' "

"Stop. You're kidding."

"You think that's bad? Then there were the various stories about someone—friend, relative, pet, you name it—dying of some disease or being hit by a car. One student described his granddad dying of 'amonia.' A-M-O-N-I-A. Amonia."

I shook my head. "You're just making this up," I said, laughing.

"I wish I were," Rick said. "And then there are the run-of-the-mill college hookup stories. Boy meets girl at frat party. They get drunk. They get high. They shag. They cheat on each other. They have a messy breakup. Et cetera. What a load of crap."

I nodded. I could only imagine what kind of wincingly bad story I would've written had I

been in Rick's creative writing class as an under-grad. His cigarette resting between his fingers, he looked totally at ease, his thick blond hair falling over his forehead and his brow furrowed as he regaled me with stories—everything from his meeting with the Dalai Lama ("a tiny old man, but with a great sense of humor"), to his account of visiting Mandela's jail cell on Robben Island, to harrowing tales of how he'd once gone undercover to chase a story during the Iraq War and had nearly been captured and beheaded.

"These kids today haven't experienced any-thing," he was saying. "They're coddled nitwits. What do they call them again? Millennials."

At the end of the evening, Rick offered to walk me back to my apartment, and I let him. He insisted on walking on the curbside ("I'm old-fashioned that way"), and I felt myself relaxing, enjoying Rick's courtesies and easy banter. He placed his hand on my waist as we climbed the porch steps to my house, and I felt a thrill at the steady pressure.

"I really enjoyed that," he said, pausing at the doorstep. "I hope I can take you out to dinner next time." Before I could answer, he leaned over and kissed me, and I caught a faint whiff of smoke and some cologne. I felt my chest seize up and a sudden rush of heat overcome me. His hand was still in my hair, and I didn't want him

to take it away. I didn't want him to leave, didn't want to spend the evening alone in my desolate apartment. I wanted him to kiss me again.

"Do you want to come in?" I stammered, pushing the door open.

"I'd been wondering when you'd ask," he said.

chapter eight

"WHERE ARE YOU GOING?" Rick asked, still lying in bed. It was Saturday morning, and I'd spent the night at Rick's place. He was stretched out on the sheets, one arm behind his head, smoking a cigarette. I paused to enjoy the view, and he winked at me flirtatiously.

"I'm supposed to meet my sister and her family in half an hour," I said. "We're taking my dad to the Fall Fest. Want to come?" I looked in the mirror and tried to fix my hair, wondering if I had time to shower and change my clothes when I got home.

"I'll pass," Rick said, yawning lazily. "I don't do kids or animals."

I leaned over to kiss him good-bye, and he pulled me in playfully. "Call me later," he whispered into my ear.

I jogged home, feeling sheepish in my rumpled clothes. Rick and I had been together for less than a week, and I still felt secretly embarrassed to be hooking up with a colleague. I was glad it was the weekend and that the chance of bumping into another professor or—God forbid—a student

was practically nil. As I rounded the corner to my place, I made sure to give the President's House a generous berth, keeping my head lowered and my hair partially covering my face. From the corner of my eye, I noticed the house was being painted, with some scaffolding covering one wing. An American flag hung from the porch, and the flower beds had been refreshed with new plantings. In the driveway, obscured by a hedge, I could make out the top of two people's heads. Without thinking, I crouched behind a tree.

This is ridiculous, I thought. There was no other route to my apartment, which was on a cul-de-sac, and I'd have to walk past the mansion without having a panic attack. I straightened myself up and emerged from behind the tree. The heads were bobbing out of sight, and I heard the sound of a door open and close.

Phew, I thought, and continued on my way, glancing furtively at the driveway as I passed by. There was a white BMW convertible parked there, with a rhinestone-studded license plate frame that spelled out "Kappa Kappa Gamma." I stared at it incredulously. Tiffany.

Tiffany was one of Pam's favorite people to gossip about. She was always dating someone, and that someone was always tall, handsome, and athletic. Why she hadn't settled down was the source of Pam's unending curiosity. "She's a

man-eater!" I'd hear Pam tell one of her friends on the phone. "She just loves all the attention." Someone had told me Tiffany had been married once before, to a professional surfer, and they'd traveled the world, living in places like Hawaii and Australia and Costa Rica. At some point, the two had parted ways, maybe because Tiffany was tired of living in surf shacks and fishing villages. "I'm totally a Cali girl," Tiffany liked to say. She lived in Santa Monica, by the beach, but kept a small place in Fairfax, where she stayed during the week.

What was Tiffany doing at the president's mansion, and on a Saturday, no less? Maybe they were having a breakfast meeting? Or maybe they were heading off to play some tennis? I scolded myself for even wondering. It was none of my business, anyway.

I had just arrived at my place and fed Jellyby when Lauren pulled up in her black SUV and honked.

"You're early!" I said, dismayed.

"Did you just wake up?" Lauren yelled from the car.

"Um, I overslept."

"You look like it," Lauren said, wrinkling her nose. "Hurry up—jump in."

I peeked into the car and saw my father in the back seat, staring vacantly out the window as Lauren's three kids quarreled beside him. Brett,

Lauren's husband, was in the driver's seat, trying to broker peace.

"Hayes ruined it," Tate wailed, holding up a torn piece of construction paper covered in glitter.

"I did not, dumbass," Hayes said, trying to punch Tate in the arm but accidentally grazing Archer, the oldest. With a yelp, Archer lunged at Hayes and yanked a fistful of his hair.

"STOP IT RIGHT NOW," Brett bellowed. "You doofuses better behave or I will KILL you. NOW SAY HELLO TO YOUR AUNT."

All three kids sulkily settled down and mumbled hello as I climbed into the car, wedging myself between Tate and Hayes. The car was huge, with three rows of seats and a built-in DVD player. Lauren switched on a show for Hayes, then handed Tate and Archer their own individual iPads as Brett pulled out of the driveway and floored it through the streets of Fairfax.

"You smell like smoke," Hayes said, sniffing the air conspicuously.

"Cigarettes cause cancer, you know," Archer said.

"Since when do you smoke?" Lauren asked, turning around.

"I don't!" I said. "I was, um, at a party last night. I, uh, didn't have a chance to take a shower this morning."

"That better just be cigarette smoke I smell,"

Brett joked, sucking on an imaginary joint while my sister looked on disapprovingly. He chuckled loudly and then reached over the back of his seat to give me a fist bump. "Just kidding, Prof. I know you're an upstanding citizen."

Brett and Lauren had met in business school a decade earlier, and he now worked for some large hedge fund in Irvine. He was built like a refrigerator, with a thick neck and huge shoulders, looking like the rugby player he once was. The older he got, the more hulking he became, with all the weight seeming to go directly to his upper body. I rarely saw him because he was always working, though he did always make time to attend his kids' Little League games, screaming profanities from the bleachers while taking business calls.

"How are you doing, Dad?" I asked, glancing over my shoulder.

"I think someone's stealing the Q-tips from my bathroom," he announced.

"He's been hung up on these Q-tips since we passed Monterey Park," Lauren said, shooting me a look.

"Q-tips? Why would anyone want your Q-tips?" I asked.

"How should I know? I'm also missing my blue towel."

"Augh, can we get off the blue towel already?" my sister groaned.

"Are you sure it's not being washed?" I asked.

"No, it's gone. Someone took it."

"Dad," Lauren interrupted. "Why would anyone want your ratty old towel?"

"It's a very nice towel, Lauren," my dad said testily.

"Wait, what's *that?*" Lauren asked, pointing to a scabby purple bruise on my dad's forearm. "How'd you get that?"

"I don't know. I must've bumped into something in the middle of the night. Damn prostate keeps me up."

"Don't *touch* it, Dad!" Lauren yelled. "You're just going to make it worse!"

"I wan' diff'ent show," Tate suddenly cried, waving his iPad around.

"What's wrong with the show you're watching?" Brett asked.

"It's *bo-wing,*" Tate pouted. "I wan' surprise eggs."

"Tough luck, kid," Brett said. "You get what you get and you don't get upset."

"Diff'ent show!" Tate yelled, louder this time.

"Suck it up, Tate," Brett growled.

"Daddy—you are *bad man.* You are *bo-wing.*"

"I think you need to check the dictionary, kid. That's not what 'boring' means."

"You guys let the kids watch too much TV," my dad interjected. "I just watched something on

Dateline. It's not good for their brain development."

"*Not now,* Dad," Lauren said. She turned to Tate. "Now, honey," she said, using a singsongy voice. "I *know* you want to watch a different show. You must be very *frustrated.* I know it must feel very *irritating.*"

I looked at Lauren like she was crazy.

"It's in a book I read," Lauren whispered. "You're supposed to acknowledge their feelings. They just want to be heard."

"I don't think it's working," I said as Tate started screaming and flung his iPad on the floor.

"Tater-Tot," Lauren said, turning around and grabbing his flailing leg. "You have a choice. We can pull over and put you in Stop and Think, or you can finish watching your show. It's up to you. Let's make good choices, OK?"

"Are we there yet?" my dad asked.

"I'm feeling carsick," Archer said.

"I have to pee," Hayes said.

"Fuck me," Brett muttered under his breath.

Lauren picked up the iPad and switched to a new show. "OK, here. Now shut up," she said, handing it to Tate. Tate immediately stopped crying, grabbed the iPad, and zoned out.

IN PREVIOUS YEARS, THE Fall Fest had been a half-hearted affair, with a handful of sororities

and fraternities participating as part of their community service requirement but scant attendance by local residents. This year, I was surprised by how packed the place was, with people from miles around, it seemed, converging for a day of games, live music, and performances. Every student group on campus seemed to have sponsored a booth—the International Students Organization, the Black Students Union, the Cooking Club, the LGBTQ Alliance. The Hawaiian Club was holding a traditional luau pig roast, digging a pit in a corner of the field and smoking an entire pig under a layer of banana leaves. Wisps of smoke escaped enticingly from the underground oven.

While Brett and I helped my dad out of the car, Lauren and the boys made a beeline for the bathroom. "Meet us by the Ferris wheel!" she yelled over her shoulder.

Brett bought tickets, and we headed toward the rides, passing an outdoor stage where student performances were taking place. A Mexican folk dance group had just left the platform and an MC was at the mike. "Listen up!" he yelled. "Help us raise money for our local Boys and Girls Club! Don't miss your chance to take a shot at dunking President Martinez! It's all happening *right now!*"

Some kids sprinted past us, joining a raucous crowd that had gathered around the dunk tank.

From where we stood at the back, we could see Adam, dressed in a Fairfax T-shirt and swim trunks, climb into the cage and begin egging the kids on, pretending to be scared when a ball got a little too close, raising his arms in triumph when he escaped dunking.

"You can't dunk me, Jasmine!" Adam teased a little girl who stepped up to the podium, a ball clutched in her tiny fist.

"Wanna bet?" she shouted back, winding up for her pitch. Her first ball went wide and landed in the grass, and the crowd gave a disappointed groan. Her second ball glanced against the tank and rolled away into some bushes. But the third ball was a direct hit, smacking the target with a satisfying clang and releasing the platform where Adam was sitting. He hit the water with a tremendous splash, and the crowd went crazy, kids rushing up to watch Adam bob to the surface, shaking the water from his hair and eyes. Jasmine was jumping up and down and shrieking, and Adam gave her an affectionate high five as he climbed out of the tank.

"You got me," he said, reaching for a towel and wiping his face. "You've got a deadly aim. I hope you come to Fairfax one day and pitch for our softball team."

Jasmine's face lit up, and Adam gave her a big hug.

"That kid has a good arm," Brett observed.

"How long are we going to be standing here?" my dad asked. "I'm hungry."

By the time we got to the Ferris wheel, the kids were eating cotton candy and popcorn and arguing over which ride to go on first.

"I wanna ride ponies!" Tate yelled.

"Bounce house!" yelled Hayes.

"Ferris wheel!" yelled Archer.

"Should we divide and conquer?" Lauren suggested.

"I'll do the Ferris wheel with Archer," Brett said.

"Dad and I'll take Hayes to the bounce house," Lauren said. "I can't stand the smell of horses."

"I guess that means you and I are doing the ponies," I said to Tate, who immediately seized my arm and started to pull me toward the pony corral.

The line for the pony rides snaked halfway around the perimeter, and Tate spent the next thirty minutes hanging off the fence and whining, "When is it gonna be *myyyyyyyyy* turn?"

"Which one do you want to ride?" I asked, trying to distract him by pointing to the different-colored ponies plodding around the dirt track. "I like the white one with brown spots."

"NO!" Tate said. "I want the BIG ONE."

"Which one is that?"

"*THAT* one," Tate said, pointing to a mangy-looking gray pony with a half-bitten ear. While

we watched, the pony took a dump, leaving a trail of dung pies in its wake. "Ewwwwwwww!!!!" Tate screamed delightedly. "The pony did a big POOP!"

When we finally got to the front of the line, Tate was given a docile brown pony with a star on its forehead. "This one's good with the little ones," the pony's handler told us, but Tate was despondent. "I want the POOPING PONY!" he wailed. He threw himself on the dirt-and-straw-covered ground. I winced.

"He's three," I apologized. "Is there any chance we can get that gray pony? Otherwise, he's going to be on that ground for a while."

"Sure," the handler said, looking at Tate with a pained smile. "Hey, kid," he said to Tate. "The ground's kinda nasty. You might want to get up."

"Sorry, sorry," I said, sheepishly rolling Tate over to one side and letting the people behind us cut us in line.

The gray pony finally trundled in, looking bored and unimpressed as Tate bounced up from the ground, covered in dust and straw, and clambered into the saddle. I watched them head off, a handler guiding the pony on a lead and Tate bouncing excitedly up and down, yelling, "Giddyup!!" They did three slow revolutions of the track, and I waved each time he passed by. He stuck his tongue out each time.

As Tate headed in after the final circuit, I steeled myself for another tantrum. He'd insist on staying on the pony, I thought. He wouldn't relinquish the pooping pony to the next child in line. He'd fling himself off the horse and onto the ground and maybe break a bone in the process.

Instead, Tate happily gave up his pony without complaint. And rather than flinging himself on the ground, he flung himself onto my head, wrapping his stout legs around my neck and using my hair as reins.

"Go, horsey!" he screeched as I stumbled out of the corral and tried to make my way to an open space.

"You're choking me, Tate," I said, trying to pry his legs from around my neck. Tate only pinned them tighter against my throat and then clapped his grimy fingers over my eyes.

"Seriously, Tate!" I said, getting frantic. "This isn't funny! I can't see!"

From behind me, I could hear Brett's voice. "Hey, knucklehead!" he yelled. "Get off your aunt *right now*." But Tate ignored him, cackling loudly and yanking my hair. "Go faster, horsey!" he shouted, jabbing his heels against my rib cage.

"I'm SERIOUS, Tate!" Brett yelled. "YOU LISTEN TO ME!!"

I felt someone pull Tate off of me. "Stop!" I heard Tate shriek, his arms and legs pinwheeling

wildly through the air. I was sweaty and covered with brown streaks of dirt, and my throat felt tight and sore.

"Thank *God,*" I sighed, turning to thank Brett. "I thought I was going to suffocate."

But it wasn't Brett standing there. It was Adam, looking at me amusedly as he kept Tate from trying to lunge at me. He was dressed in a black sport coat with a crisp shirt and a red tie, a small Fairfax College pin on his coat lapel.

Brett ran up, Archer in tow, and grabbed Tate by the elbow. "You're busted, kid," he bellowed. To Adam, he said, "Thanks, man. I owe you."

"Not at all," Adam said. "I could tell Anne needed some help." I stood there, trying to clean Tate's shoe prints from my day-old shirt and smooth my hair. *I must look like a wreck,* I thought.

"You guys know each other?" Brett asked.

Just then, Lauren appeared with my father and Hayes. She looked confused and then surprised when she recognized Adam standing with us. "What's going on?" she asked. "Did I miss something?"

"This guy just saved your sister from being choked to death by your son," Brett said. "We should buy him a beer."

"Hi, Lauren," Adam said, extending his hand. "Nice to see you again."

"Adam," Lauren said, her voice tinny and

falsely cheerful. "How funny to bump into you!" She looked him up and down in a not very subtle way. "Thank you *so much* for coming to the rescue," she said, gathering her kids to her. "This is my husband, Brett, and my three sons— Archer, Hayes, and Tate, who I take it you've met already."

I couldn't believe how ingratiating Lauren was being. The last time they'd met, Lauren had virtually interrogated Adam: Where was he from? What did his parents do? What was he planning to do next year? How was he planning to make a living doing that? When I'd told her we were engaged, she'd blown up at me, calling me naive and "even dumber" than she'd realized. Adam was a loser, she'd declared, with crappy career prospects and even crappier taste in rings (she'd taken one look at my cameo and sniffed, "You're kidding. No diamond?"). Now, though, Lauren was ladling on the charm, smiling with all her teeth and practically falling over herself to introduce Adam to everyone.

"Oh, and of *course* you must remember my father, Jerry," she simpered, gesturing to my father.

"Mr. Corey?" Adam said, shaking my dad's hand. "It's been a long time. Welcome to Fairfax."

"What was your name again?" my father asked, looking at Adam blankly.

"Adam Martinez."

"Huh," he said. It was clear he had no memory of ever having met Adam before.

"Adam and I went to college together," I lamely explained to Brett. "He's the new president of Fairfax College."

"Wait a minute—didn't I just see you get dunked?" Brett said. "That was epic!"

Adam laughed. "Yeah, that was me. I went and got dried off."

"So president, huh?" Brett said. "Think you can get my kids into Fairfax in another ten years? I promise the two older ones aren't as bad as *this* little monster." He tipped his head toward Tate, who was now tearing fistfuls of grass from the ground and trying to pelt his brothers with them.

"Adam!" someone called out. I looked up and saw Tiffany bouncing across the grass toward us, wearing a gingham sundress and espadrilles, her hair in a high ponytail. A black-and-white shepherd mix was bounding beside her, snapping playfully at the ribbons tied around her ankles.

"Stop it, Charlie!" she said sternly.

Adam whistled, and Charlie immediately left Tiffany and trotted to Adam's side.

"Good boy, Charlie," Adam said, giving his dog an affectionate pet. "I'm sorry—he's a little hyper. But he's great with kids."

"Is he hypergenital?" Tate asked Adam.

149

"*What* did you say?" Lauren asked, looking mortified.

"Is he hypergenital? Like our neighbor's dog?"

"You mean *hypoallergenic,* dude," Brett said.

"Here, Tate," Adam said, kneeling beside Tate and pulling a chew toy out of his pocket. "Why don't you throw this around for Charlie to chase?" Tate and his brothers took off, tossing the chew toy to each other like a football as Charlie ran around in exuberant circles.

While Tiffany introduced herself to my family, I turned to Adam. "Thank you so much for your help," I said quietly. "Tate can be sort of a handful."

"It was the least I could do. How's your father adjusting to his move to Fairfax?" he asked, glancing at my father.

I sighed. "He's not happy about it. I'm hoping he'll settle in soon. I try to visit him as often as I can."

Behind us, I could hear Lauren yelling at my dad. "I *told* you to stop picking at your scab! What did I tell you? Didn't I *say* it was going to bleed?"

Adam was smiling at me sympathetically. Poor Anne, he must have been thinking, covered in dirt and dried horse manure and bits of hay, tagging along with her judgy sister, her three awful nephews, and her senile dad.

"Hey, Adam! Let's go get some lemonade!"

Tiffany interrupted, grabbing his hand. "I'm *dying* of thirst."

"Oh, don't let us keep you," Lauren chirped. She was still smiling too hard at Adam. "*So* good to bump into you. I'm really impressed! You're really something—" I could hear the unspoken "now" hanging in the air and wanted to strangle her. Even when she was on her best behavior, she couldn't help but be condescending.

I watched as Adam and Tiffany headed off to the concession stands, Tiffany's arm curled around Adam's waist, her ponytail swinging jauntily, Charlie at their heels.

"Seems like a cool guy," Brett said to Lauren.

"I always knew he'd do great things," she replied. "Anne should've never broken up with him. I could just tell he was going places."

I felt an ugly stab of jealousy as Adam and Tiffany disappeared into the crowd. That could have been us, I thought, happily coupled, with a dog and maybe even some kids by now. Why had I given all that up? What had I been thinking?

Before I could drown under a wave of what ifs, I shook myself angrily.

No, I said to myself. *I have a career. A book manuscript. Students who count on me. I am not a failure. I am not a failure!*

With a sigh, I turned and followed my sister back to the car.

From: <Jack_LindseyTiger@gmail.com>
To: Anne Corey <A.Corey@Fairfax.edu>
Subject: hey
Date: September 29

hey ann, bex told me ur a professor. I just wraped a film called jane vampire. i know u guys read it in ur book club. im playing rochester, hes based on a character in a book called jane eyre, have u heard of it? im about to start doing press and wanted to ask u questions about my character and backstory, in case i get questions i want to be prepared. the roles a stretch for me, i dont usually do period stuff, but i hope to make the jump from tv and think this will put me in good position for a franchise. i can get u a postproduction consultant credit, let me know if ur interested. jack

From: Lawrence Ettinger <L.Ettinger@Fairfax.edu>
To: Anne Corey <A.Corey@Fairfax.edu>

SQUEEEE!!!! His messages are adorbs! It's like reading an e. e. cummings poem!

On September 29, Anne Corey <A.Corey@Fairfax.edu> wrote:

I think he's illiterate.

---------- Forwarded message ----------
From: <Jack_LindseyTiger@gmail.com>
To: Anne Corey <A.Corey@Fairfax.edu>
Subject: hey
Date: September 29

(. . .)

From: Library Circulation Desk
<circulation@Fairfax.edu>
To: Anne Corey <A.Corey@Fairfax.edu>
Subject: URGENT: Library Items (3rd Overdue
Notice)
Date: October 3

Dear Anne Corey,

The following Library materials are overdue.
Please return them as soon as possible to
avoid accruing more late fees. You currently owe
$691.20.
   Your borrowing privileges will be suspended if you
do not settle your account. If you have any questions
or would like to work out a payment plan, please
contact us at—.
   You can check your online account by visiting our
website at: http://www.Fairfax.edu/ChandlerLibrary/
AccountInfo.

This is a system generated e-mail.
Please do not reply directly to this e-mail.

Total Overdue Items: 98
Due Date: September 1

(. . .)

From: <Jack_LindseyTiger@gmail.com>
To: Anne Corey <A.Corey@Fairfax.edu>
Subject: Re: hey
Date: October 4

hey ann, thanks for agreeing to help out, i had a question that's been bugging me. Why do they say jane vampire takes place in "—, north –shire, 18—" why don't they tell u the exact place + date. is this a typo. j-dawg

From: Ursula Burton, Acquisitions Editor
<UABurton@oup.com>
To: Anne Corey <A.Corey@Fairfax.edu>
Subject: Manuscript request
Date: October 5

Dear Professor Corey,

We would be interested in seeing a complete manuscript of *Ivory Tower: Nineteenth-Century Women Writers and the Literary Imagination.* You can e-mail the manuscript to this address (MS Word only), and we will send it out for review as soon as possible. We should receive two reader's reports by December. If you haven't heard from us by then, please e-mail me.

All best,
Ursula Burton

_____
Acquisitions Editor
Oxford University Press
Academic Division

chapter nine

D IDN'T I TELL YOU Oxford would come through?" Rick said, playfully nuzzling my neck.

"Don't jinx it!" I said. "I still have to wait for the reader's reports. If they're negative, I might have to kill myself."

"Oh, Anne, don't fret so much," Rick said, massaging my shoulders. "What if I told you that the editor at Oxford is a good friend of mine?"

"Ursula Burton? You *know* her?"

"We dated briefly at university. In fact, to be honest, I think she may still fancy me. I told her that she must absolutely request your manuscript, that it was a terrific piece of scholarship. She was very intrigued."

I blushed. "But you haven't even read my book!"

"Doesn't matter. I already know you're brilliant. And beautiful, too." He nibbled my ear.

Rick and I were sprawled on a blanket at the local botanical gardens, playing hooky from a department meeting. The weather had

turned slightly cool—not cold, by any means, but brisk enough for a sweater or light jacket. We'd ridden on Rick's motorcycle, an experience that left me simultaneously enthralled and exhausted. I couldn't believe I'd done something so reckless—I was the kind of person who got anxious just getting on a bicycle. Yet Rick made it seem a great adventure, the two of us hurtling through life while everyone else was just dully shuffling along.

I reached into my bag and pulled out a stack of papers.

"Put those away," Rick said, reaching for my hand. "Let's play instead."

"I've got to finish grading these," I apologized. "I promised to hand them back two weeks ago!"

Leaning over, Rick picked one of the papers from the pile and began to read aloud:

> Since the beginning of time, many people have dealt with the immortal question of love. According to Webster's English Dictionary, "to persuade" means "to cause someone to do something by asking, arguing, or giving reasons." The famous authoress Jane Austen wrote her magnificent book *Persuasion* in 1817. In it, she talks about the everlasting mystery that is love.

"My goodness," Rick mused. "It's got the trifecta: an opening that begins with 'Since the beginning of time,' a Webster's Dictionary definition, and an assortment of empty clichés and editorializing. Not a very *persuasive* essay, if I do say so myself."

"That's one of the better ones," I said. "Only ten more to go."

"Just do a bullshit sandwich. One sentence about how it's clear Johnny worked very hard on this paper, two sentences about everything that's wrong, then one sentence saying 'Good effort!' "

I laughed, swatting Rick's hand away as he tried to grab the paper from my hand. He sighed and pretended to pout.

"You know, I have something terrible to confess," he said.

"What is it?"

"I've never really cared for Jane Austen."

"What?" I said. "How could you say that?"

"It's true. I mean, how many guys do you know who actually like reading her?"

"Larry adores her."

Rick gave me a look. "She's pretty much writing oldfashioned chick lit," Rick said.

"And what's so wrong with that?" I asked.

"Come on, Anne—it's a bunch of women yakking about frivolous stuff like eligible men and parties. Honestly, I've never been able to finish one of her books. There's something about

her that rubs me the wrong way, something I don't trust—"

"Shut up!" I said, punching him in the arm. "I'm personally offended! This might actually be a deal breaker, you know."

"OK, I take it back," Rick said, grinning. He pushed the papers away, moving in for a kiss. "Now forget about Austen. This is much more interesting."

PAM WAS SITTING AT her desk when I returned to the office, putting together a department mailing while talking loudly on the phone.

"I just knew she had her eye on him," she was saying. "Tiffany's practically moved into the President's House, from what I hear. I bet they're engaged by Christmas. A handsome guy like him and a pretty gal like her? It's too perfect! Do you think she'll take his name? Tiffany Martinez has a nice ring to it."

Spying me trying to edge past her desk, she cupped her hand over the phone receiver and hollered, "Anne! Anne, come over here!"

"Yes, Pam?" I said. "Is it important? I'm kind of in a hurry . . ."

"I didn't see you at the department meeting this morning—" she said.

"Oh, yeah—um, I had a doctor's appointment I couldn't reschedule. Sorry about that."

"I wanted to ask you—my friend in HR says

she saw you chatting with Richard Chasen at the student union last week. Is something up? He's c-u-t-e! He's got that David Beckham kinda look, don't you think? The undergrads won't stop talking about him. They're in here all the time, asking when his office hours are, looking all googly-eyed . . ."

"Nothing's going on," I said. "We're friends. That's it."

"Are you sure? You promise to tell me if something changes?"

"Sure," I said, while thinking, *HELL NO.*

"By the way," Pam said before uncupping her phone. "You look great! Did you lose weight or something?"

I hurried past Steve's office and darted into Larry's office, closing the door behind me.

"So where were *you* this morning?" Larry asked, arms folded reproachfully. "You missed a scintillating department meeting. Steve started reciting *The Canterbury Tales* in Middle English."

"Sorry I missed it," I said guiltily. "Rick and I ditched and went to the park."

"You two crazy kids. Better keep it on the DL—Pam's starting to get suspicious."

"I know. She practically jumped me on my way in." I sidled up to Larry and whisper-screamed, "Oxford requested my full manuscript this morning!"

"Wait, what?! *Oxford University Press?*"

"I got the e-mail this morning—Rick knows the editor there, and he put in a good word for me. You gotta cross your fingers that the reader's reports are positive."

"OMG, Anne!" Larry said, doing a happy dance with me. "This is *amazing* news! I'll cross my fingers *and* toes."

After a celebratory whirl, Larry bumped my hip and winked at me mischievously. "Soooooooo, I have some big news, too," he said. "But it's a secret."

"A secret?" I yelled.

"Shhhhhh!!!! I will literally have to kill you and stuff you under the floorboards if you breathe a word to anyone."

"What is it? Tell me!"

"It's about Jack Lindsey." Larry began to beam. "We've been e-mailing each other."

"Oh God," I groaned. "Did he ask you to be a historical consultant, too?"

"No! Even better—we're kind of dating!"

"Wait, *what?* What do you mean 'kind of'? He's married! And straight!"

"*Is* he?"

"*Isn't* he?"

"He told me he and Bex have an open relationship," Larry said. "They apparently haven't slept together since their kid was born." He couldn't stop smiling. "You should see your face. Now

don't go running off to TMZ or anything. It's a secret."

I shook my head in disbelief. "How long have you been seeing him?"

"Oh, just a few weeks. I've been sneaking down to LA and meeting him at random dive bars and hotels."

"So is *that* where you've been going on weekends?"

Larry nodded impishly. "It's all very exciting," he said. "In fact, I think we might meet up later this week." He pulled a cheap plastic flip phone from his pocket and started scrolling through his text messages.

"Wait, what's that?" I asked. "Is that a burner phone? What is this, *The Wire*?"

"Jack gave it to me, just in case, you know, someone tries to tap his phone." He paused to read a message. "Hey—what are you doing Friday?" he asked me.

"I'll be at the Huntington," I said. "One more set of Brontë letters to read, then I'm sending the full manuscript off to Oxford."

"Can I hitch a ride with you?"

"Sure," I said. "Why? Are you meeting Jack at the Huntington?"

"No, not exactly—I was wondering if I could drop you off at the library and then borrow your car for the day. I'll pick you up whenever you're ready."

"Wait—why don't we just take your car then?"

"Jack's paranoid," Larry sighed. "He doesn't want the paps to be able to trace my plates. He specifically asked that I borrow someone else's car, or even get a rental."

"Oh, great—so now the paps are gonna think *I'm* the one having an affair with Jack Lindsey?"

"You *wish.*"

"The things I do for you," I said, laughing and heading to the door.

"Hey—where are you going?" Larry asked. "I still have more to tell you about Jack!"

"Sorry, Lar. I've got to run—I've got a fundraising meeting with Tiffany, then I have to somehow get ninety-eight books back to the library *and* sweet-talk them into waiving my late fees. Wish me luck."

"Aw, poor baby," Larry said. "Good luck!"

TIFFANY HAD RESERVED A large conference room for the training session, placing shiny red Fairfax binders and Fairfax-branded bottles of water at each seat. She gave me a thumbs-up as I came in and slid into a seat toward the back. I tuned out as she launched into a slick slide-show presentation, then walked us through our binders full of numbers and factoids, renderings of prospective buildings, and a thick booklet of phone numbers. I was in charge of supervising a phone bank, heading a team of volunteers who

would cold-call alums and parents to wheedle for donations. Tiffany had included a sample script to follow.

1. Hello! May I please speak to_____?
2. This is_____from the Thrive! Fairfax Capital Campaign! I am an alum/ professor/friend of Fairfax College. Is this a convenient time to talk? I promise it will only take a few minutes.
3. [If alum has given before:] Thank you for your past support of Fairfax College. We appreciate your generosity.
4. We're calling alumni tonight to speak to them about our exciting new capital campaign to help support financial aid and fund library and dormitory renovations. I know Fairfax College means a lot to you, just as it means a lot to me. [Include personal story about what Fairfax means to you.]
5. Would you consider a gift of $_____ to support the Thrive! Capital Campaign and future generations of Fairfax students?

I blanched. I was terrible at asking for money. "I can't do this," I texted Larry. "Can I quit?"

A few seconds later, Larry texted back: "Lean in, bitch!"

"Remember, it's not the amount that counts," Tiffany was yelling. "We just want sky-high

participation numbers! Are you all with me???"

There were a few feeble yeahs.

"I can't HEAARRRR you!!!" Tiffany theatrically cupped one of her ears. "I said, ARE YOU ALL WITH ME???"

"Yeah!" a few more people joined in.

"Go Wolverines!" Tiffany screamed, doing a fist pump with her right hand.

Adam had come in during Tiffany's mini pep rally and was standing to one side, watching her jump up and down. He now whispered something in her ear and then took the microphone from her.

"I just wanted to thank all of you personally for volunteering in our campaign," he said. "Asking people for money is one of the hardest parts of my job, but I also know how important it is. I was a scholarship kid, and I wouldn't have been able to attend college if it weren't for people like you—alums, staff, faculty—pitching in their time and money. With the money we raise, we can help attract and retain those who wouldn't necessarily consider Fairfax a possibility. So thank you on behalf of the college but also on behalf of our future students."

His speech reminded me why Adam had initially dropped out of Princeton. The story didn't appear in any of his official PR materials, but he'd confided in me that summer we'd exchanged letters. Adam had been working in

the dining room one evening, scraping food off plates coming down the conveyor belt, a job that was both messy and relentless and left him, at the end of his shift, "smelling like steamed garbage." His friends had long since quit their dining hall jobs for easier gigs working in the library or doing office work for departments, but the dish room paid the best and Adam needed the money. He was in the middle of his shift, stacking dirty plates into plastic racks, when some jerks from his hall spied him through the kitchen door. Smirking, they took syrup jugs and ketchup bottles from the commissary and poured the contents into cereal bowls and dishes, watching as the plates made their way down the belt to Adam. As he tried to dump the contents into a garbage can, spattering himself in the process, the guys burst out laughing. "I requested a leave of absence soon after," he'd written to me.

There was a ripple of applause, and I watched Adam start circulating around the room, shaking people's hands. Watching him now, I wondered what he was thinking. Did he even remember telling me the story?

"Hi, Anne," Adam said when he got to my seat. "Listen, thanks for helping out. I really appreciate it."

"It's a great cause," I said. "Your personal anecdote was really moving."

"It's all true. I often think of how different things would have been if I hadn't gone to college."

"You don't regret it at all? I know how hard it was, at times . . ."

Adam shook his head emphatically. "No, going back and finishing was the best decision I ever made. For lots of reasons."

His words hung in the air. I wanted to reach over and touch his hand, let him know I understood because I'd been there. Adam, too, seemed to recognize the strange intimacy of the moment. His hand went to his mouth for a second, as if he were wondering whether to say more. I caught his eye, and he smiled slightly.

"What about you?" he asked. "Do you have regrets?"

"Me?" I asked, a little taken aback. "I— Well, every month, when I see I have another thirty-odd years of student loan payments remaining . . . yeah, I have some regrets."

Adam looked surprised. "I thought your dad paid for college."

"He cut me off, just like he threatened to," I murmured.

"Because you went to graduate school?"

I nodded. "I took out loans, maxed out my credit cards, deferred payments for as long as I could. Grad school wasn't exactly cheap, either," I said with a bitter laugh. "My stipend barely

covered my rent, so I had to take out more loans to cover living expenses. I figured I could pay it all off once I landed a job—but then the economy crashed and, well, you know . . . I guess I have no one to blame but myself—it's what I wanted to do."

"So would you do it over again?" Adam asked. "Knowing everything that you know now?"

"What do you mean?"

"I mean, was it worth it? Are you happy?"

Now it was my turn to be tongue-tied. I thought of the piles of grading, the manuscript to submit, the fund-raising calls. I thought of the years bouncing around from temporary position to temporary position, living out of suitcases and half-unpacked boxes. I thought of how lonely I'd been, how many nights I'd spent in the library, surrounded by nothing but books. I blinked at Adam, then forced myself to smile.

"Of course," I said brightly. "Like you said. It was all worth it."

I turned away before Adam could see the doubt clouding my face.

AFTER THE TRAINING SESSION, I headed to my office to collect my overdue books and return them to the library, piling as many as I could into two large file boxes and then struggling to get them downstairs to the book return bin. As I took

a break to catch my breath, I heard the whine of a motorcycle and Rick pulled up to the curb next to me.

"Hey!" he said, taking off his helmet. "I was just taking off for the day. Do you need help with those?"

"That would be great," I panted. "They're heavier than I thought."

Rick easily hefted up a box and carried it to the bin, tipping the box over and letting the books cascade into its maw.

"How was your fund-raising meeting?" Rick asked as we returned for the second box.

"Oh, you know. It was pretty much what I expected. Lots of rah-rah Fairfax speak."

"Speaking of which—" Rick muttered under his breath.

I turned around and saw Adam and Tiffany walking toward us.

"Hello," Adam said, glancing at Rick and then at me. His voice was aloof.

"I don't think we've met yet!" Tiffany said, smiling broadly at Rick and introducing herself. "Whatcha guys doing there?" she asked, glancing at the remaining file box resting at my feet.

"Rick's helping me return some overdue library books," I said.

"It looks like you've got half the library in there!" she joked. She turned to Rick and winked.

"That's our Anne. Always got her head stuck in a book."

"You should've seen the other box she had," Rick said. "That was the other half of the library."

Listening to their friendly banter made Adam's stiff posture all the more striking. He just stood there, making no move to contribute to the conversation and looking eager to go. I tried to catch his eye, but he only gave me a polite half smile and then avoided my gaze altogether, glancing at the footpath or off into the middle distance, where some students were noisily heading to the dining hall. After a minute more of small talk, they wished us a good evening and left.

"What a jackass. He couldn't even look me in the eye," Rick muttered, hoisting up the second box and dumping it into the bin.

"That was awkward," I said. "What happened? You must've done something to really piss him off."

"Oh, you know—I stood up for the rights of the faculty. Resisted the corporatization of the university. Helped unionize university employees. Terrible, terrible things." Rick laughed ironically.

"Well, looks like he's carrying a grudge."

"Oh, I don't doubt it. He pretty much single-handedly ousted me from Houston. I was really happy there, getting some decent writing done,

enjoying my teaching, plus making some real political headway with the union. He put an end to all that."

"How?" I asked. "Could he really fire you over something like that?"

"He wanted to, and he did. He was clever about it, though. He knew I'd have legal standing to sue, so he used the excuse of 'budget cuts' and 'reorganization.' But I knew—everyone knew. He's a bad guy. Very vindictive. You've got to be careful around him."

"That's awful," I said. "And scary. I can't believe he'd do that."

"Oh, believe it," Rick said, pulling me in for a kiss. "But don't be scared of him. He's a bully, that's all. He gets off on making people feel small and pathetic. You can't let him get to you. Always remember this: You must never back down from a bully. Never."

Rick took my hand and brought it to his lips, and I couldn't help but smile at the gesture. He wanted to protect me, and I was touched by his concern. While I still couldn't quite believe Adam was capable of such terrible things—was Rick getting him mixed up with someone else? had there been some terrible misunderstanding?—I also wondered why I was even defending him. I barely knew Adam anymore.

From: Jerome Corey <jerrycorey1944@aol.com>
To: Anne Corey <A.Corey@Fairfax.edu>
Subject: PLEASE BRING MORE AA BATTERIES
  NEXT TIME YOU VISIT
Date: October 3

I ALSO NEED
1) 2 LITER BOTTLES PEPSI ONE (NOT DIET PEPSI)
2) MICROWAVE POPCORN
3) MORE PLASTIC GARBAGE BAGS
4) ALMOND ROCA

From: <Jack_LindseyTiger@gmail.com>
To: Anne Corey <A.Corey@Fairfax.edu>
Subject: Re: hey
Date: October 5

whats a governess ? is that like a governer? what's a
governer?

From: Lauren Corey Winston <lauren@toteally.com>
To: Anne Corey <A.Corey@Fairfax.edu>
Subject: Dad
Date: October 6

The nurse at the facility mentioned that Dad has
a new girlfriend? Named Margie??? I know it's

supposed to be about companionship etc but I'm totally skeeved out. Since when does Dad date???? Do you think she's out for his money? You need to talk to him.

I can't come visit this weekend. Hayes has soccer and Tate has speech therapy. I'll be in DC the week after to chaperone Archer's class trip and then we're busy with his school's fund-raiser/silent auction. FYI, Archer's selling raffle tickets for $10/ticket. I told him you'd buy a couple books (10 tickets/book). Send a check made out to St. Andrew's Academy ASAP— he's trying to sell the most tickets in his class.

Lauren

From: Library Circulation Desk
<circulation@Fairfax.edu>
To: Anne Corey <A.Corey@Fairfax.edu>
Subject: URGENT: Library Items (FINAL Overdue Notice)
Date: October 7

Dear Anne Corey,

The following Library materials are overdue. Please return them as soon as possible to avoid accruing more late fees. You currently owe $702.55.

Your borrowing privileges will be suspended if you

do not settle your account. If you have any questions or would like to work out a payment plan, please contact us at—.

You can check your online account by visiting our website at: http://www.Fairfax.edu/ChandlerLibrary/AccountInfo.

This is a system generated e-mail. Please do not reply directly to this e-mail.

Total Overdue Items: 4
Due Date: September 1

(. . .)

chapter ten

"OH GOD, I'M SWEATING," Larry said, fanning himself in my car. We were on our way to the Huntington Library, and Larry had pointed all the vents toward his face. "Can you crank up the AC?" he begged.

"It's already up all the way," I said. "Sorry. Old car."

"I've honestly never felt this way before," Larry sighed, mopping his brow with a handkerchief. "I'm totally besotted with Jack. I'm just worried he's going to break things off."

"Why?"

"He's worried about his image. *Jane Vampire*'s his shot at the big time—he doesn't want to jeopardize it. He warned me we might have to cool things off when the movie premieres and he's doing wall-to-wall press."

Larry lifted up his sunglasses and glanced nervously at the rearview mirror.

"Is anyone following us?" he asked.

"No, Larry. I don't think there are any paps tailing a 2001 Honda Accord."

"You never know," Larry said. "I mean, OK,

fine. Jack's kind of B-list right now. I'd say he's *maybe* higher on the food chain than the Real Housewives. But if his movie's a hit? All that's going to change—there'll be people stalking him 24/7!"

"You need to stop freaking out," I said, flashing my reader badge to the security guard at the parking kiosk. "Jack's clearly into you. I mean, isn't he risking his career right now, meeting up with you?"

"Maybe he's a masochist. Maybe *I'm* a masochist. Ugh, I just can't stop."

I pulled into a loading zone in front of the library and hopped out.

"See you in a few hours?" I said as Larry climbed into the driver's seat. He flashed a peace sign and drove away.

I headed into the library, checked my bags, and made my way to the reading room.

An archivist was ready with my requested documents, presenting me with a large, flat file that she carried in both hands like a tray. Placing it carefully onto my desk, she whispered, "We just catalogued these, Dr. Corey. You're literally the first person to see them!"

"Are they Brontë's letters to Monsieur Heger?" I asked. I'd put in a request weeks ago and been waiting impatiently to see them. The archivist smiled and nodded.

I reached for the letters eagerly. For years, they'd

been in private hands, preserved by the descendants of Constantin Heger, Brontë's French tutor and the founder of a school in Brussels where she'd gone to teach in her twenties. Though he was married and had children, Brontë had fallen in love with Heger, writing him as often as twice a week after she returned home. Madame Heger was, predictably, unamused. She instructed Brontë that she could only write twice a *year*. Undeterred, Brontë continued to send letters, but Heger responded curtly, infrequently, and then not at all. Most of Brontë's love letters to Heger had been destroyed—burned or tossed out—and the handful that had survived had been sewn back together from scraps retrieved from the trash can. Experts speculated that Monsieur Heger had torn up the letters and his wife had fished them from the garbage.

The letters were sealed in a stiff, clear envelope to prevent further deterioration. I held my breath as I looked at them for the first time. The pages were yellowed with age, spotted with stains, pieced back together like a crossword puzzle. Brontë's script, demure and even, crossed the page. As I looked more closely, I realized Brontë was writing in French—French because, as she wrote in a short postscript, it was the language "most precious to me because it reminds me of you—I love French for your sake with all my heart and soul."

I, on the other hand, did not love French with all my heart and soul, but only with enough force of will to pass my PhD language exam. Borrowing a French dictionary from the reference desk, I began, arduously, to translate. For the next few hours, I transcribed Brontë's letters to my computer, stopping only for a quick bite to eat at lunchtime.

As promised, Larry picked me up a few hours later, honking from the curb in front of the library and startling several tourists and a flock of pigeons.

"You look happy," I said, sliding into the passenger seat. "How was Jack?"

"Dreamy," Larry said. "How about you? Did you get a lot of work done?"

"I have to tell you about these letters I just read," I said. "You'll die. They're Brontë's letters to her tutor Monsieur Heger."

"Who's that?"

"Her tutor when she was living in Belgium. She was desperately in love with him, but he was married and had kids."

"That sounds awfully familiar," Larry said, looking at me sideways.

"No, no, no—it's not like you and Jack. Brontë was obsessed with Heger, but he didn't love her back. She wrote him all these love letters, pretty much spilling her guts to him, and get this—*his wife was reading all the letters.*"

"Shut. The. Front. Door."

"I'm serious! And Brontë knew—but she didn't care! She just kept writing him, even when he didn't write her back, even when his wife wrote her to say, 'Cool it.' Can you imagine? I mean, how incredibly *sad* is that?"

"Why sad?" Larry asked, his voice turning serious. "She was in love."

"But I wish she'd just pulled herself together and moved on."

"Oh, Anne," Larry said, looking at me fondly. "Haven't you ever been in love? It makes you do crazy things."

"But she was old enough to know better!"

"Um, look at me! I'm forty years old and carpooling to LA with my best friend so I can use her car as a decoy to meet my much-younger, married, closeted boyfriend in Best Westerns around the city. I don't know about you, but that sounds pretty *sad,* to use your word."

"Larry!"

"It's true, though. Isn't it? I'm a loser. I'm old enough to know better."

"Larry, stop it. You're not a loser. You're a lover. You're a hopeless romantic."

"I guess you're right," Larry sighed. "I just wish I'd find the right guy."

"You will," I said. "I think you're highly lovable."

"Thanks," Larry said, giving me an affectionate

shoulder bump. "I think you are, too. And trust me—one day, you'll fall in love, and you'll understand what I'm talking about."

I instantly thought of Adam and felt my ears burning. I didn't say anything, though, and let Larry ramble on about Jack for the rest of our drive to Fairfax.

HAD I BEEN IN love with Adam? At the time, I would have said yes. There was nothing I felt more sure of, no doubt in my mind that what we had was the real thing. Now that I was older, though, I wasn't so sure. The love letters, the engagement, the heated declarations of love—they all seemed so melodramatic now. In the end, we'd broken up in such a predictable way—on grad night, a final prom-like celebration held in the school gym the night before the commencement.

Adam's mother had been scheduled to fly in later that night, and he was fretting about whether her plane would be on time, how she would get from the airport to his dorm room, whether she'd agree to take his bed or insist on sleeping on the floor, how she would react to the pomp and circumstance of commencement.

I'd been so consumed with my own family drama that I was hardly listening to him. Lauren was staying in New York with some new boyfriend of hers and taking the train in in the

morning. My father had flown in that afternoon, but I hadn't told Adam, wanting to minimize any interaction between the two. "I'll see you in the morning," I told my father over the phone, and he seemed perfectly happy to avoid a strained dinner at Chili's where he would ask me, once again, to reconsider law school.

"Are you listening to me?" Adam asked as we arrived at the gym, which was festooned with orange and black balloons and fronted by a large, melting ice sculpture that spelled out "2003." Inside, a DJ was playing cheesy dance music and hordes of drunk soon-to-be grads were milling around the dance floor.

"Uh-huh," I said, looking around to see if I recognized anyone. The atmosphere felt desperately festive. This was it—the last hurrah, the final bender before all of us were expelled into the real world. Commencement was for the parents, but grad night—grad night was supposed to be for us. Yet already, things had changed. You could sense it in people's dazed looks, the forced levity in their voices. Parents had flown in by now, siblings and grandparents and other random relatives, and even if they weren't at the party that night, their presence hung in the air.

"I was saying that I want our parents to meet tomorrow," Adam said. "Maybe we could meet for brunch right after the ceremony? The Center for Jewish Life does a really nice spread, and I'd

like my coworkers to meet my mom. There'll even be champagne!"

"Yeah," I said vaguely. "I'll check with my dad tomorrow. He might want to leave for New York right after the ceremony. God knows my sister will want to get out ASAP."

"This is important, Anne—when else will they get a chance to meet before we get married?"

"There'll be plenty of other chances," I said vaguely. Adam and I had talked of eloping that fall, maybe during one of my planned trips to California. He'd even scoped out San Francisco city hall, excitedly telling me how beautiful the building was, how we could get married under the rotunda at the top of a sweeping staircase. Adam had wanted our immediate families to be there, but I'd convinced him to keep the ceremony intimate—just the two of us. Later, once we'd saved some money, we could host a reception for friends and family.

"I just think this is a perfect time," Adam was saying. "Everyone's here."

"I know, I know. It's just—my sister's bringing her new boyfriend along, and you know how difficult she is, and how difficult my dad is, and he's already complaining about how he doesn't trust his manager to watch his properties while he's gone—"

"When did he get in?"

"This afternoon," I said without thinking.

"He's here already? Why didn't you have dinner with him?"

"I wanted to have dinner with you," I babbled, feeling my face redden. "Besides, he was tired and wanted to turn in early."

"We could have had dinner together," Adam said softly. "Why didn't you tell me he was already in town?"

"It's no big deal. I just wanted to enjoy our last day together without stressing out about my dad and all—"

Adam was walking around the side of the building, away from the noise of the speakers, away from the throngs of people dipping strawberries in chocolate fountains and shoveling shrimp from the bed of ice beneath the melting ice sculpture. He stopped by an empty bike rack beneath the feeble glow of a lamppost. Nearby, a generator droned loudly, working double time on the sticky June night.

"What's the matter—Adam, what's going on?" I said, following him.

His hands were in his pockets, and he was hunched over. I touched his elbow and felt him stiffen.

"Are you mad at me?" I asked. "What did I do?"

Adam turned to look at me. His hair had gotten long, and he brushed it from his eyes as he spoke. He didn't look angry. He looked sad.

"Are you ashamed of me?" he asked.

"Ashamed? What are you talking about?"

"Not wanting me to have dinner with your father. Not wanting my mother to meet your family. Not telling me things."

"You're overreacting, Adam. This has nothing to do with that. This is about me and my screwed-up family! I'm trying to protect you from them!"

Adam didn't reply. He tipped his head back and took a deep breath, staring at the cloud of gnats hovering around the lamppost. I waited for him to say something, gripped with anxiety. Adam and I never fought. He'd never even raised his voice with me before.

"Your father and sister don't like me," he finally said.

"They just don't know you."

"And Dr. Russell thinks I'm a distraction."

"She never said that. She just wants to make sure I don't make decisions I'll later regret."

"*I* want to make sure you don't make a decision you'll later regret." Adam looked at me, his face questioning, and I felt my stomach turn over queasily.

"Maybe we should take a break," Adam said.

I felt my eyes fill with tears, but not from sadness. I was furious. "You mean, *you* want to take a break."

"That's not fair," Adam said. "I've tried to

make this work all year! I went to Florida with you, I didn't push you on the engagement, I let you go to Yale—"

"You *let* me go to Yale?"

"That's not what I meant," Adam snapped. "I bent over backwards—"

"*You* bent over backwards? What about *me?* I supported you when you suddenly decided you wanted a fancy job instead of going to grad school. I listened to you talk about being wined and dined by those corporate tools. I *let* you take that job in San Francisco. Don't talk to me about trying to make it work!"

Adam shook his head. "You think I sold out, don't you?"

I nodded, angrily wiping the tears from my eyes.

"It's easy to think that when you've never had a real job, Annie." Before I could interrupt, he added, "Working for your dad doesn't count. And neither does work-study at the library."

I felt myself go cold with rage. "So you think I'm spoiled. You think I'm a princess because I'm choosing to be a broke professor instead of selling my soul to some consulting firm? You think that teaching isn't a real job? God, you sound just like my father!"

"Your father isn't wrong. You've never had to be practical. You've never left the ivory tower. You can live a life of the mind because you've

got a safety net. Your dad, your sister—they might drive you crazy, but they'll never abandon you."

"I feel like you're abandoning me," I said bleakly. I pulled the cameo ring off my finger. "Here," I said, handing it to him. "I guess you want this back."

"No, keep it," Adam said. "I don't want it anymore."

In the distance, I could hear Kool and the Gang's "Celebration" playing. Someone was smoking pot nearby. Adam said something about keeping in touch and tried to give me a hug, but I pushed him away.

"Go," I said. "Your mom is probably here by now."

I turned and walked away. I half expected him to come running after me, to feel his hand on my shoulder and his voice in my ear, apologizing and begging me to stay. But he never came after me, and I was too full of rage and pride to look back. I walked back to my dorm, alone and in the darkness.

"ARE YOU DOING OK?" Larry asked, as we pulled off the freeway and drove down the dark streets of Fairfax. "You've been awfully quiet."

"I'm just tired," I said. "It's been a long day."

I arrived home once again to a dark apartment, with no one but Jellyby waiting for me. As I

filled her bowl and tried to decide whether to open up a new bottle of wine, my phone buzzed. It was a text message from Rick.

"Are you back yet?" it read.

"Just walked in the door," I texted back.

"Are you free tonight?"

I paused. "Yes," I finally typed back. Then, impulsively, I texted, "Want to come over for a drink?"

"Be there in ten," Rick texted back immediately. "I'll bring over some snacks."

I settled onto my couch, looking forward to seeing Rick despite my low mood. Our relationship was so easy and uncomplicated. Rick was attractive, funny, and smart. He was great in bed. He was there when I wanted company, but he didn't crowd me.

Maybe it wasn't full-blown, tempestuous love—at least, not yet—but that was OK with me. I wasn't going to make the same mistake twice. I didn't want to prostrate myself to another person, didn't want to suffer like I had in the past. Let Larry and Brontë wallow in their lovesickness. I was done.

chapter eleven

IT WAS ALMOST NOVEMBER, and the black-tie gala to launch the capital campaign was fast approaching. Tiffany was now sending almost daily e-mails full of updates and pep talks. She ran the campaign like a telethon host, and I might as well have been a robocaller, dialing up alums for dollars, giving my canned sales pitch, and, 90 percent of the time, being hung up on.

"I feel like I'm working at a call center, not a university," I complained to Larry.

"Suck it up, buttercup," Larry said. "Someone's got to sing for their supper, and I've got tenure."

I invited Rick to attend the gala with me, and he leapt at the invitation. "A chance to have steak and wine on the college's dime?" he said. "I'm in!" He joked about how he'd wear his motorcycle jacket and jeans instead of the black tie stipulated on the invitation.

"I can't wait to piss off some posh trustee," he said. "These parties are just an excuse for rich people to dress in monkey suits."

At the last minute, though, Rick was called

away to New York for a meeting and Larry stepped in as my date. Larry was the only person I knew who actually owned a tuxedo—and not just a tuxedo, but a complete set of tails.

"You don't have to go overboard," I warned him. "It's a college fund-raiser, not the Oscars."

"I *love* fancy balls," he said.

"It's not a ball. It's like a really bad prom."

"No, it's not," he said. "My prom took place at the local Howard Johnson. This *gala* is taking place at the Bel-Air. The *Bel-Air!*"

Through some magic or connections, Tiffany had managed to book the Hotel Bel-Air for our Fairfax College gala. Lauren and her crowd were the type of people who frequented the Bel-Air— for weddings, for baby showers, for brunches. I'd never been, but Lauren talked endlessly about how intimate and tasteful it was, how Oprah could take meetings there without being hounded by the hoi polloi, and how the lake had actual, real-life swans paddling about.

"I can't wait," Larry said. "Should I get you a corsage?"

"No," I said. "But you *can* help me find a dress to wear."

The day before the gala, Larry dragged me to Saks on Rodeo Drive in Beverly Hills, where tourists mingled with well-manicured locals and people hardly batted an eye when a bright yellow Lamborghini or tricked-out Ferrari roared by.

Inside the store, I gravitated toward the cocktail dresses, but Larry sniffed disapprovingly at my selections.

"Long," he said. "You need to wear a long gown."

"I'll be overdressed," I said. "And besides, I'm not dropping a ton of money for a dress I'll only wear once."

Larry refused to listen to me, selecting several floor-length dresses and pushing me to the dressing room. He sat on a tufted brocade bench outside as I tried on each dress and modeled for him.

"Too busy," he said when I tried on a gown in a bright floral print.

"Too mother-of-the-bride," he said to a pale pink gown with elbow-length sleeves.

"Too pageanty," he said to a gown with sequins and illusion netting.

"I kinda like this one," I said, sucking in my stomach in the three-way mirror. "It's giving me Mariah Carey vibes."

I practiced striking a classic Mariah pose, hair flung back, hands placed on my hips for the illusion of slimness. I gave my best paralyzed Mariah smile. "Lambily, what do you think?" I asked.

"Meh," Larry said. "You're no elusive butterfly."

"I'm tired," I complained, exhaling and

stepping off the pedestal. "Can I just get a plain black dress and be done with it?"

"That's so boring!" Larry said. He mused for a second, his hand at his lips. "I see you in Valentino red," he decided.

"Larry, I can't afford Valentino. In case you forgot, I'm a professor, not an heiress."

"I'm talking about the color, not the couturier." He dashed out of the dressing room and came back carrying an armful of bright red dresses. I blanched, looking at them. "They're so . . . *look at me,*" I said. "What is this? *Pretty Woman*?"

"Please," Larry said. "You're no hooker with a heart of gold."

"Yeah, and I'm no Julia Roberts, either," I sighed, and reluctantly took one of the dresses and tried it on.

"Now *that,*" Larry said when I emerged from the dressing room, "is a real gown."

I contemplated myself in the mirror. The dress fit remarkably well, making me look somehow taller and leggier than I was. It was more form-fitting than what I was used to wearing, but it still looked like my style—simple and under-stated. My biggest fear—that I'd look like one of the fashion victims in *Glamour* magazine, a black bar of shame over my eyes—subsided as I modeled the dress, checking it out from all possible angles. I looked good, I thought, feeling unexpectedly delighted.

"Practice smizing," Larry said, and I obliged.

"It's perfect," Larry said. "You have to get it."

I looked at the price tag and practically choked. "I can't," I said. "I've never spent so much money on a dress in my entire life."

"Charge it!" Larry said. "As Oscar Wilde once said, 'Anyone who lives within their means suffers from a lack of imagination.' "

"I guess I have no imagination."

"And I, alas, have too much. I'd buy the dress for you, but I'm still paying off my imaginative excesses at an extortionary annual percentage rate of 21.5 percent."

"Well, my birthday *is* coming up . . ." I reasoned.

"There you go," Larry said. "It's a sign. The universe *wants* you to buy this dress. Live a little! How old are you turning?"

"Thirty-three," I said.

"Jesus died at age thirty-three, you know," Larry pointed out. "Jesus would want you to buy the dress. Come on!"

I started laughing so hard that Larry began fretting that I might split the dress. A saleswoman appeared as Larry was trying to unzip me from my gown.

"Do you need any help?" she asked.

"I'd like to buy this dress," I said, handing her my credit card before I could change my mind.

• • •

THE NIGHT OF THE gala, Larry picked me up in his Mini Cooper for the hour-long drive to Los Angeles. I'd plucked a white camellia from the bush outside my house and tucked it behind my ear, leaving my hair loose and wavy and keeping my makeup simple except for a deep red lipstick.

"Va-va-va-voom," Larry said as he opened the door to his car and helped me in. As promised, he was wearing his tails, a green carnation in his lapel, and he looked dapper and handsome.

"Too bad Rick isn't here to see you," Larry said. "His eyes would fall out of his face."

"I can't move," I groaned. "I'm wearing two pairs of Spanx and I can barely breathe. How the hell are you supposed to go to the bathroom in these?"

"You're not supposed to," Larry said, pulling away from the curb as I tried to sit in such a way so that my dress didn't wrinkle.

"I'm starving," I said, opening up Larry's glove compartment and rummaging around. "Do you have any food?"

"Why didn't you eat before we left?"

"I forgot. Oh, wait, I did eat. I had half a box of Girl Scout cookies."

"And you didn't share? *Why do some people get all the cookies?*"

"Come on, Larry, can we please stop by

In-N-Out? I'll just order some French fries and then we can hit the road again."

"Anne—you're supposed to get In-N-Out *after* the party, not before. Besides, In-N-Out French fries suck."

"Not when you get them animal style."

"You are *not* ordering French fries animal style. You'll get sauce all over your dress!"

But after listening to me moan pathetically every time we passed an In-N-Out on the side of the freeway, Larry finally relented and took me to a drive-thru. I covered my entire dress with white paper napkins and happily munched on fries for the rest of the trip, occasionally feeding one to Larry, who kept complaining that his car was going to smell for days and that I better not drop any fries between the seats.

As we made our way to the hotel, I started to recognize the winding streets and wooded hills from when we'd visited Bex's house for book club. The Bel-Air wasn't quite as far up the hill as Bex's home, nestled into a quiet street among residential homes. An old-fashioned green-and-white awning with "Hotel Bel-Air" printed in cursive script marked the entrance to the hotel. As we pulled in, Larry said, "Look!" A handful of paparazzi, cameras poised from across the street, scanned inside our car to see if we were anyone important.

"Unbelievable," Larry said, sounding excited.

"I wonder if there's someone famous staying here!"

The gala was being held outside in the hotel's famed gardens, surrounded by its distinctive pink Spanish-style buildings. A waiter greeted us with crystal flutes of champagne. An old-fashioned big band was playing in the background, and the whole soiree had the feel of an old Hollywood party.

"Where are the swans?" Larry asked, walking toward the lake. "I read that there're three of them: Athena, Hercules, and their baby, Chloe." He teetered on the edge of the water, pushing aside some thick ferns and flowering daylilies.

"Careful!" I said, holding Larry back by his tails.

Larry cleared his throat and began to recite Yeats's "The Wild Swans at Coole" into the night:

> The trees are in their autumn beauty,
> The woodland paths are dry,
> Under the October twilight the water
> Mirrors a still sky;
> Upon the brimming water among the
>   stones
> Are nine-and-fifty swans.

"There are only three swans, Larry," I pointed out.

"But it's still an uneven number," Larry said mournfully. "Swans pair off for life, but one poor swan is stuck alone. Poor Chloe. Where is she going to find a mate?" He sighed dramatically.

He caught his breath and pointed. "There they are!" he whispered. Hidden in the rushes were Athena and Hercules, little Chloe trailing behind them, the three of them glowing white in the dusky darkness. Larry whispered to me:

> Unwearied still, lover by lover,
> They paddle in the cold
> Companionable streams or climb the air;
> Their hearts have not grown old;
> Passion or conquest, wander where they
>   will,
> Attend upon them still.

We watched as the three swans drifted away. I felt a pang as they disappeared.

"You know, I first read that poem in Dr. Russell's class a million years ago," I told Larry as we made our way back to the festivities. "I understand it so differently now."

"Your heart's grown old," Larry said sadly. "So has mine."

A crowd of people were gathered around cocktail tables, drinking and laughing and greeting one another. I hardly recognized anyone. Everyone looked flushed and prosperous, decked out

in their best clothes. Here and there, I spied a faculty member or an administrator, looking lost, wearing an ill-fitting tux or a cheap dress and too much makeup. I self-consciously smoothed down my own dress, checked my hair, craned my neck to see if I'd missed delinting a patch of Jellyby's hair.

"Do I look OK?" I asked Larry. "I don't look silly?"

"You look fine," Larry said. "But you smell like French fries."

He suddenly stopped to stare at someone across the courtyard.

"Oh shit," he said. "Jack's here."

I followed his gaze and saw Bex and Jack standing beneath a wooden gazebo spangled with lights. Bex was dressed in a creamy silk slip dress with delicate straps crisscrossing her elegant back, her hair pulled back with a feathered comb. Jack stood next to her, his arm cradling her waist, dressed in a beautifully tailored tuxedo that looked blue-black under the light.

"I thought he wasn't coming," Larry murmured. "She must have insisted on dragging him along."

Bex and Jack were talking to Adam and Tiffany, who was wearing a hot-pink taffeta gown with an enormous bow on one shoulder. Tiffany seemed to have some sort of sixth sense because she caught sight of us looking at them and motioned us over with an enthusiastic wave.

"Larry! Anne! Great to see you!" she called out. "Come join us!"

Bex and Jack had turned around and seen us, and now we had no choice but to go over. "You look so pretty," Bex said as I approached. "I've never seen you so dressed up!" I felt like a fraud in my new red dress and lipstick, looking like a fire hydrant next to Bex's tall, slender frame. I shouldn't have worn such a bright color, I told myself. Only someone like Tiffany, who already had a loud personality, could pull it off.

"Bex, Jack, you remember Larry," I said. "He was at the book club with me."

"Oh, yes!" Bex said, giving Larry a kiss on the cheek. "It's wonderful to see you again!"

"Yes, it's good to see you, Larry," Jack said, shaking Larry's hand. I could see sweat springing to Larry's forehead, but Jack was relaxed and unperturbed, greeting Larry like a passing acquaintance. I was impressed. Maybe he was a better actor than I gave him credit for.

"I can't believe you all knew each other in college!" Tiffany tittered to me. "Such a small world! And now here we are, getting ready to announce Bex's incredibly generous gift to the school! Can you believe it? *Twenty million dollars?*"

Larry choked on his champagne, and Jack leaned over to pat him on the back.

"I *know,* isn't it *incredible?*" Tiffany asked.

"Apparently Adam here was so persuasive in his vision for the school that Bex decided to double her gift at the last minute." Tiffany beamed at Adam.

"You know, Anne here was really great in helping me figure out my role in *Jane Vampire*," Jack told the group. "She gave me a lot of historical background and even talked me through *Jane Eyre*. The movie's coming out over Thanksgiving, by the way," he said, turning to me. "You should check out your name in the credits."

"Honey, you should see if you can get Anne tickets to the premiere," Bex said. "It's going to be held in Westwood. You and Larry should both come!"

I looked at Larry, who opened his mouth in seeming protest.

"I'll see what I can do," Jack said, and I swore I saw him wink at Larry.

Bex turned to me. "I never got a chance to thank you personally for putting me in touch with Tiffany," she said. "And for helping Jack with all his questions. I really appreciate it."

"Sure," I said. "It was no big deal."

"You know, I'd love to know more about what you're working on," she said. "I heard you tell Marni at the book club that it's not a novel. What is it about, then?"

"Oh," I stammered. "It's not that interesting. I mean, it's pretty academic."

"Please—indulge me. Let me live vicariously through you." Bex gave me a disarming smile.

I launched into a description of my book project and was struck by how genuinely interested Bex was. She'd read most of the novels I worked on and wanted to know more about my research and writing process. Once again, I thought of how she really would have made a wonderful teacher and scholar.

While I was engrossed in conversation with Bex, I tried to keep an eye on Larry, who had flagged down a waiter for another flute of champagne and looked like he was well on his way to getting drunk. Over the din of the party, I could catch bits and pieces of his conversation.

"Really? I didn't realize you and Curtis used to work together!" Larry was saying to Adam. "He just got married and moved to Ohio. He's running for state attorney general . . . Yes, to a woman named Susan. She's perfectly nice. . . but let's be honest, she's no Anne Corey."

Adam said something I couldn't catch.

"Oh, Curtis dated Anne for over a year, back when he was in law school," Larry continued. "He was head over heels for her, wanted to marry her and everything, but she made it clear she wasn't interested . . . she wanted her own career. Can you believe we could've been sister and brother?"

Jack interrupted and said something. I cringed

as I heard Larry respond, "She kind of broke Curtis's heart. I mean, *you* know—you used to date her, right? Anne's tough. She's got high standards."

I stole a quick glance at Adam while pretending to be listening to Bex. I'd never seen him in a tuxedo before. We'd never attended a formal or house party together in college—neither of us had joined an eating club, and we'd broken up before the wave of weddings and holiday parties that might have required such formal wear. Adam was fiddling with his cuff links distractedly and leaned over to whisper something in Tiffany's ear.

"It looks like we should probably get seated," Tiffany announced. "They're about to serve dinner and get the program started." To Bex and Jack, she said, "You're at our table—come follow me!" The four of them walked toward a round table decked with flowers and situated in the place of honor next to the podium.

Larry and I were seated in a far corner of the garden, along with other faculty members and employees who didn't fit neatly into the guest list. I vaguely recognized some of them from working at the phone bank or attending campus meetings, but after quickly introducing ourselves to each other, we all fell back to chatting with our dates.

"Oh my God," Larry moaned. "I had no idea

he was going to be here. Was I a total mess? Seriously—tell me. Was my face bright red? Was I sweating like a beast?"

"I won't lie—you were a little sweaty—but Jack's a celebrity. Everyone probably assumed you were just nervous."

"Ugh, I haven't seen Bex since that book party. Do you think she knows? Do you think she hates me? I could barely look her in the eye."

"I thought you said they had an open marriage," I said.

"That doesn't mean she wants Jack to shove her face in it! Oh God, I'm terrified of her."

"She seemed completely gracious," I said. "Seriously, Larry, I don't think you have anything to worry about."

The salad course was served, while various university officials and trustees got up to speak. Just before the main course was brought out, Adam took the microphone and announced Bex's gift, sending a loud gasp through the crowd. He invited her to the podium, and she glided up in her silken dress, pausing to exchange an affectionate kiss on his cheek before taking the microphone.

"God, she's a knockout," one of our tablemates whispered. "Did you know she's married to Jack Lindsey? He's over there sitting at the table." Everyone craned their necks to get a look. Larry quietly whimpered beside me.

Bex's speech was short and modest. She spoke of her cousin who had graduated from Fairfax, pointing to a silver-haired lady in pearls sitting at her table, and she briefly touched on her family's long commitment to education. "I feel incredibly privileged to join President Martinez and the entire board of trustees in opening this new chapter in the life of the college," she said. "I look forward to seeing what great things are on the horizon."

There was a tinkling of glass as everyone toasted Bex, followed by a phalanx of waiters sweeping in to serve us our filet mignon or roast chicken. My Spanx were cutting off my circulation, and I was starting to regret the fries. I wondered if I could convince Larry to leave early and let me shimmy them off in his car. From the corner of my eye, I could see Tiffany's bright pink dress moving from table to table, making sure all the donors were happy, that no one needed a refill of wine or an extra napkin or a vegetarian entrée. The night felt like her own personal triumph. I could hear people congratulating her on choosing such a fine venue and organizing such a lovely gala, and she barely seemed to sit down the entire night.

"I'll be right back," Larry whispered to me, standing up, his burner phone in hand.

"Where are you going?" I asked. "Are you going to call Jack? Are you crazy?"

"Calm down," he said. "I promise I'm not going to do anything stupid."

"Hold on—are you coming back soon?"

"Of course! Could you make sure I get an espresso? And don't let them forget my dessert!"

I watched him walk away, tapping on his phone. *Please, God,* I thought. *Please let him not make a scene. Please let him not humiliate himself—or me—publicly.*

I picked at the rest of my steak, not bothering to make small talk with my neighbors, who were debating whether or not they'd have to pay for the valet. Across the garden, I saw Adam leaning over to talk to Bex. She had her hand clasped under her chin and was gazing intently at him, nodding her head, breaking into a smile at something he said. Tiffany's seat was empty—she was chatting with guests at an adjoining table—and Jack's was, too. I looked around the party to see if I could locate him, but people had started milling around and it was hard to make anyone out.

The big band struck up a dance number, and some people started to gravitate toward the dance floor. I looked around for Larry, wishing he'd hurry up and get back. Behind me, the lake was now shrouded in complete darkness, and I wondered if Chloe the swan was peeking through the rushes, watching everyone pair off. I glumly

watched the festivities, trying to keep my face neutral even though I was feeling unspeakably lonely. A couple of guests from my table got up to leave. "We've got a long drive to Fairfax," they said, wishing us a good night. The table was now half empty, so I decided to get up and find Larry.

I made my way across the grass, wishing I'd brought a wrap now that the sun had set and the night had turned cool. I paused in front of a round stone fountain decorated in pretty blue-and-yellow Spanish tiles and lit from within so that the water glowed like lava. I stood for a moment, mesmerized by the sight and sound of the burbling water. Rubbing my hands along my arms, I shivered.

"Are you cold?" someone asked. Startled, I looked up and saw Adam a few feet away, half veiled by the darkness.

"You scared me," I said.

"Here," he said. "Take my coat." Despite my protests, he took off his tuxedo jacket and draped it around my shoulders.

"Thanks," I said, the jacket swallowing me up like a blanket. The lining was silk and still warm from his body.

Neither of us talked for a minute. The jacket smelled of wool and the faint, familiar scent of Adam's body, mixed with a perfume I didn't recognize. *Probably Tiffany's,* I thought.

"This was a great party," I said lamely. "And what great news about Bex's gift!"

Adam nodded. "It's all Tiffany's doing," he said. "She organized the whole gala, and she really deserves the credit for cultivating Bex. I just closed the deal."

"Uh-huh," I said. Adam was so close to me that I could feel the heat from his body.

"Is that a real flower in your hair?" he asked.

"Yes, it's a camellia," I mumbled. He leaned toward me, and I felt his hand graze my hair as he touched the petals. Involuntarily, I turned my face toward him and felt his palm brush my cheek. Adam was now so close that if I just bent forward slightly, we would be kissing. I caught his eye and felt my breathing stop.

"Very pretty," he said.

Then he abruptly let his hand drop and stepped away.

I was stunned. Was he messing with me? Testing to see if I still had feelings for him? I felt a sudden flare of anger.

"Where's Tiffany, anyway?" I asked. "She's probably looking for you, you know."

I saw that my question annoyed Adam. Still, he responded smoothly, "She's talking to some donors, the last I checked. What about you? I thought you'd be here with Rick."

"He was called out of town at the last minute,"

I said. "I think it had something to do with the Booker."

"I see," Adam said. He paused for a moment. "I knew him when I was at the University of Houston."

"I know," I said. "He told me."

Adam looked surprised. "He did?" he said. "Then you know he and I had our differences."

"Yes, I know all about it."

"I wanted to warn you to be careful. Rick's not—How do I say this? He's not trustworthy."

"He's been nothing but a gentleman with me," I said testily. "You don't have to slander him just because you don't like him."

"He's an opportunist, Anne. I've seen him do things—"

"What things? Unionize workers? Defend academic freedom? Resist the corporatization of the university?"

"I don't know what he's told you, but he wasn't some champion of the people. If anything, he only looked out for himself."

"You're wrong," I said, shaking my head. "Maybe from up there in senior administration, you think you know what's best for everyone, but you don't. You're totally out of touch."

"I know more than you realize, Anne."

"Don't condescend to me, Adam!" I said. I pulled his jacket off. "Thanks for letting me borrow this, but I should get going."

"Anne," Adam said. "I don't want to see you get hurt."

"Could you stop being so patronizing?" I said. "You don't *know* me anymore. You know nothing about my life. A lot's happened since we were togeth— since we were in college. I mean, look at you. I barely recognize you anymore, talking about 'cultivating' donors and 'closing deals.' "

"I don't understand why you're getting so upset, Anne—"

"Just—just leave me alone. You do your own thing—raise money, hobnob with donors, whatever it is you do. Don't butt into my life!"

I pushed the jacket into Adam's hands. He took it from me but didn't put it on, standing there in his shirtsleeves and cummerbund. I was freezing, but I clenched my teeth and stood up straight, trying to look dignified.

"Annie?" I heard from one of the hallways running along the buildings. It was Larry, looking tipsy and flushed. "I've been looking for you," he said. Spying Adam, he doffed an imaginary top hat but lost his balance and had to steady himself on a pillar.

"Is he OK?" Adam asked.

"He's fine," I said shortly. "We were just leaving." I marched up to Larry but nearly toppled over when one of my heels caught in the grass. The only way I avoided a complete wipeout was

by grabbing Larry by the arm. "Ow!" he said as I tried to right myself. He smelled like scotch, and his eyes fluttered as if he wanted to go to sleep.

"What happened to you?" I whispered fiercely. "Where'd you go?"

"I want to go home," Larry said, smiling sweetly and slumping against my shoulder. Without looking back to say good-bye, I helped walk Larry down the corridor and to our car, where the valet helped me load him into the back seat and where he promptly vomited all over himself and fell asleep.

chapter twelve

L ARRY ENDED UP SPENDING the night on
my couch, where I'd dragged him, still
covered in vomit, and dumped him without
bothering to take off his shoes or cover him
with a blanket. Jellyby took one sniff of him
and fled, reproachfully meowing at me as I
finally wriggled out of my dress and Spanx and
collapsed into bed.

The next morning, I heard Larry groan and roll
off the couch, landing with a crash on the floor.

"Unnnhhhhhhh," he moaned. "Holy Jesus
mother of God."

He was still lying on the floor when I came in a
few minutes later to feed Jellyby and make some
coffee.

"You need some help?" I asked.

"Just leave me here," he groaned. "Put me out
of my misery."

"Can you at least move so I can get by you?"

Larry rolled over obediently, lying on his back,
arms splayed open. I poured two cups of coffee,
stepped over his body, sat on the couch, and
handed him a cup.

"So thanks for ditching me last night," I said. "What the hell happened?"

Larry slowly pulled himself up on one elbow, taking a sip of the coffee and pinching his nose between his eyebrows. He noticed the film of dried vomit on his coat lapel and grimaced. "I'm *crunchy,*" he said.

"You should see your car," I said. "It's Barfalona in there."

"Someone must've slipped roofies in my drink."

"Larry, we were at a gala, not a frat party. You just drank too much."

"You're mad at me."

"You met up with Jack, didn't you? You ditched me at the party so you could hook up with him."

Larry hung his head in shame.

"Thanks," I said. "You're officially the worst date ever."

"I couldn't help myself!" Larry cried. "You know me. I can resist everything but temptation. Jack texted me to meet him at the hotel bar ASAP—he said he had something important to tell me. I couldn't *not* go."

"What did he say?"

"Terrible news. We have to stop seeing each other for the next few months. A total blackout period. His people are adamant—the studio's got a ton of money riding on his new movie. He just

can't risk being found out cheating on his wife."

"So he's breaking up with you?"

"He swore it's not a 'breakup.' It's just a 'break.' I told him that was just a question of semantics, but he insisted nothing had really changed and that we could still text each other."

"And you believe him?"

"What choice do I have? I love him!" Larry moaned. "I was just so happy to see him last night and so distraught that it was the last time I'd see him for God knows how long. It made me reckless. I had a double scotch and then another one and another one and soon I was sloshed. We ended up in his hotel room—at least I think it was his hotel room. I can't remember. All I can say is that the Bel-Air is much, *much* nicer than a Best Western." He reached over to grab my hand and kiss it apologetically. "I'm sorry, Anne," he said. "I'm a sucky friend. Will you ever forgive me?"

"I guess so," I said. "But you owe me big time."

"Anything. I'll do anything to make it up to you."

"Anything?"

"Yes, I swear."

"Well, Tiffany *does* have another phone drive scheduled for next week. You're in charge."

Larry winced.

"You said anything."

"OK, fine, I'll do it." He dropped my hand and

lay back down. "Now I have to rest a little. Do you have smelling salts? I think I'm having the vapors."

The next day, Larry had an enormous bouquet of flowers delivered to my house, along with a card that read:

Roses are red
Violets are blue
Your friend is a jerk
Who can't hold his booze

"YOU WERE RIGHT ABOUT Adam," I told Rick. "He's not a good guy."

I was at Rick's house, getting ready for class. He'd gotten back from New York the previous night and had brought a bag of coffee beans from his favorite coffee shop in Brooklyn, offering to brew me a cup in his Chemex before I took off for campus.

"What happened?" Rick asked.

"Nothing," I said. "He was just his usual patronizing self at the gala. I can't believe I ever tried to defend him."

"So the gala was a bust, huh?"

Rick handed me a cup of coffee and sat next to me on the couch, affectionately putting his arm around me. "I'm sorry I couldn't be there," he said. "I'm sure you looked absolutely smashing."

I sighed. We were into the final stretch of the

fall semester, and I felt swamped with work. I took a sip of coffee and scrolled through my phone, suddenly stopping at an e-mail message from Ursula Burton with the subject line: "Oxford UP Reader's Reports."

"Oh God," I said.

"What is it?" Rick asked, drawing my hair back and resting his chin on my shoulder.

"It's my book," I said. "The reports are in. I wasn't supposed to hear for another month!" I tremblingly opened up the e-mail, feeling myself tense up with anticipation.

Dear Anne Corey,

You will find attached two anonymous reader's reports on your manuscript, *Ivory Tower: Nineteenth-Century Women Writers and the Literary Imagination.* As you will see, both readers recommended publication of the manuscript, with reader #1 praising its "originality," and reader #2 calling it a "valuable contribution to the field." Both readers felt your profiles of the six women writers brought new light to the inner workings of the nineteenth-century publishing industry and advanced existing feminist scholarship by figures such as Ellen Russell and Philippa Conrad-Jones. Reader #2 felt a bit more could be added to the Introduction regarding the Married Women's Property Act (1884) and the regulation of female desire, and Reader #1 wondered if an epilogue might make sense, tying your research

to the current wave of literary and cinematic retellings of novels by Austen, Brontë, and the like. Both readers praised the manuscript as "highly readable" and "blessedly free of jargon."

If you could write a short (1–2 page) response to the reader's reports, addressing concerns and laying out anticipated revisions, I can bring your materials to our board at our next meeting, scheduled for December 10. Once we receive board approval, I can immediately draw up a contract and send it to you for your signature. We are anticipating a publication date of next December.

Please contact me with any questions, and congratulations. I look forward to working with you.

All best,
Ursula Burton

Acquisitions Editor
Oxford University Press
Academic Division

Attachment 1: CoreyReader'sReport1
Attachment 2: CoreyReader'sReport2

I screamed, startling Rick and, I'm sure, the whole neighborhood. "Oh my God! My book's getting published! I'm going to be a real author! It's happening!" I showed Rick the e-mail, doing a little dance in his living room and cackling.

"Nicely done," Rick said, giving me a big hug. "It feels great, doesn't it?"

"You pulled strings, didn't you?" I said. "I know you did." I felt a twinge of guilt and even shame at being beholden to Rick, but I shook it off. A book contract was a book contract, and I desperately wanted to keep my job.

Rick shrugged innocently. "Ursula has good taste. What can I say?"

"I'm sure it's no big deal for you," I said. "You publish stuff all the time. But this is my first *real* book. I've spent half my life writing about women writers—and now I'm one of them!"

"It never gets old," Rick said, "but you always remember the first time." He pulled me over and gave me a kiss, and I felt myself thrill as he ran his hands over my back and fumbled at the zipper of my dress.

"Want to celebrate?" he asked.

"I have to run to class," I said, pulling away and laughing. "But maybe later."

"Promise?" he asked, letting me go with a flirtatious squeeze.

"Promise."

I ran to class feeling elated and invincible. A book meant I'd get to keep my job. It meant I wouldn't have to move. And it meant I was a "real" writer, someone worthy of having her words in print.

Larry wasn't answering his phone, so I barged

into his department office, yelling, "I have *awesome* news, Lar!"

Larry was sitting at his computer, engrossed in something on the screen. He looked startled and embarrassed as I came in, minimizing whatever he was reading with a nervous click of his mouse.

"Oooooh, Larry—are you watching *porn?*" I asked. "Bad, bad boy."

"Of course not," he said. "This is a school computer. I don't want to get *fired.*"

"Then why're you looking so sneaky?" I teased.

"OK, you busted me," he said, raising his hands up. "I was watching old YouTube videos of Jack doing the ice bucket challenge."

"I heard from Oxford!" I screamed. "The reader's reports were positive!!! They're going to publish my book!!!"

Larry's face broke into a huge smile. "I *knew* it, Annie," he said, getting up to give me a bear hug. "I knew it would work out."

"Thank you, Larry," I said. "I don't know what I'd do without you. I owe you so much." I felt tears spring to my eyes and brushed them away with a happy laugh.

He spun me around his office. "You don't owe me anything. You're a rock star."

I arrived in class in a great mood, feeling giddy and magnanimous. As if sensing this, one of my students raised her hand and said, "Professor Corey, have you seen the ads for *Jane Vampire?*"

"Of course," I said. They were impossible to miss, plastered on bus shelters and billboards around town and featuring a young actress whose name I couldn't remember wrapped in a passionate embrace with Jack Lindsey. They were both spattered with blood, and Jack stared sullenly at the camera, his forearms bare and clutching the starlet's bare back. "Can you love someone to death?" the ad copy read. "*Jane Vampire*. In theaters November 20th."

"Can we get extra credit for watching the movie?" the student asked. "Pretty please?"

"I don't know," I said. "We didn't read the book in class."

"But we read *Jane Eyre*! What if we write a review comparing the two? If the movie sucks, we can talk about why it sucks. Please, Professor Corey???"

My students looked at me eagerly. I felt myself relenting. I'd have to watch *Jane Vampire*, too, in order to write that requested epilogue to my book. Maybe I'd learn something from what my students had to say.

"OK, why not?" I said. "I'll give you extra credit, but the review has to be in by the last day of classes."

The class cheered.

"And please no fanboying or fangirling over the actors. I want a real review, not some random gushing about how hot someone is." I gave a

knowing smile, and there was a burst of laughter.

"I've read the whole *Jane Vampire* trilogy," I heard them say to each other.

"Me, too! I stayed up all night!"

"Jack Lindsey is *so hot.*"

"What did I just hear?" I interrupted, cupping my ear.

"Oops!" the student laughed. "Um, yeah, I meant Jack Lindsay *inhabits the character* of Edward Rochester with, uh, *smoldering physicality.*"

"Much better," I said.

I let class out early and headed back to my office, practically skipping along the way. I even smiled at Pam as I walked past her desk.

"My, it looks like *someone's* in a good mood," Pam teased me as I passed by. "And I have a feeling I know why!"

I looked at her in surprise. No one besides Rick and Larry knew about my book acceptance yet.

"Oh, honey, it's no use pretending anymore. People have seen you riding around campus on Rick's motorcycle. You know people can still recognize you under that helmet, so don't act all innocent!"

"Oh, that," I said. "We're just having fun. It's casual."

"Sure, hon. Just be careful. You know what they say . . . Why buy the cow when you can get the milk for free?"

"Pam," I said, trying not to sound exasperated. "I'm in my thirties. It's the twenty-first century. And I'm not a cow!"

"It's a *metaphor*," Pam said. "You're not getting any younger, and as I always tell my girls, it's better to be safe than sorry." She lowered her voice to a whisper. "I mean, look at what happened to Tiffany."

"What happened to her?" I asked. I hadn't seen Tiffany since the gala, and I assumed she was off lining up more multimillion-dollar donations.

"You didn't hear? She and President Martinez *broke up*."

"What?" I said, trying to hide my surprise. "What happened? I thought they were serious."

"See?" Pam said. "That's what Tiffany thought, too! But President Martinez thought it was just—what was the word you used? 'Casual.' Luckily, she figured it out, and now she's engaged to a Boeing exec. My friend in the development office saw the ring. It's huge!"

"*That* was fast," I said. "What happened? Did he propose to her after a week?"

"Oh, Tiffany's no dummy. She didn't put all her eggs in one basket. She'd been dating this Boeing guy since last year, and once she saw that President Martinez was stringing her along, she moved on. You might take a page from her handbook," she said, "is all I'm saying." Pam looked at me keenly.

I saw Tiffany the next day at a fund-raising meeting, basking in her newly engaged status, happily flaunting her ring and telling anyone who would listen the story of how her fiancé proposed to her over the Jumbotron at the Staples Center during a Lakers game.

"When's the wedding going to be?" someone asked.

"Next winter, sometime," she said. "I'm thinking destination wedding in Cabo, barefoot on the beach, all-white color scheme with teal accents."

Catching sight of me, Tiffany motioned me over, putting a chummy arm over my shoulder.

"Congratulations," I said.

"Oh, thanks," Tiffany said, giggling. "So I see that you and Rick Chasen are getting close," she said, lowering her voice. "That was so sweet of him to help you carry your books."

"Yeah, it was," I said.

"You guys are so perfect for one another! You're both so . . . bookish. So tell me—is it serious?"

I shrugged. "We're dating. It's only been a couple months."

"You only need a couple months to know," she said coyly. "Take my advice. If he's serious, tell him to put a ring on it."

Rick and I began meeting at Chandler Library regularly for writing dates—I had to revise my

manuscript, and Rick had a draft of his novel due to his publisher in the spring. The building was old and drafty, with questionable plumbing and spotty Internet service, but it was still the best place on campus to get work done and so impressive-looking that it was often used as a setting for movie shoots. On the first floor was a large, sun-drenched reading room with leaded windows and long wooden desks, full of Fairfax students with their headphones on and laptops open, cramming for their upcoming finals.

Rick was seated at one of the tables, waving me over to an empty seat beside him. I slid in next to him, plugging in my laptop next to his and unpacking my bag. As I was about to turn on my computer, I heard Rick curse under his breath.

"What's the matter?" I whispered.

Rick was studying his computer with disgust. "It's this wanker who's been sending me these harassing e-mails. Claims I've been recycling some of the writing for my blog."

Rick had recently started writing a weekly column for the website of an acclaimed literary magazine. While the gig was prestigious and well paid, he'd been complaining to me about the frenetic publication schedule.

"What do you mean?"

"He claims I'm self-plagiarizing. Have you ever *heard* of such a thing? It's like accusing

me of raiding my own fridge! So what? Who cares if I'm recycling earlier work? It's a *blog*."

"What does he want you to do?"

"Who the hell knows? Print a retraction? I mean, what a prick. Some people just have too much time on their hands." Rick's voice rose in anger, and some students now looked up from their work.

"Don't worry," I said, trying to calm him down. "He's a troll. Ignore him."

"Let me give you a piece of advice," Rick said. "*Never ever* read the comments section. It's a cesspool of illiterate bile."

Noticing the students staring at us, he lowered his voice and smiled at me wryly.

"Sorry," he whispered. "See what you have to look forward to once you become a published author? Suddenly everyone's out to get you."

We heard a rustle as a group of people walked into the reading room, led by a man in shirt-sleeves and a tie. For a moment I thought it was a campus tour for prospective students, but as they came closer I saw that it was a group of architects, engineers, and administrators carrying large rolls of plans and clipboards. The school paper had recently reported that Bex's gift would help fund a major renovation and expansion of the campus library and that Bex, with her background in art and design, would assume a significant role in

the process. Toward the back of the group, I saw her standing with Adam, her golden hair pulled back in a loose bun, nodding seriously at what the architect was saying.

"Look who's making the rounds," Rick whispered to me. "Your favorite person. Who's that blond lady beside him?"

"Bex Lindsey. She went to college with us. She just donated a huge amount of money to the school."

"Well, Martinez is certainly cozying up to her. That's one thing I have to give the man—he's sly, that one. Knows how to charm dollars out of donors."

"Shhhhh," I said. Adam and Bex were walking over.

"Sorry to bother you while you're working," Adam said, "but I wanted to introduce Professor Chasen to Elizabeth Lindsey. She was very excited to hear you're teaching here."

"It's such an honor to meet you," Bex said, shaking his hand. "I just finished *Subterranean City*—I couldn't put it down."

Rick smiled modestly. "Thank you so much," he said. "I'm delighted you enjoyed it."

"Are you working on anything else now?" Bex asked, glancing at his open laptop. "I hope that's not too invasive a question to ask—I know some writers don't like talking about their current projects."

"Oh, not at all," Rick said. "I'm not precious about that kind of stuff."

As they continued to talk, Adam leaned over to me and whispered, "About the gala—I wanted to apologize."

"It's fine," I said tightly, not looking at him and pretending to pay attention to Bex and Rick's conversation.

"No, it was out of bounds. I was wrong to say anything."

"I don't want to talk about it."

"Please—Anne, don't do this. Look at me."

I grudgingly turned toward him. "To be honest, I *was* pretty upset," I confessed. "I can take care of myself, you know."

"I know. It's all my fault. I was being stupid. Not for the first time."

Rick was laughing at something Bex had said. I watched as she fished into her handbag to give him one of her cards.

"Things are going really well for me right now," I said. "I need you to let me be happy."

"You're absolutely right. I'm an idiot. Please— will you forgive me? Can we be friends?"

I softened in spite of myself. Adam seemed genuinely contrite.

"OK," I relented, finally looking him in the eye. Adam smiled at me with relief, and I let myself smile back.

"It was a pleasure to meet you," Bex was

saying. "I'm sorry we have to run now and catch up with our tour." She looked wistfully at Rick and me. "It must be so lovely to work in the ivory tower," she said. "All your time spent together, reading books and writing. It seems like heaven."

As they walked away, Rick reached over and squeezed my hand.

"If she only knew," he said.

"YOU SURE RICK DOESN'T want to join us?" Larry asked. He'd gotten us tickets to the opening night show of *Jane Vampire* at our local Cineplex.

"I'm sure," I said. "He called it a piece of 'Hollywood dreck.' "

"Doesn't he realize he's missing out on a cultural phenomenon?"

"Um, I think his tastes run more toward the French New Wave."

"Well, *la-di-da,*" Larry said. "His loss."

Now that we were in line for popcorn, I was glad Rick had decided to stay home. The place was packed with women—and not just young girls, but also middle-aged women and grand-mothers, all chattering excitedly, some even dressed in period costume. "My God," Larry said, looking around. "I'm the only guy in this theater."

We wedged ourselves into our seats, between a group of women on a "moms' night out" and a

229

clique of Fairfax sorority girls in matching pink sweatshirts.

"I'm still *so* bitter Jack couldn't get us tickets to the premiere," Larry complained.

"Whatever happened with that?" I asked, reaching over for a handful of popcorn.

"The studio ran out, apparently. Too many VIPs requesting seats. I think he's lying. He's the star of the movie! How can he not get a couple extra tickets to the premiere? He just doesn't want me around. I know it."

"He's still texting you, though," I pointed out.

"Not for the last week, he hasn't. He's in Asia doing press and said his phone might not work from there."

"You don't think Bex found his phone, do you?"

"God, I hope not," Larry said, flinching. "Whatever." He suddenly turned defiant. "Who cares if she did? She knows their marriage is a sham!"

The lights dimmed and we sat through several previews, including a remake of *Cruel Intentions*, a trailer for a movie about male strippers, and a *Downton Abbey*–esque period drama. The cat-calls began with the opening credits, as Jack appeared in the mist, dressed in a waistcoat and cravat, blood trickling from his dagger.

"Be still my heart," Larry sighed.

The movie was a mix of campy violence, over-

acting, and really bad special effects. Jack's Yorkshire accent went in and out, sometimes sounding Australian, sometimes Southern. He spent most of the movie in various states of undress, his shirt torn to shreds or his breeches half falling off, glaring broodingly at the camera when he wasn't trying to slay were-wolves. Rachel's hair was dyed blond for the role, and she was wan and expressionless, with little sexual chemistry with Jack. Still, when she finally sank her teeth into Jack-slash-Rochester, the whole audience squealed in unison. There was a final torrid sex scene, a trembling declaration of love, and then the movie was over. As the lights went up, I looked around. Some girls and even women were wiping their eyes. "That was *so good*," I heard them say. "It was so romantic!"

I turned to Larry, ready to make fun of them, but he was sitting back in his seat, a look of utter bliss on his face. "That was incredible," he said. "I don't think I've seen an adaptation as good since—well, since *Clueless*."

"You're joking, right? Didn't you think it was a little over-the-top?"

"Moderation is a fatal thing," Larry said. "Nothing succeeds like excess."

"I thought Jack's performance was awful," I said. "He sounded like he was still acting in *Days of Our Lives*."

"Oh, Anne," Larry sighed. "Can't you stop being so critical for a minute? You're going to miss your name!"

The credits were rolling by so fast that I was sure we'd already missed it, but Larry suddenly exclaimed, "There it is!" He pointed to the words "Historical Consultant," followed by my name, "Ann Corey." He began clapping wildly.

"They misspelled my name," I noted sourly. "It's probably Jack's fault. He could never be bothered to spell my name right."

Larry ignored me, his eyes still fixed on the screen. We stayed until the bitter end, and as we were filing out of the theater, Larry turned to me and asked, "Want to see it again? I think there's a midnight showing."

From: Stephen Culpepper
<S.Culpepper@Fairfax.edu>
To: <English Department Faculty and Staff>
Subject: Sundry Deadlines
Date: December 2

Dear Esteemed Colleagues,

As the semester comes to a close, *nota bene* the following deadlines:

December 3: Course evaluations distributed in your department mailboxes. Please follow the instructions regarding dissemination and collection

of said evaluations. You **cannot** be in the room while evaluations are being completed.

    December 10: Sealed course evaluations due to Pam
    December 17: Final Grades due to Registrar
    The office will be closed for winter break from December 18 to January 3.

    Happy Holidays and Best Wishes for a Prosperous New Year.

As ever,
Steve

From: Ursula Burton, Acquisitions Editor
<UABurton@oup.com>
To: Anne Corey <A.Corey@Fairfax.edu>
Subject: Manuscript request
Date: December 10

Dear Anne Corey,

I am delighted to report that your manuscript has passed our board review. I will issue you a publication contract shortly. Please sign and return to me at your earliest convenience.

    In the meantime, if you could submit your **final** revised manuscript (including complete Table of Contents, Bibliography, Notes, and Acknowledgments) by **February 1**, we should be able to adhere

to our planned publication schedule. I will send you a house style guide shortly. Please do not hesitate to contact me with any questions or concerns. Welcome aboard!

Ursula Burton

_____

Acquisitions Editor
Oxford University Press
Academic Division

From: Fairfax Retirement Home <info@fairfaxhome.org>
To: <undisclosed recipients>
Subject: Secret Santa Holiday Party
Date: December 12

Please join us for our annual holiday party on Sunday, December 22 from 1-3 p.m. in the rec room. We will exchange Secret Santa gifts and enjoy cookies, punch, caroling, and even a special visit from Santa Claus!
   RSVP to Mimi at Margaret.Payton@fairfaxhome.org by December 18.

From: Lauren Corey Winston <lauren@toteally.com>
To: Anne Corey <A.Corey@Fairfax.edu>
Subject: Secret Santa
Date: December 16

Can you deal with the Secret Santa gift? I'm too busy dealing with the kids' school stuff. We'll be in Chicago from 12/20 - 1/3.

FYI, the boys want iTunes gift cards for Christmas. You can just mail them to us. I'm buying them a trampoline and saying it's from Dad.

chapter thirteen

I T'S THE MOST WONDERFUL time of the year!"
Larry sang out.

"What, Christmastime?" I asked.

"No! Course-evaluation time!"

Larry was the only person I knew who actually
looked forward to reading his student evals.
He was one of the most popular professors on
campus, with his own Facebook fan club and
a string of departmental and college teaching
awards. Even his Rate My Professor reviews
were over-the-top effusive. "Professor Ettinger
is seriously the best prof I've had at Fairfax," a
typical review read. "He's tough, but you'll learn
a lot. I heart him." One of Larry's favorite things
to do was to go through his reviews and count
how many chili peppers he got.

"Don't you feel like you're a restaurant on
Yelp?" I once asked him.

"Oh, yes," he said. "It's wonderful! Apparently
my students find me absolutely flaming."

"I *loathe* course evaluations," I said, pulling my
package of evals from my department mailbox.
"I never remember the good ones, only the bad.

Like the time someone wrote, 'If I had an hour to live, I'd spend it in this class because it felt like ETERNITY.' "

"Oh, everyone gets an occasional doozy. You just have to laugh at them. I've memorized my favorites."

"Like what?"

"Like the time someone called me a 'flaming douche nugget with a messed-up sense of humer'—h-u-m-e-r."

"That's awesome," I laughed. "You win. I've definitely never been called that before."

I walked over to the Xerox machine to run off copies of my upcoming final exam, placing my original on the glass and hitting start. Nothing happened. I pushed the button again. Still nothing.

"Goddammit," I said.

"Another paper jam?" Larry asked.

"Some idiot played ding-dong-ditch with the copier."

"Ooooh, let me take a wild guess who it was . . ."

I unlocked some levers, opened a flap, and removed several sheets of paper that had accordioned on the rollers. Part of the sheet was still legible:

Dr. Stephen Culpepper
ENGL 431: Medieval Morality Plays
Glossary of Literar—

"It was Steve," I said.

"Of course it was," Larry laughed. "Did you even have to look?"

"How is someone capable of reading Anglo-Saxon and not understand how to clear a *paper jam?* Or at least leave a Post-it note apologizing?"

"Oh, you know Steve—he thinks his copies just magically disappear in the bowels of the machine. Like medieval sorcery!"

Steve was in his office setting up a miniature nativity scene when I swung by to deliver the news about my book contract.

"My, my, my! Congratulations, Anne," Steve said, adjusting the manger. "Just barely in the nick of time! Truthfully, I was starting to get a bit nervous for you. So when will the book be out?"

"In about a year, if everything goes smoothly."

"I hope you'll get a chance to celebrate a little over the holidays. Are you going anywhere?"

"No, I'll be around," I said. "Working on book revisions." Rick had floated the possibility of my joining him at a writer's colony in Costa Rica, but I'd had to decline. For one thing, the plane ticket would have cost close to a thousand bucks. For another, Lauren was going to be visiting her in-laws for the holidays, which meant I was in charge of celebrating with my father.

"And when are these revisions due?" Steve asked.

"Beginning of February."

"Well, you better get cracking," Steve said, putting on a CD of medieval Christmas carols and starting to hum along. "As soon as we get back from break, I'll get in touch with HR about extending your employment contract. In the meantime, I'll need a copy of your book contract and, come February, proof that the entire revised manuscript has been submitted."

Seeing me start (what else did he want? my firstborn child?) Steve gave a little shrug. "Writers break their contracts all the time. You wouldn't believe the stories—I know a fellow who managed to be promoted to *full* professor on the strength of a book that never materialized." He shook his head. "We want to make sure everything's airtight before we proceed."

"Oh," I said. "Thanks." As I turned to leave, I added, "I found some of your handouts stuck in the copy machine. I left them in your box."

"Ah, thank you," Steve said, chuckling. "Some little elves must have left them there."

THE CAMPUS EMPTIED OUT completely over the winter break. The dorms closed, the library shut down, and even businesses on Main Street shuttered their doors for the two-week holiday. Rick had left for Costa Rica, and Larry was on his way to Paris, where he'd booked a last-minute getaway to distract himself from his Jack travails.

I went to the Christmas party at the assisted-living facility, bringing my dad some new socks and two boxes of See's chocolates—one for him and one for his Secret Santa. The place was decorated with tinsel and a large artificial Christmas tree hung with plastic gold ornaments and candy canes. All the staff members were wearing Santa hats, and some of the residents were wearing Christmas sweaters and reindeer antlers. My father was sitting in a chair, dressed in a robe with his leg propped up on a stool and swaddled by a flesh-colored bandage. An aide dressed in holiday scrubs stood beside him, checking his dressing.

"What happened?" I asked, rushing to his side.

"Oh, nothing," my father said, pooh-poohing my concern. "Some idiot pushed me."

"Now Mr. Corey, you know that's not true," the aide said, giving him a bemused look. "You tripped and hurt your shin."

"OK, fine. But my story sounds better." My dad winked at her, and she made a show of rolling her eyes.

"Has your father always been such a trouble-maker?" the aide asked me, grinning. "The *real* story is that he was walking to the rec room and lost his balance. Knocked his leg against one of the side tables. The doctor's already checked it out. It's not broken—just bruised."

"Is he OK? Does he need a walker or something?" I asked.

"We're keeping an eye on him—he may need a cane for added stability."

"I don't need a cane!" my father bellowed. "The only thing that's bruised is my ego!"

I shushed my father and handed him a paper cup filled with punch, and he settled back in his chair. Over the next hour, he held court as a steady stream of old ladies approached us to see how he was doing and offer their sympathies. "Are you Jerry's daughter?" they asked me. "Are you the single one or the one with kids? Jerry's such a sweetheart. Always cracking jokes, that one."

"Wow, Dad, you're really popular," I whispered.

"There are only four men in this entire facility, and one just had a heart attack," my dad said, deadpan. "The odds are with me."

I couldn't believe it. As far as I knew, my father had never dated anyone after my mother died. I was four when she passed away from ovarian cancer and I had only the dimmest memories of her—a certain rose-scented lotion, a soft set of hands. They were the only constants against a backdrop that seemed perpetually to be changing. Back then, we'd moved frequently, staying at a place just long enough for my father to fix it up and rent it out before we moved to the next place. I never learned to memorize my home address because six months later, it would inevitably change.

After my mother died, my father made one concession to us. He didn't make us move anymore. He bought a modest tract home in a good neighborhood and let us, for once, put pictures on the wall. He was always working, and Lauren and I soon learned to take care of ourselves, keeping the place tidy, doing the grocery shopping, cooking our own meals. Our mother receded into the background, and Lauren assumed her spot in the household.

Now, freed from responsibility, my father seemed lighter and happier than I'd ever seen him. He even cracked jokes and smiled every once in a while. He introduced me to a silver-haired woman named Georgia, then a redhead named Helene. They were each vying for my father's attention when Helene suddenly squealed, "Is that a *baby?*"

A young woman had just entered the room, carrying an infant in a carrier on her chest. Around me, there was a ripple of excitement. "Did someone say 'BABY'? I want to see the BABY!"

The young mother looked startled as she was surrounded by a bunch of frantic old ladies. I'd never seen anything like it. Even the ladies snoozing in their wheelchairs suddenly perked up and started rolling their way over.

"Is that your BABY?" one of them asked, her frail arms outstretched. "Can I hold your

BABY?" The baby started to cry and the mother tried to shush him.

I watched in morbid fascination from across the room. Turning to my father, I asked, "Are they always like that?"

My dad shrugged. "Who knows?" he said. "Even I can't compete with a baby."

I chuckled at my dad's joke. For a second, I considered telling him about my book contract but then thought better of it. A contract would mean nothing to him. He'd want to see an actual book, something he could hold and touch. As far as he was concerned, nothing I'd ever done had worked out. I thought back to how he'd dismissed Adam and scoffed at my career aspirations, and I was sure he would see this book contract as another foolish scheme of mine that was bound to fail.

Best to wait until the book was out to share the news, I decided. Anything could happen between now and the book's publication, and I didn't want to rile him up unnecessarily. With his leg hoisted onto the stool, he looked frailer than normal, swallowed up by his huge armchair.

I stood up. "Want more punch, Dad?" I asked.

I WALKED HOME THAT evening after promising my father to visit again on Christmas Day. The sky had turned dusky, and I could smell the smoky, sweet smell of a wood-burning fireplace.

As I turned down my cul-de-sac and walked up to my apartment, I saw an explosion of leaves and then a flurry of barking coming from the front yard of a nearby house. A couple of squirrels darted up a tree, chased by a black-and-white dog with a speckled snout and light-colored eyes. The squirrels chattered excitedly above, sending down a shower of leaves, while the dog circled below, paws scrambling against the trunk.

Is that Charlie? I wondered, making my way over. The dog ran over to me, snuffling around my ankles and leaping up for kisses. I leaned over and managed to get ahold of his collar. On the small blue tag, I read:

CHARLIE
ADAM MARTINEZ
76 WELLESLEY ROAD
FAIRFAX, CA

I looked around, but the street was deserted. Charlie must have slipped out of his house and gotten lost.

"Come on, Charlie," I said. "Let me take you home."

Charlie followed me without much coaxing, pausing now and again to sniff at someone's lawn or perk up his ears when a bird flew by. As we approached the president's mansion, he broke into a run, leaping up the steps and to the

front door, where he started barking to be let in.

I ran up the stairs after him, noticing how the porch had been decorated for the season, with large pots filled with red and white poinsettias and a lush holly wreath on the door. A white porch swing hung to my right, covered in dark green cushions, along with some matching rattan furniture.

Before I could ring the doorbell, Adam had opened the door.

"There you are, you rascal!" he said as Charlie jumped up to greet him. "You nearly gave me a heart attack!"

"Hi," I said. "I saw him running around my neighborhood just now and figured he'd gotten lost."

"Thanks so much for bringing him home," Adam said, shaking his head with relief. "I'm so glad he didn't get hit by a car. We were just about to head to LA."

"Luckily he ran *away* from the main thorough-fare instead of toward it," I said. "When I found him, he was in the middle of terrorizing some squirrels."

"Of course," Adam laughed. "He's absolutely convinced that one day he's going to catch one."

"Did you find Charlie?" someone asked, coming up behind Adam. Bex.

"Oh, hi!" I said, startled. "I didn't realize you were still in town."

"I'm just here for the day looking at some real estate," Bex said, smiling. "Fairfax is just so charming—I'm thinking of maybe buying a place. Do you live around here?"

"Yes—just around the corner, in one of those old Victorians."

"Oh, I love those! Which one?"

"The yellow one with peeling paint and green shutters. I live at the top."

"How darling! My dream is to buy one of those houses and fix it up. Could you imagine? Let me know if your landlord is ever interested in selling."

"Sure. Well, happy holidays to both of you," I said, heading back down the steps. "Have a safe drive."

"Are you going anywhere for the holidays?" Adam called out.

"No—just staying in town with my dad."

"Well, happy holidays," Adam said, waving. "And thanks again."

WITHOUT CLASSES TO TEACH, I found myself reverting to a nocturnal schedule, waking up at noon, visiting my father for a couple hours, then heading home to write late into the evening and night. I subsisted on a typical grad school diet of ramen and countless cups of coffee, sometimes not bothering to get out of my pajamas or even take a shower. Rick sent me photos of dazzling

Costa Rican sunsets and a shot of him resting on a surfboard. Larry sent me photos of macarons at Ladurée.

The days blurred together. I felt like I was in a submarine, isolated from the rest of the world. I knew the process of revision was slow and painful, but this was slower and more painful than anything I'd ever worked on before. Every time I took a break to eat or make another cup of coffee, I felt myself flooded with self-doubt. This was it, I thought. I was going to fail. The contract was a fluke. I was an imposter. The only reason I'd even gotten the contract was because of Rick. Who did I think I was anyway?

I'd choke back the doubts and force myself underwater again, back into the bubble of writing and revising. The sun set, my coffee got cold, and Jellyby kept trying to sit on my keyboard. I wrote into the night, and when I was finally too tired to keep my eyes open, I dropped onto the couch and slept, but even then I dreamed about what I had to fix still and how much more I had to do. I woke up troubled and anxious, made myself another pot of coffee, toasted some bread that I immediately forgot about, and sat down again at my computer.

On New Year's Eve, I sat down at my desk around three p.m. and had been working, uninterrupted, for a couple hours or so when I heard a volley of barking outside. I walked over to my

window and peeked out, blinking into the setting sun. It was Charlie, pulling Adam up the steps of my porch.

"Adam!" I said, opening the front door, frantically trying to smooth my hair and look somewhat presentable. "What are you doing here?"

"Sorry to barge in on you like this," he apologized. "I was taking Charlie on a walk and saw the light on. I wasn't sure if it was your place, but Charlie seemed convinced. Yellow Victorian with green shutters, right?"

"That's right." Charlie wiggled past me and into my apartment.

"Charlie!" Adam yelled. "Get back here! I'm so sorry—he's got terrible manners."

"It's fine—come in. Um, sorry about the mess. I've been working." I'd been deep into my chapter on Brontë and now felt disoriented seeing Adam walk into my living room. He looked out of place in my small apartment, too tall and too pulled together. I wondered if my place smelled. I wondered if my breath smelled. I wondered if I could surreptitiously change out of my pajamas and put on a bra. Behind me, I could hear Jellyby hissing. Charlie had cornered her under the bed and was barking at her excitedly.

"You have a cat?" Adam asked.

"Yes, named Jellyby."

"That's Dickens, right?"

"Yes! You know me too well."

As soon as the words came out of my mouth, I wished I hadn't said them, but Adam was grinning at me affectionately. I felt myself getting flustered, listening to the cacophony of Charlie's barking and Jellyby's retaliatory yowls.

I finally managed to lure Charlie from my bedroom with a scoop of Jellyby's kibble and quickly shut the bedroom door behind me, hoping Adam hadn't seen my unmade bed and the pile of unfolded laundry I'd dumped onto a chair. Years of being a grad student meant most of my furniture was still secondhand or from IKEA. Nothing—from my towels to my bedsheets to my dishes—matched. While I liked to think my place looked boho chic in an Anthropologie sort of way, I now suspected it looked more like a grown-up dorm room, haphazard and cluttered.

"Please sit!" I told Adam, trying to tidy up the living room a little. During the break, my apartment had fallen into a state of squalor—my sink was full of dirty dishes, the coffee table covered in empty mugs, the couch blanketed in Jellyby's fur. I found a lint brush and tried to clear a spot for Adam to sit on.

"Sorry," I muttered. "I swear, I'm not usually such a slob." I felt strangely vulnerable having Adam in my private space. We'd practically lived together in college, but now he was a stranger and I wondered what he was thinking. That he

couldn't imagine having to live in such filth? That I could still barely take care of myself?

"What are you working on?" Adam asked, looking curiously at the pile of books and papers on my desk.

"I'm finishing up my book," I said. "I just landed a book contract and need to finish up some revisions."

"Wow!" Adam exclaimed, practically bounding from his seat in excitement. "Why didn't you tell me? That's a huge accomplishment! Congratulations!"

"Thanks," I said, blushing. "Though I've still got a lot of work to do."

"This is huge! We need to celebrate." Adam paused. "I know—what are you doing tonight? Do you already have plans?"

"I was just planning to write," I stammered. "I'm kind of in the zone. Besides, everyone's out of town."

"It's New Year's Eve. You deserve a break. I have an idea—why don't you come over and we'll toast your book? I have some champagne left over from a reception. And my mom sent me home with about ten pounds of tamales."

"Oh, you really don't have to do that," I said. "I'm sure you've got other plans—"

"Nope—no plans. I just got back into town an hour ago and was planning to watch a movie and go to bed. Very exciting stuff."

I hesitated. Adam leaned toward me, his elbows resting on his knees. "Please let me do this—it's the very least I can do after you brought Charlie home safely. Deal?" Hearing his name, Charlie trotted up and nosed his way between us, demanding pets.

"I guess so," I finally said. Charlie rewarded me with a sloppy kiss.

Before I could change my mind, Adam had whistled for Charlie and was heading for the door.

"I'll see you around eight or so," he said. "No excuses."

AT 8:12 P.M., I walked up the porch to Adam's house and knocked, feeling slightly tipsy. Just before leaving my apartment, I'd impulsively knocked back a double shot of tequila, something I hadn't done since college. It had burned a trail into my stomach, where it sat like a lump of coal, radiating heat and self-confidence.

Liquid courage! I said to myself as I did one last mirror check before leaving the house. *You can do this.*

"Perfect timing," Adam said when he opened the door, a bottle of champagne in his hand. "I was just about to open this!"

I smiled a little too widely at Adam and then leaned over to pet Charlie, noticing he was wearing a silver bow tie.

"What's this?" I laughed.

"He got all dressed up for you," Adam said, leading me into the house. He'd changed into a fresh T-shirt and jeans and was barefoot. I'd changed into what I thought was a casual but festive top but now wondered if I looked like Charlie—silly and overdressed. I followed Adam through the public rooms, now dimly lit and deserted, and into the main kitchen. It was a cavernous space, more like a professional catering kitchen than anything else. Adam didn't stop there, though, but made a slight turn into an adjoining room.

"Where are we going?" I asked, as we entered a breakfast nook with a view of the backyard and then a second, more traditional home kitchen.

"These are the private living quarters. Most of the rooms in the front are for public events, but this is where I really, actually live. It's weird, huh? Two kitchens in the same house and this whole other section that no one really sees."

Adam popped the champagne and poured me a glass while I looked around. It was our first time really alone together, and I tried to mask my nerves with a steady patter of superficial questions and observations. I tried not to appear too nosy or stare at anything for too long, but I felt Adam watching me and tried to act casual and nonchalant.

The kitchen and dining area were comfort-

able and minimally adorned, a bowl of oranges on the breakfast table and a small stack of books piled neatly beside it. To the right was a writing alcove covered with Fairfax memorabilia—name badges, pennants, a stuffed wolverine with a red ribbon around its neck. The bulletin board was thick with invitations, programs, and business cards, interspersed with photographs from official campus functions. I peered more closely. There was a photo of Adam posing with the board of trustees, another from convocation, a third from some kind of alumni function, with Bex smiling beside him.

"Nice pictures," I said lamely.

We moved into the adjoining living room, where a small fire was burning in the fireplace. Adam held the door open for me and switched on a lamp, which bathed the room in a low, golden light. Through a side door, I caught a glimpse into Adam's library, the bookshelves wreathed in shadows.

"Please sit," Adam said, handing me the glass of champagne. I sat on one end of the couch, and Adam took a seat across from me, our knees almost touching. Charlie settled, with a dramatic sigh, into a heap at my feet.

"Cheers!" he said. "To your book!"

We clinked glasses and sipped. Adam found some mixed nuts and chocolates in a holiday gift basket and set them out on the coffee table.

"It must be strange living here," I said, surveying the carved mantelpiece and the tasteful neutral-colored furniture. "It's so . . . grown-up." I thought of Adam's college dorm room, with its shelves made of plywood and Yaffa blocks and its battered, faded futon. I thought of my own apartment, with its mismatched furnishings and chipped dishes and tumbleweeds of cat hair.

"It *is* weird," Adam said. "It's just me and Charlie rattling around in this huge space. Sometimes I talk to myself just to hear someone's voice."

The house *was* awfully quiet. The sound of the fire crackling in its grate seemed magnified by the silence.

I took a chocolate and bit into it. It was filled with cherry liqueur and I tried not to gag, taking a big swig of champagne to wash it down. "How was your Christmas?" I asked, coughing as the bubbles went up my nose.

"It was relaxing—I went to LA to see my mother. I try to get down to see her at least once a week."

"Is she doing OK?"

"Yes, she's doing great. I've been trying to get her to stop working so hard, but she won't listen to me. She retired a few years ago, but you'd never know from looking at her—she barely sat down the whole time I was there."

"Has she been up here to visit you yet?"

"Just once, for the inauguration. I'd like her to come more often, but she says she doesn't want to bother me. These official college functions—they can be overwhelming for her. All these strangers, this big old house . . . and, well, she's still self-conscious about her accent."

I nodded. The whole time we'd been in college, Adam's mother had never visited. Partly it was because plane tickets were expensive and she couldn't take the time off work, but partly, Adam explained, it was because she was intimidated by the campus. During one of our first dates, Adam had told me his mother had been nineteen when she fled Guatemala, taking an infant Adam with her. About his father, Adam said he knew little—his mother refused to talk about him, but Adam suspected he'd been a member of the local militia. Mother and son were understandably close, and they were drawn even closer when Adam was fourteen and his mother informed him that college was out of the question, not because of tuition but because they were undocumented. What followed was a harrowing year of visits to law offices, his mother crying beside him, Adam aware that at any moment they could be deported to a country he did not remember. After nearly two years of desperate prayers, along with letters of support from his school principal, his mother's employers, and even the archbishop

of Los Angeles, Adam and his mother were granted asylum, with a path to a green card and, eventually, citizenship.

"She must be so proud of you," I said.

"She is—though honestly, at this point all she wants are grandkids." He laughed ruefully.

"Is that her in the photo?" I asked, getting up to look at a small framed picture on the mantel. It showed Adam beaming beside a slightly built, dark-haired woman in front of a pretty Craftsman house covered in bougainvillea.

"Yes, that's her. We took that picture a few years ago."

"Where were you? It looks just like Fairfax!"

"It's actually in Altadena. I bought her a house there a few years ago."

"You bought her a *house?*" I gulped.

"I saved up for a long time," Adam said, looking embarrassed. "It's something I'd always wanted to do for her."

"Wow. You're like the greatest son ever. All I got my dad for Christmas was a ten-pack of Costco socks."

Adam laughed. "I'm sure he appreciated them. Very practical, just like him." Before I could protest, he'd reached over and refilled my glass of champagne.

"How about you? How was your Christmas?" he asked.

"Oh, it was low-key," I said, taking another

sip. "I just spent it with my dad at the retirement home. Luckily, he seems to be adapting better to the environment. He even has a couple of girlfriends."

"No kidding," Adam said.

"Yeah, it's crazy," I said. The mixture of champagne and tequila was making me feel witty and expansive. "The ratio there is like ten women to each man, so my dad kind of has his pick. Lauren's freaking out—she thinks it's weird."

"Is she up here often?"

"Every once in awhile. She's busy with the kids, though, so she kind of depends on me to keep an eye on him during the week. It's the least I can do—I mean, she's paying for everything else and all." I thought again about the Costco socks and cringed.

"Your dad is lucky to have you so close by," Adam said. "Just being able to see you regularly—that's a huge gift."

Adam left to heat up some of his mother's tamales, switching on the television for me to watch while he was gone. I helped myself to a third glass of champagne, tossed it back, and immediately regretted it. What had I eaten for dinner again? I couldn't remember, but I was pretty sure it wasn't much more than a piece of toast or can of soup. The room had started to swirl a little, and I settled back farther into the couch, trying to focus on what was going on on

the television. Ryan Seacrest was interviewing people in Times Square, and I suddenly realized it was almost midnight in New York. The camera zoomed in on the ball, and I felt my eyes cross.

Adam returned, and I tried to eat some tamales as daintily as I could, hoping to soak up some of the alcohol.

"These are really good," I heard myself say. "Tell your mom I said so." I dropped some food on the carpet and tried, surreptitiously, to wipe it up while Charlie waited at my elbow, eager to help.

The one-minute countdown began, and Adam and I fell silent, watching as the camera panned across the crowds of people in New York.

"It looks cold there," I said. I tried to think what I should do when the clock hit midnight—wish Adam a Happy New Year? Give him a hug? Clink glasses again? Would Adam kiss me? He was sitting right across from me, our knees practically touching, his arm resting casually beside him. How badly I wanted to reach over and take his hand or, better yet, slip onto the couch beside him and rest my head on his shoulder. My fondest memories of our relationship had been of sitting with him just so, secure and content, his hand in mine. We'd spent one New Year's in college in just such a way, huddled under a blanket and drinking hot chocolate, ignoring the

hoots and hollers of drunken partygoers outside.

"Yeah—I don't miss New York winters," Adam said. His fingers drummed the couch cushion softly, and his eyes remained fixed on the television screen.

Definitely no interest here, I thought. He was just waiting impatiently for the ball to drop. I cursed myself for having drunk all the champagne, eyeing the empty bottle and Adam's still half-full glass. In slow motion, I watched as the ball dropped, followed by fireworks and shot after shot of couples, young and old, kissing each other to ring in the new year. I had just turned toward Adam when my phone buzzed. A text from Rick.

"Happy New Year!"

"Hppy nqq yard!" I texted back. That didn't look right.

"Doing anything tonight?" he wrote back.

"Nkthing."

"Are you drunk?"

"N

O

O

!

☺ "

As I fumbled with my phone, I heard Adam go into the library to answer a call from his mother. "*Prospero Año Nuevo, Mamá!*" I heard him say. "*Te quiero.*"

While I waited for Adam to return, I suddenly realized I was, indeed, horrifyingly, embarrassingly drunk. So drunk I needed to rest my head on a pillow for a minute lest I throw up the contents of my stomach. I closed my eyes and forced myself to take deep breaths, counting my breaths aloud.

The last time I'd been this drunk was the night Adam and I broke up and I'd gone back to my dorm room and downed an entire bottle of peach schnapps that I found under my bed. I'd gone to bed at six a.m. and nearly slept through graduation, saved only by the angry knocking of my sister at the door. She was furious with me, as was my father, who looked at my swollen face and disheveled hair and shook his head sourly. They left right after the ceremony, skipping my graduation brunch and making no mention of the fact that I'd graduated magna cum laude, marked by a little asterisk by my name in the commencement program. I'd killed myself for that dumb asterisk, wanting to make Professor Russell and my father proud.

In the other room, I could hear Adam continue to talk to his mother, his voice soft and soothing. He must have had a wonderful graduation, I thought enviously. I could just imagine the two of them at brunch, Adam handsome in his cap and gown, his mother beside him, bursting with pride. While they'd been celebrating, I had

slipped away, alone, to the post office in Palmer Square. There, I'd dropped the engagement ring Adam had given me into a plain envelope, sealed it shut, and addressed it to Adam care of his mother. I didn't bother insuring the contents or requesting delivery confirmation, so I never found out if Adam ever got the package. He never tried to contact me, and I was too angry and proud to reach out to him.

From the other room, I could hear Adam wish his mother good-bye and then step out of the library and back into the living room. I forced myself to an upright position but kept my eyes closed.

"Are you OK?" I heard Adam say from far away.

"Yeah," I said. "Just resting my eyes a little. Don't mind me. Ima little drunk."

"The bathroom's down the hall," he said.

"Thanks, 'preciate it. Just gimme a minute."

I heard Adam walk into the kitchen and place some glasses into the sink.

How long ago it all seemed, I thought wearily. I'd been so angry at Adam for so long, but now I just felt embarrassment and shame. I'd behaved badly. I'd humiliated myself. In the years following our breakup, I stopped searching for him online, not wanting to be reminded of the past. Best just to forget it all, I told myself. Adam's letters, which I'd carefully saved in a

shoebox, I eventually tossed into the garbage, along with every other vestige of our relationship—class notes we'd shared, movie ticket stubs, a card tucked into a bouquet of flowers Adam had gotten me for Valentine's Day. I was sure Adam had done the same. The only thing I couldn't bear to throw away was the copy of *Persuasion* Adam had given me—not so much (I told myself) because he'd given it to me but because it was a *book,* and I never threw away books. To toss a Jane Austen novel into the trash? Now *that* would be sacrilege.

I must have fallen asleep because the next thing I knew, it was dawn and I heard the sound of sprinklers going off outside. I sat up, disoriented and hungover. For a split second, I thought I was back in my college dorm room, fooled by the dim slant of light through the lead glass windows and the rattling sound of an old radiator. *Where am I?* I thought. Dully, I realized I was stretched out on Adam's couch, and he had taken off my shoes and put a blanket over me. A glass of water and a small trash can had been placed next to my head.

I felt my head throb painfully. I'd drooled all over the pillow, and the fabric had left indentations down the side of my face. I couldn't remember lying down, much less falling asleep, and I wondered if there was anything else I didn't remember. Had I said or done anything else

embarrassing? My face burning, I quickly folded up the blanket, collected my shoes, and crept into the kitchen to see if Adam was up. The kitchen was dark, our two empty glasses of champagne in the sink, the champagne bottle in the recycling bin. I chugged a glass of water, spilled some on myself, tried to mop up the mess with a paper towel, then couldn't find the trash can before eventually locating it under the kitchen sink. Everything was so tidy and organized, and I found myself stifling the urge to look through the rest of the cupboards. I peeked around the corner and saw a small laundry room with a narrow staircase leading up to the second floor. A minute later, I heard the rustle of Charlie's tags as he appeared on top of the landing, looking down at me.

"Shhhhhhh!" I said, putting my finger on my lips. "It's just me."

Charlie scurried down the stairs and I gave him a quick pet. "Sorry I was such a lousy guest," I whispered. I found a memo pad on the kitchen table and jotted down a quick note.

"I let myself out. Happy New Year. Anne."

Before I left, I took one last look at Adam's living quarters. The place looked immaculate, as if I'd never been there. Satisfied, I eased my way out the back door and picked my way across the damp lawn, Charlie watching me from the window all the while.

From: Britnee <brit.brat.bro@yahoo.com>
To: Anne Corey <A.Corey@Fairfax.edu>
Subject: ENG 220 grade
Date: January 3

dear mrs. cory,

i just checked my grades online and i was very disappointed that you gave me a d+ in your poetry class. i worked really hard and wrote all the papers. i know i missed a lot of classes, but i had an undiagnosed case of mono that i'm only getting over now.
    i lost my syllabus so if you could let me know what i missed and what extra credit I can do to make it up, that would be awesome. i just applied to law school and this could really mess up my gpa. I think i at least deserve a b.

brit

✳

From: Stephen Culpepper <S.Culpepper@Fairfax.edu>
To: Anne Corey <A.Corey@Fairfax.edu>
Subject: Britnee Brown
Date: January 6

Dear Anne,

Happy New Year! Hope you had a wonderful and recuperative winter break.

I'm sorry to bother you, but one of your ENG 220 students from last semester, Britnee Brown, has been leaving endless messages on my office phone about changing her grade. I told her she could file a grade appeal, and that seemed to satisfy her, but then her father called this morning and threatened to sue if her grade wasn't amended. The department will, of course, stand behind you, but I would very much appreciate it if you could forward me Ms. Brown's grade breakdown as well as a list of absences to refer to, as needed.

I am, yours faithfully,
Steve

Editor, *"Piers Plowman" Reader*
(Cambridge UP, 2011)
Coeditor (with Ron Holbrook),
Early Medieval Grammar (CLIO Press, 2006)
Editor, *Journal of Anglo-Norman Studies*
(2005–present)
Member, Medium Aevum, the Society for the Study of Medieval Languages and Literature

From: Lawrence Ettinger <L.Ettinger@Fairfax.edu>
To: Anne Corey <A.Corey@Fairfax.edu>
Subject: little miss b
Date: January 6

You want a better GPA? You want a JD/MBA?
  You best not be MIA. You better work bitch.
  You better work bitch. You better work bitch.

chapter fourteen

I MISSED YOU," RICK SAID, giving me a bear hug. He was tan and even blonder from his time in Costa Rica.

"Did you get a lot of writing done?" I asked.

"Tons. It was really quite therapeutic. It's too bad you couldn't join. How were things over here?"

"I'm completely exhausted," I said. "I need a vacation from vacation. I don't know how you make writing seem so easy—this book's killing me."

"Just wait until you start your second book. That one's the real killer."

"Second book? Ha! Let me finish this one first."

We were in my office, prepping for the start of the spring semester. Rick had another pile of applications to read for his writing workshop, and I was belatedly trying to finalize my syllabus. Usually I liked nothing more than writing up syllabi—it was like ordering a nine-course meal of all my favorite dishes—but now I was feeling uninspired and burned out.

"What do you think if I call my nineteenth-

century novel class 'Scribbling Women: The Rise of the Female Author'?" I asked Rick.

"You want my honest opinion?"

"Of course!"

"No offense, but *I* wouldn't want to take that class."

"Why not?" I asked, hurt.

"Well, for starters, I'm a guy. It sounds like it's all about gender and feminism."

"Well, it *is*."

"You're not thinking like a nineteen-year-old undergraduate. A nineteen-year-old undergrad doesn't care about scribbling women, or the rise of the female author, or anything other than what time the class meets and if it requires too much reading and writing."

"Really?" I protested.

"What does Larry call his Oscar Wilde class?"

I thought for a moment. "I think he titled it 'Girls Gone Wilde' the last time I checked."

"There you go. Take it from me. Sex sells."

I sighed and turned to my computer, taking a break from my syllabus to scroll through the posts on my favorite celebrity blog. I clicked on a new blind item, posted under a big pink question mark:

Has she had enough?

They were longtime sweethearts, the golden couple. He's an actor who's

finally broken through, playing against type in a big Hollywood blockbuster. She's a civilian, but in some ways bigger than he is because of her Family. Think Rockefeller, not Corleone. There were rumors that the two of them were taking a break, a "conscious uncoupling," as it were. Discretion was key. He had certain urges. She looked the other way. She assumed he was like one of the characters he'd once played, the one whose family she knew from summering on the Cape.

Except he swings both ways. He likes them young and he likes them buff, though he's not overly discerning. She's fine being his beard, so long as he keeps his s— tight. But he's getting reckless. Maybe it's the fame going to his head, maybe the relationship has just run its course. The only problem is that he needs her more than she needs him. She could walk at any time and be fine, but he's got two sequels lined up and an image to protect. She's given him an ultimatum. Three strikes and you're out.

Hint: *Not* Bradley Cooper

I gasped.
"What is it?" Rick asked.

"Read this," I said, pointing to the screen. "Can you tell who it is?"

Rick glanced at the item and shrugged. "Am I supposed to know?" he asked.

"It's Jack Lindsey. I mean, it's obvious."

"I can't believe you read that crap, Anne," Rick said, turning back to his reading. "Don't you know those tabloid rags just make stuff up? You have a PhD—you should know better."

"Some of these gossip blogs are really well written," I protested. "And they're right, a lot of the time!"

"So if they wrote that Bigfoot was discovered on Mars, you'd believe them?"

"That's ridiculous. These blogs focus on celebrities."

"OK, so if they wrote that Tom Cruise was gay, you'd believe them?"

"Tom Cruise *is* gay."

"What about John Travolta?"

"He's gay, too."

"Christ, do you think *everybody* is gay?"

"Not everybody. Just Jack Lindsey. And Tom Cruise. And John Travolta. And Bradley Cooper. And—"

"OK, stop," Rick said. "You're just proving my point."

I ran over to Larry's office to show him the post. As soon as I walked in, I noticed that his Keanu *Speed* poster was no longer on the wall,

replaced by a poster of Jack in his *Jane Vampire* getup.

"You broke up with *Keanu?*" I cried.

"It was time," Larry said, sorrowfully. "I told him I think we should see other people."

"You're heartless!"

"We're just on two different paths right now. You know, if you really love someone, sometimes you just have to let them go."

"I can't believe I'm saying this, but Keanu is *such* a better actor than Jack."

Larry clapped his hands over his ears.

"Hey, look," I said, pulling up the blog post on his computer. "I just read this. What do you think?"

"Oh, fudge," he said, scanning the article. "It sounds like Jack, doesn't it?"

"I mean, a lot of the details fit . . . the wife from a prominent family, the Kennedy reference, the sequels—"

"But it says he 'likes them young and he likes them buff.' That's not me. I'm old and skinnyfat." Larry flexed his bicep for sad effect. "Oh God, what if he's stepping out on me?"

"OK, hold on, it also says he's 'not overly discerning.' "

"Oh, great. Awesome. Thanks, Anne. That makes me feel *so* much better. He likes them young and buff, but he'll settle for a middle-aged fatty patatty."

I ignored Larry. "And then there's the 'three strikes and you're out' reference," I said. "Jack used to play baseball in college. It's gotta be him."

"Wow," Larry said admiringly. "You sound just like you're close-reading a poem. Your students would be *so* impressed."

"I wonder who's leaking the info. Do you think it's someone in his camp?"

"I should text him," Larry said, reaching for his burner phone.

"Don't!" I said. "What if your phone's compromised?"

"Oh my goodness, Anne! You're worse than Jack. I just want to check in, NBD."

"You should be careful," I said. "You never know who might be hacking your phone."

"OK, Little Miss Paranoid," he said, putting his phone aside. "I mean, what's a little gay rumor, anyway? Jack should be thrilled. Every great actor's been suspected of being gay—it means he's finally made it!"

LARRY HAD MANAGED TO download a bootleg copy of *Jane Vampire* from the Internet, and for the next several weeks, the two of us watched and rewatched *Jane Vampire* from a makeshift theater Larry had set up in his living room. He would draw the drapes over all his windows, project the movie onto a blank wall, and pop

fresh popcorn that he'd place in a bucket between us. After the third viewing, I tried to beg off, but Larry chastised me. "But it's research! For your epilogue!" he cried. At our next viewing, he assigned himself the role of closed-captioning assistant, pausing the video so I could record the dialogue while Larry ogled Jack.

"You can press play again," I'd tell Larry.

"What?" he'd ask. "Oh! You sure you don't need to see it again?"

"There's no dialogue in this part, Larry. You can fast-forward it."

"What?! And skip all the best parts? Absolutely not."

I soon discovered there was no need for a written transcript anyway because Larry had memorized all the lines.

"Am I hideous, Jane?" Jack/Rochester would say on the screen, and Larry would respond, in a quavering voice, "Very, sir, you always were, you know."

"You must stay! I swear it!" Jack/Rochester would cry.

"I tell you I must go!" Larry would wail, pitching himself onto the couch and launching into a sobbing soliloquy. "Do you think I am a zombie? An undead being without feelings? Do you think because I am poor, obscure, plain, and little, I am soulless and heartless? You think wrong! I have as much soul as you—and

full as much heart! Let me go!" He would gaze despairingly at Jack/Rochester on the screen and pantomime stabbing himself in the heart.

"I feel like I'm at *The Rocky Horror Picture Show*," I said in the middle of one such performance.

"Keep working on your epilogue," Larry said, hushing me.

"Ugh, don't remind me," I groaned. "I still have to write my acknowledgments, too."

"You better make them good," Larry said, his eyes still glued to the screen. "It's the only part of your book that I'm guaranteed to read, word for word."

I'd always figured the acknowledgments would be the easiest part of the book to write, a welcome break from the intellectual heavy lifting I'd been doing. Instead, with twenty-four hours remaining until my deadline, I found myself in my office, staring at the empty screen, wondering how not to sound long-winded or trite or, worst of all, ungrateful. I'd pulled several all-nighters to complete the manuscript and felt woozy with fatigue. Taking a deep breath, I began by giving the requisite thanks to my editor and publisher. I thanked all the librarians and archivists who'd facilitated my research and tracked down sources. I thanked the fellowship committee that gave me a small research travel grant. I thanked my department chair and dean.

I thanked Ellen Russell. I thanked my father and sister. I thanked all the students who had taken my classes and helped me think through my ideas.

Then, I got to the "good part," as Larry called it.

"Finally, I must express my especial gratitude to the following people," I wrote. "First and foremost is my beloved colleague Lawrence Ettinger. For years now, Larry has been my trusted confidante, TV buddy, and friend. Without his faith in me, I would have given up on this project long ago, and I owe to him my career and, more importantly, my sanity." I pondered what I'd written for a few minutes. It didn't quite capture my relationship with Larry, but it would have to do. I forged ahead. "Last but not least, I'd like to express my gratitude to Richard Chasen, who came into my life at exactly the right time." I hesitated, then added, "You helped me believe I could be a writer." The last sentence was borderline cheesy, but in the end, I decided to keep it.

Satisfied, I sent the manuscript off via e-mail to Ursula Burton. I felt light-headed with relief. My part was complete. I'd handed in the manuscript, fulfilled my end of the book contract, met Steve's stipulations. While there was still copyediting and indexing to complete, for all intents and purposes, the bulk of the work was

done. In about a year, I would have a physical copy of the book in my hands.

I locked up my office and headed over to Rick's office around the corner, feeling simultaneously elated and exhausted.

The door was closed and I could hear Rick murmuring to someone inside. I knocked briskly, and a minute later, Emily appeared at the door, lugging her tennis rackets and school backpack.

"Emily!" I said, surprised. "What are you doing here?"

"I'm taking Rick's workshop again this semester," she said, smiling happily.

"She couldn't get enough of me," Rick joked, appearing at the doorway behind her. "I don't usually accept repeat students, but she did such fantastic work last semester that I made an exception."

Emily blushed at the compliment. "I've been working on some short stories," she said. "Rick's been helping me polish them for submission to some journals."

"I think she has real potential to get into a top MFA program," Rick told me. To Emily he said, "Professor Corey was the one who insisted I accept you into my workshop last semester. She called you a superstar. I'm glad I listened to her!"

Emily beamed. For a second, she reminded me of a child basking in the approval of her parents.

"Heard anything yet from grad schools?" I asked.

"Not yet," Emily said. "I should know some-time next month, I think. I'll let you know as soon as I hear anything!"

Emily excused herself to run to practice, and I followed Rick into his office, settling into his leather couch. His shelves were overflowing with books, so much so that he had books stacked in leaning piles on the floor and some even balanced on the arms of his couch. Every day, it seemed, publishers were sending him galleys, hoping he'd agree to blurb some new young author. The rest of Rick's office was filled with an assortment of toys and gadgets that helped him "get into a creative mind-set." There was a soccer ball in one corner, an acoustic guitar leaning against a meditation stool, and a modified skateboard-scooter that Rick liked to use to get around campus. I picked up a book that had toppled facedown onto the floor and placed it carefully back on one of the stacks.

"I just sent in my manuscript!" I announced. "Let's celebrate!"

Rick looked distracted by something on his computer. He raised a finger up while he scanned the screen, then looked up. "What was that?" he asked.

"I just finished my book," I said, deflated by

Rick's tepid response. "I sent it off to your friend Ursula five minutes ago."

"Right," he said. "Kudos! That's wonderful news. Sorry I'm so spacey—I just got an e-mail from my agent. He needs me to fly out to New York ASAP."

"What's wrong?"

"Oh, just more crap having to do with our good friend President Martinez. Despite my best efforts, it appears I'm no closer to landing a permanent position here at Fairfax. My agent's trying to light a fire under his ass. He just lined me up an interview with NYU and wants me there pronto. Maybe the prospect of losing me to another school will get Martinez to finally come through with a real job offer."

"NYU?" I said, crestfallen. "That's so far away from here."

"It's gamesmanship, Anne. Don't worry. We're playing a game of chicken, but he'll blink. I know it."

I felt a fresh surge of resentment toward Adam. I knew he didn't like Rick, but this was ridiculous. It wasn't just Rick's life he was playing with—it was mine. I'd worked so hard the past few months, writing into the night, focused single-mindedly on finishing my book, and now it all felt pointless. What had I been working for anyway? If Rick ended up leaving Fairfax . . . I felt my lip start to tremble.

Rick gave me a kiss. "Don't look so gutted," he said. "I promise it'll be OK. Now come on—let's go grab a bite to eat."

THE FOLLOWING MONDAY, RICK flew to New York for his interview. Carrying a heavy winter coat over his arm, a cashmere scarf draped around his neck, he looked intrepid and dashing as he left for the airport. Even though it was dawn, I got out of bed to wish him good-bye, padding outside in my pajamas and watching him load his bags into the waiting taxi.

"Good luck," I said. "I'm sure you'll do great."

"I'm coming back, you know," Rick laughed. "I'm going to New York, not some war zone."

"I know," I said ruefully. "I just wish I could go with you."

"You're not missing anything," Rick said. "I'm sure it's just going to be some dog and pony show. Besides, how could I give up all this?" He swept his arms around to include me, his charming rental house, and the San Bernardino Mountains turning peach-colored in the early dawn light. I watched his taxi drive away, feeling desolate and abandoned.

With my manuscript finally submitted, Steve had forwarded my new employment contract to HR, and I stopped by their offices to sign the final paperwork. I'd finally been converted from contingent faculty to tenure track, and

with my book's publication, I'd be eligible for early tenure and lifetime job security. Staring at the executed contract, signed by Adam and Steve, I could hardly believe the document was real. I wasn't going to be unemployed in the fall. I had a career. I had a book. My life was falling into place, except for one important thing. I shoved my copy of the contract into my bag.

I want more cookies, I said to myself.

Impulsively, I decided to walk past Adam's office to see if he was in. The president's office occupied the entire east wing of the administrative building, through grand walnut-carved doors with the Fairfax motto, "Veritas et Virtus," etched in gold on the lintel. The waiting room was empty and the receptionist had stepped out for lunch, and I was about to leave when I saw that Adam's door was ajar.

"Hey," I said, knocking tentatively on the door and peeking in. "Do you have a minute?"

"Come on in!" Adam said, smiling and pushing a pile of papers to one side. "I'm just working through lunch."

I'd only seen Adam's office in the *PAW*. It was bigger and more corporate than I expected, with glass plaques arranged on a side table and shelves of what looked like law textbooks lining the walls. All of Adam's framed diplomas, embellished with gold seals and ribbons, hung above

the shelves. Sitting across from him, I felt like a student who had just been summoned to the principal's office.

"I just signed your contract for next year," Adam said, reaching over his desk to shake my hand warmly. "Congratulations!"

"Thanks," I said, smiling in spite of myself. "And listen—about New Year's . . ."

"Don't think of it," Adam said. "I just hope you weren't feeling too awful the next day." He gave me a knowing look.

I laughed nervously, then took a deep breath. "I came by because, well, I had a favor to ask. I was hoping you could help with Rick's situation."

"His situation?"

"Yeah," I said, shifting uncomfortably. "NYU's trying to poach him, but I know he really wants to stay here at Fairfax. I don't know if you can do anything to help him stay . . ."

"Hiring decisions aren't up to me, unfortunately," Adam said, his manner suddenly formal. "Has he talked to the dean?"

"I'm not sure," I admitted. "But he says his agent's been in discussions with you—"

Adam frowned. "His agent?" he said cagily. "Not that I'm aware of."

"Listen—I know these things are confidential. I just wanted to say that whatever your personal feelings about Rick, I hope you won't let them

cloud your judgment. He's an incredibly talented, respected writer—any school would be lucky to have him."

"Perhaps, then, you should have Rick come speak to me directly instead of communicating through you," he said crisply.

I stared at Adam. "Just so you know, he didn't send me here," I snapped. "This was my own idea. In fact, he'd probably kill me if he knew I was talking to you."

"So he didn't send you?"

"No! He'd never ask me to do anything like this. He's way too modest." I stood up abruptly. "Forget it. I thought we could discuss this in a reasonable way, but clearly I was wrong."

"Stop—Anne—I'm sorry if I offended you," Adam said, leaping to his feet. "I just wanted to be clear on why you were doing this."

"I owe a huge debt to Rick," I said quietly. "He went above and beyond to help me get my book published. I know you don't believe me, but he's a really good person. He's allowed me to have a writing career—and a life." I felt my throat tighten painfully.

Adam was looking at me thoughtfully. "I see," he said. "That changes things."

"You're going to lose him if you don't make an offer soon," I said weakly.

"Let me think through some options," Adam said. "I can't make any promises, but I'll see

what I can do." He walked me to the door and then reached out to shake my hand.

"And you don't have to worry, Anne," he said. "I'm perfectly capable of separating the personal from the professional. You have my word."

chapter fifteen

"T HE VISIT WAS PHENOMENAL," Rick exclaimed when I picked him up from the airport. He'd been on his phone talking to his agent when I pulled up, so I'd had to idle at the curb as he finished his call.

"Sorry about the wait," Rick apologized as he threw his bag and coat into the back seat and climbed into the car. "Things are moving very quickly."

"So everything went well?" I asked, pulling away from the curb and trying to avoid pedestrians weaving through traffic.

"Incredibly well. They've got some fantastic writers on their faculty, it's a top-notch MFA program, and NYU is absolutely filthy loaded." Rick stretched out in his seat, trying to work out a kink in his neck.

"So the people were nice?" I asked.

"Absolutely lovely—the kind of people I'd actually want to grab a drink with. Regular folks, not hoity-toity snobs. Real artists, all of them." He listed a series of bold-faced names, among them the famous writer who had told me, long

ago, that seminar was a "fucking waste of time."

"So where did they take you?" I asked, wincing inwardly.

"Oh, all over—we ate at this great little Ethiopian restaurant, and afterwards we heard some jazz at a club. I hit the Strand and Zabar's, of course, and took a walk through Central Park. God, I hadn't realized how much I missed New York."

I didn't say anything. I hadn't visited New York since grad school, when I spent the night sleeping on the floor of a friend's fifth-floor walk-up and then got stuck in a blackout while riding the train back to New Haven. We'd sat on the tracks in the sweltering heat for two hours before some buses arrived to rescue us.

"And Christ, you should've *seen* the apartments that NYU subsidizes for faculty. They're insane—hardwood floors, doorman building, overlooking Washington Square Park. *Easily* worth twice what they charge faculty in rent! And the pay's not shabby, either. I'm telling you—it's nice to work for a school with resources. They understand you have to pay top dollar to attract talent, unlike *some* places I know."

I sighed. Fairfax was a respected small liberal arts college, but it wasn't in the same league as a research behemoth like NYU. "Fairfax can't really compete," I mumbled.

"No kidding. Did you know NYU has cam-

puses all over the world? I could teach a semester abroad in Abu Dhabi or Shanghai, all expenses paid. I'd get regular sabbaticals, too, to write and travel. Could you imagine? It would be absolutely perfect."

"It does sound incredible," I said.

"Hold on," Rick said, pulling out his phone. "It's my agent again—I've got to take this call."

I tried to concentrate on driving as Rick chatted on the phone. I told myself I was happy for him. From the beginning, we'd agreed that we were just having fun—no pressure, no expectations. We'd never talked about what would happen if one of us moved away, whether we'd still date long-distance or let the relationship fizzle out. It seemed foolish and pathetic to bring it up now.

"It's such an amazing opportunity," I told him when he got off the phone. "You have to take it."

"You think so?" Rick asked.

"Yes! It's NYU! It's in the heart of the Village! You'll have amazing colleagues and students!"

"That's true," Rick said, leaning over to give me a kiss. "Thanks for being so supportive. It's too bad Fairfax couldn't get its act together."

"They still could—you never know," I ventured, thinking of my conversation with Adam.

Rick scoffed. "I'm not holding my breath," he said. "Besides, this is a *much* better job than Fairfax. I'd be a lunatic to turn it down."

• • •

"COULD WE *PLEASE* WATCH anything but *Jane Vampire?*" I begged Larry. "Otherwise, I might have to stab *myself* in the face."

"Sheesh—you're in a bad mood," Larry said, tossing me the remote control and settling back with his tub of popcorn.

"I am. Rick's being courted by NYU."

"He *is?*" Larry said. His popcorn missed his mouth and tumbled down his shirt. "Wow—*I* want a job at NYU."

"Yeah, well, if he takes it—"

"How could he not take it?"

"Exactly. How could he not take it? He leaves, I stay, and our relationship's toast." I clicked angrily through the channels, trying to find *Law & Order: SVU*.

"You could always do long-distance . . . There's FaceTime, and e-mail, and . . ." Larry suggested.

"Like what you're doing with Jack?" I said without thinking. Larry's face fell. "I'm sorry," I said. "I know how hard it is for you. I just don't know how you do it—I don't think I could."

"It *is* hard," Larry conceded. "You both have to be on board to make it work."

"Yeah," I sighed. "And I don't know if Rick's on board."

I found NBC finally and we waited for the last few minutes of *Extra* to wrap up. Mario Lopez,

dressed in a shiny black suit with his hair slicked back, was introducing a final segment when a *Jane Vampire* movie poster swooped onto the screen behind him.

"Don't you dare change the channel!" Larry said, leaning forward in anticipation.

"*Jane Vampire* smashed box office records this holiday season," Mario was saying, "taking the top spot for an impressive six weeks in a row. It broke even more records when it opened worldwide, racking up nearly seven hundred *million* dollars in ticket sales."

The camera cut to a clip of Jack Lindsey and his costars at the London *Jane Vampire* premiere, posing for photographers under a barrage of exploding flashbulbs.

"The movie has turned its stars, Rachel Lynn Evans and Jack Lindsey, into household names, catapulting them onto the A-list." The camera pulled in on Rachel and Jack, posing together on the red carpet. Jack leaned over to whisper something into Rachel's ear, and she smirked in response.

"There were rumors that Rachel and Jack were getting a *little* too close to one another on set," Mario continued. "Rachel had recently split from her boyfriend, Nigel Marks, a member of the boy band All for One, and Jack was said to be undergoing a trial separation from his wife, the lovely heiress Elizabeth Beckington, eldest

daughter of one of the wealthiest families in the country."

The camera panned to the right, showing Bex trailing behind Jack. Next to her, Rachel looked like she needed some sleep and a shower.

"But *Extra* has discovered there's more to the story," Mario said, his voice turning ominous. "We recently obtained some never-before-seen footage of Jack Lindsey in Paris on a secret *rendezvous* with his lover . . . and it's *not* who you think it is."

Some grainy, badly lit footage appeared, taken from a cell phone camera outside a restaurant window. Cheesy French accordion music played in the background. The camera zoomed in shakily, revealing Jack's handsome profile, laughing and drinking from a glass of wine.

"We have proof that Jack's been stepping out on his wife—and it's not with Rachel Lynn Evans. On the contrary, Jack's taste seems to be of, shall we say, a *different* persuasion."

The cell phone video pulled back slightly, revealing the fuzzy outline of Jack's dinner date, his back to the camera. Jack leaned over and gave the man a kiss. The man moved slightly into the light, and it became clear that he was balding.

"We were just as surprised as you are," Mario said, "when we discovered Jack's lover was follicularly challenged. Who would have thought

that Mr. Movie Star would fall for someone—ahem!—*lacking* in the hair department?"

I turned to Larry. He was holding his head in his hands and rocking back and forth.

"Larry," I gasped. "Is that . . . is that *you?*"

Larry was quiet for a second. Then he raised his head up and howled, "That *little shit.* Calling me 'follicularly challenged'? How'd you like it if I called you a *circus midget,* Mr. *Saved by the Bell?*"

"Have you been seeing Jack *this whole time?* And you didn't tell me?"

"I knew you wouldn't understand, Anne. We just couldn't stay away from each other."

"Oh my God. You met up with him in Paris, didn't you?"

Larry nodded.

"I'm such an idiot," I groaned. "I actually bought your BS about finding a crazy last-minute deal on Groupon."

"Well, I *did* find a crazy amazing fare, but no, the trip was planned. It was divine. We stayed on Île Saint-Louis, at this adorable little pied-à-terre. You should stay there sometime—we found it on Airbnb!" Larry sighed happily at the memory.

"Are you *crazy?* You're gonna ruin Jack's marriage! And what about his career? What about *your* career?"

"Eeesh, Anne. See, this is why I didn't want to

tell you! You're being so Judgy McJudgerson!"

"What do you want to happen?" I asked. "Do you want him to run off with you? Do you really think that's going to happen?"

"Why not?" Larry asked pitifully. "It's better than sneaking around like this. I still don't know how they got that video of us at that restaurant. We were being *so* careful."

"Apparently not careful enough."

"Someone must have tipped them off. There was no one else in there!"

"I can't believe this is happening," I said, shaking my head. "I can't believe you're not freaking out more. Let's hope people don't put two and two together and figure out you're the guy in that video."

"Maybe it's for the best," Larry said stubbornly. "Jack needs to stop living a lie. He needs to step up and declare the truth—declare the love that dare not speak its name!"

Larry was getting worked up, beating his chest with his fist.

"I am not ashamed!" he roared. "I might be a hairless nobody, but I've got nothing to hide! I've got nothing to lose! I publicly declare my love for Jack Lindsey!"

I sat back and gave Larry a polite golf clap. "Nice speech," I said as he graciously accepted my applause. "Now please promise me there isn't a sex tape. *Please.*"

"Ewwww!" Larry yelled, pelting me with popcorn. "Anne! Who do you think I am? Sex tapes are *so* 2007."

OVER THE NEXT FEW days, the tabloids were flooded with pictures of Jack and Bex having a romantic dinner at Katsuya, Jack and Bex taking their daughter out for ice cream, Jack and Bex bringing their daughter to Disneyland. In all the pictures, the two of them were wearing their wedding rings and acting lovey-dovey for the cameras. "Jack Lindsey calls his wife his soul mate," read one headline. " 'Our marriage is stronger than ever,' " read another. "Lovebirds," read a third.

A PR rep for Jack and Bex issued a statement to *People* magazine, claiming that the cell phone video was "obviously doctored" and that the man in the video was not Jack. "Jack Lindsey is a devoted husband and father," the statement read, "and it is shameful that unscrupulous sources would try to defame his character and attack his family. This report is utter garbage and riddled with lies. We are in the process of investigating legal options against *Extra*."

"Lies!" Larry told me that night. "It's all lies! Jack told me they're doing a family media blitz until all of this dies down. I can't believe people are actually buying it!"

"Did you know he's a Virgo?" I asked, flipping through the pages of a magazine.

"Where are you reading this?"

"*Us Weekly*. They're doing a feature called 'Twenty Things You Didn't Know About Jack Lindsey.' "

"Gimme that!" Larry yelled, snatching the magazine from my hand. He read through the article and then tossed it aside. "He didn't answer these questions," Larry said dismissively. "Someone else did."

"Wait, what do you mean?" I asked. "Jack doesn't answer his own questions now?"

"The studio hired a crisis management firm," Larry told me. "He's got a PR minder who vets all media inquiries. He's also got a bodyguard shadowing him 24/7."

"Why?" I asked. "To protect him from the paparazzi?"

"No—to protect him from himself. They don't want him going rogue again." Larry sighed. "I.e., no more secret rendezvous with *moi*."

"Is he still calling you?" I asked, grabbing the magazine back.

"He's been texting. He's got back-to-back events this week, visiting sick kids at a hospital, running a 10K for charity, MC-ing an auction. They're trying to keep him busy. He's worried they're going to confiscate his phone next."

"Do you really think they'd do that?"

"I don't know," Larry said, looking worried. "I'd die if that happened." He looked at me plaintively. "Anne, I know you think I'm pathetic, but I can't help it. I really miss him. Tell me things are going to work out. Please?"

"Things are going to work out," I said, trying to sound more convincing than I felt.

IN THE WEEKS LEADING up to my book deadline, I'd skipped a few of my regular visits with my father, begging off via phone call or e-mail. Now that he'd settled into the home comfortably, I often felt like an unwanted chaperone when I did come to visit, interrupting his lunch date with Helene or his daily poker game. When I asked how he was doing, he'd roll his eyes like a teenager and then ask for more Q-tips or batteries or undershirts before shooing me away. I figured my absence would hardly be noticed.

Still, as penance, I brought my father a jumbo jar of mixed nuts and a new digital clock for his bedroom at my next visit. I found him sitting alone in an alcove that the staff had decorated to look like a 1940s drawing room, with an old-fashioned radio playing big band music, some ladies' hats displayed on shelves, and some war memorabilia. Usually the oldest residents of the home clustered here, napping or listening to music, but it was now deserted. Sitting on a

couch beside my father, I felt like I'd accidentally wandered onto a stage set.

"Where've you been?" my dad asked querulously, inspecting the new clock.

"I'm sorry—I had a deadline," I said. "It was rough toward the end—I was pulling a bunch of all-nighters."

"Are these spicy?" my dad asked, opening the jar of nuts and sniffing. "I can't do spicy. It bothers my prostate."

"I got the unsalted kind," I said.

My father carefully tried one of the cashews. "I'm almost out of Q-tips again," he added, chewing. "I really think someone's stealing them. There's no possible way I'm going through them so fast."

"Uh-huh," I said, trying not to sound impatient. "I'll bring some more next time."

"Not the cheap ones, OK? The brand-name ones. I can tell the difference."

I sighed. "I promise I'll bring you the right ones," I said. I looked around the alcove. "So where is everyone?"

"Getting their hair done," my dad said. "Hairdresser's here today."

"Are you having lunch with Helene later?"

"She's mad at me," my dad grumbled. "I forgot her birthday last week, and she's giving me the silent treatment."

"What about Georgia?"

"Who?"

"Georgia—silver hair? I met her at the Christmas party?"

"Oh, her? She moved to a different facility. I haven't seen her in a while."

I glanced at the TV mounted to one of the walls, the one anachronistic touch in the room. There was a *Law & Order* rerun on, and I saw that Jack Lindsey was guest-starring as a congressman accused of having an affair with an intern and then murdering her. I started watching in spite of myself.

"I knew him in college," I said to my dad, pointing to Jack appearing on the witness stand. "His name is Jack Lindsey. We were in the same English class."

My dad squinted at the screen. "What is he now, a lawyer?" he asked.

"No, he's an actor."

"Never heard of him."

"He's friends with Lauren," I said. "Or actually, it's more like his wife is."

"Where's Lauren anyway? I haven't seen her in months." He reached over and began scratching his leg through his trousers.

"She's in the Bahamas for her wedding anniversary." Lauren and Brett were spending a week at the same resort where they'd been married.

"She never told me that."

"Yes, she did—she sent you an e-mail."

"I never got it," my dad said. "What's her husband's name again?"

"Dad—she's married to Brett! You remember Brett!"

"Sure," my dad said vaguely. He hitched his trouser leg up. "My damn leg feels funny," he complained, scratching his bare skin.

"Dad—stop," I said, cringing at his skinny, blotchy leg. "Did you fall again?" Since his last accident, he'd been given a walking cane, a gray piece of metal with a four-fingered claw at the bottom. Seeing him so bent and frail scared me. He was still his usual irascible self, but his body no longer reflected the fierceness of his personality.

"No. It just feels weak."

"Then use your cane," I said, trying to keep the worry out of my voice. "That's what it's there for."

"The cane's no good. It just gets in the way."

"If you fall again, you might break your hip and then you'll be in a wheelchair. Do you want that?"

"Of course not."

"Then use your cane," I said, throwing up my hands in exasperation. I glanced at my phone and got up from the couch. "Hey, Dad—I gotta run to a department meeting. I'll call you later."

"I got my poker game at three. Don't call me

then. And don't forget the Q-tips next time, OK? I only have a handful left. I think someone's been stealing them from me."

I nodded, hugged him briefly, then dashed out. On the way to the meeting, I tried calling Larry. He didn't answer, so I tried a second time and then a third. As I was just about to hang up, Larry finally answered. He sounded hoarse, as if he was coming down with a cold.

"Hey!" I said. "Where are you? Are you coming to the department meeting?"

Larry sniffled.

"What's the matter?" I asked. "Are you sick?"

"It's over," Larry said.

"What's over? Are you talking about Jack?"

"They took away his phone. I'm sure of it. He hasn't texted me in thirty-six hours."

"Maybe he's out of the country?"

"No, he warned me this was coming. His last message to me was 'im sorry, please wait for me.'"

"Did you write back?"

"Of course I did! I wrote, 'i'm here for you, my lovely boy,' and then there was that little text bubble where you know the other person is typing something . . . and then poof! It disappeared. I've never been so distraught over an ellipsis! To be continued . . . NEVER!"

"Maybe he got interrupted in the middle of his text?"

"Yeah right. Dot dot dot . . . I'll be waiting forever."

"You're overanalyzing a text. Or a nontext, in this case."

"Dot dot dot . . . our love is dead."

"What? OK, stop being melodramatic."

"Dot dot dot . . . the end."

"Larry—our department meeting is in fifteen minutes. Come on. Rally!"

"Tell Steve I'm indisposed. You can be elliptical."

"Larry! This isn't funny. You can't wallow!"

"I'm hanging up on you now, dot dot dot . . ."

"Don't you dare!"

". . ."

I stared at my phone. Larry had hung up on me.

"Where's Larry?" Rick asked, waving me over when I arrived at the meeting. Steve was at the front of the room, passing out copies of the agenda with Pam.

"He's having another case of the vapors," I grumbled, sliding into the seat beside him. I switched my phone to silent and shoved it into my bag. "This thing with Jack is really messing him up."

"He still has a crush on that movie star guy?"

"It's more than a crush—they had a real relationship."

Rick raised an eyebrow. "Well, this might be a sign he needs to move on," he said.

"It's not that easy," I said. "He's pretty devastated."

"It was never going to work out, anyway," Rick said, reaching his arm around my shoulder and resting it on the back of my chair. "Better he figure that out now rather than later."

Steve cleared his throat and began going through general housekeeping while I quickly scanned the agenda:

ENGLISH DEPARTMENT
MEETING AGENDA
February 11
1. Chair's Remarks – Steve
2. Approval of Minutes for January 14
Department Meeting – Pam
3. Committee Reports – Committee Chairs
4. Undergraduate Curriculum Review – Steve
5. Hiring Initiatives – President Martinez
6. Announcements

I pointed to item no. 5. "What's this?" I whispered to Rick.

Rick shrugged. "No clue," he said, looking mystified.

I doodled on my agenda as Steve meandered through his opening remarks (a textbook rep was giving a presentation Tuesday, campus recycling week was coming up, volunteers were needed to grade comp exams) and Pam went over last

month's minutes. I was the chair and sole member of the tech committee, so I stood up to give my report: the department Facebook page had 314 members and the department Twitter account had 163 followers, a student volunteer was helping me revamp the official department home page, and next month the department was hosting its second annual "Middlemarch Madness" challenge, so everyone was encouraged to fill out their brackets online. Last year, *The Sound and the Fury* had upset *The Portrait of a Lady*, much to Larry's chagrin.

Adam turned up just as Steve was beginning his long-winded overview of our curriculum overhaul. Seeing Adam from the corner of his eye, Steve mercifully cut his presentation short and handed over the floor. I continued to doodle on my agenda, drawing curlicues around the edges of the paper as Adam stepped up to the front of the room.

"Before I begin," Adam said, "I wanted to congratulate one of the members of your department on a truly remarkable set of accomplishments. Some of you might already know that Dr. Anne Corey has a book forthcoming with a major press"—here Adam paused to acknowledge a smattering of applause as I looked up in surprise—"but I'm also delighted to announce that we have renewed her contract and she has agreed to stay with us here at Fairfax!"

Adam began clapping loudly and gesturing to me to stand up. I was startled and instinctively hung back, but Rick hoisted me up and began cheering loudly beside me. "Stop!" I hissed at Rick, embarrassed but also touched by his enthusiasm. After a few seconds, I sat down again, feeling flushed and warm from the unexpected attention.

"This is a great way to transition into my topic for today," Adam was now saying. "Namely the launch of a new college-wide hiring initiative to hire and retain exceptional faculty members. In the past, this was done on an ad hoc basis, but we've come to recognize the need for a more transparent and systematic way of supporting faculty retention."

Rick and I exchanged glances.

"I'm putting together a work group to hash out the details, and I'm soliciting suggestions from individual departments on hiring priorities and wish lists. So far, the response has been very positive, and I've already begun collecting nominations of current exceptional members of our contingent faculty who wish to stay on permanently. I'm here to enlist all of your help in identifying and recruiting promising candidates."

"!!!!!" I wrote on my agenda, nudging the paper toward Rick.

"First I've heard of this," Rick whispered.

"But it sounds promising!"

"He could be talking about someone else—"

"Who? It's got to be you! There's no one else!"

"What should I do?"

"You need to talk to him. ASAP!"

Steve was glaring at us, so I quickly shut up and hunched over my agenda, pretending to take notes as my colleagues raised their hands to ask questions, offer suggestions, or volunteer to serve on the working group. The discussion spilled over the allotted time, and Steve suspended the discussion, moving that we continue to talk through the issues at our meeting the following month. The department voted "Aye," Pam recorded the passing of the motion, and everyone immediately scrambled for the doors. As Adam got up to leave, I rushed over to catch him before he slipped out.

"This hiring initiative sounds amazing!" I blurted out. "I'm so glad Fairfax is doing this."

"Yes—it's a great idea," Rick added, appearing at my side and reaching out to shake Adam's hand. "I'm glad you've thrown your support behind this."

"Everyone's been very enthusiastic," Adam said, shaking Rick's hand firmly. "We're trying very hard to get it off the ground this year since we don't want to lose talented faculty to other institutions. In fact, I'm scheduled to meet with some donors later today to figure out immediate

funding issues. I'll hopefully have more to report sometime next week."

"Let me know what I can do to help," Rick said. "As you can probably tell, I'm quite eager to stay at Fairfax. It's my top choice—for many reasons." He touched my back lightly, and I smiled.

"Anne's been very persuasive in helping me think through this," Adam said, glancing at me. "I'm confident it's the right thing to do."

"I'm very lucky," Rick said, looking at me fondly. "She's a keeper."

As Rick and Adam continued to talk, I pulled out my phone to text Larry. With a start, I saw that I'd missed seven calls from Lauren. For a moment, I thought it must be a mistake. Lauren was in the Bahamas, and she'd already warned everyone that she'd be off the grid for at least a week. Maybe she'd butt-dialed me? But seven times?

Seeing my face, Adam asked, "Is everything OK?"

"I don't know," I said uncertainly, dialing Lauren's number. "I guess Lauren's trying to reach me."

Lauren picked up on the first ring. "Where have you been?" she screamed. "I've been trying to reach you for over an hour!"

"What's the matter?" I said, feeling dread in my stomach. "Are you OK?"

"It's Daddy," Lauren said, sobbing.

"What happened?" I asked, suddenly chilled.

"He's had a stroke."

"What?" I gasped. "When? I just saw him! Where is he?"

"Fairfax Hospital. I'm trying to get a flight back now. They wouldn't tell me anything over the phone—but it's bad. I know it."

"Oh my God," I whimpered. "Is he awake? Is he breathing? Is he alive?"

"I told you! I don't know!" Lauren wailed. "Don't ask me! I'm just trying to get off this goddamn island!" She broke into tears. "I can't do anything from over here. The reception sucks."

"OK," I said, forcing myself to stay calm. "I'm heading to the hospital now. I'll call as soon as I find out anything."

I hung up the phone, then dropped it because my hands were shaking so hard.

"What happened?" Adam asked, looking at my stricken face. "Do you need to sit down?"

"I have to go," I cried, scrambling on all fours to pick up my phone. "My dad's in the hospital." I stood up and headed for the door, then stopped uncertainly.

"I don't have my car," I said in a dazed voice. "I walked here."

"Where's your car?" Rick asked.

"At home." I looked around, frantic. "Can I borrow someone's car?"

"You can't drive like this," Adam said, putting his hand on my arm. "You're shaking."

"He's right. I'll get my motorcycle," Rick said.

"No, I'll drive you," Adam said firmly. "My car's right outside."

"Hold up, mate," Rick said, turning to Adam. "I've got this."

"She's in no condition to ride a motorcycle. She can barely stand."

"I'm fine," I said, but I wasn't fine. I felt my legs buckle beneath me. Adam caught me before I could fall.

"She clearly can't hold onto you while you're driving," Adam was saying to Rick. "Listen— just meet us there. We just need to hurry."

"Jellyby," I blurted. "Someone needs to feed Jellyby. Rick—you have my keys. Could you check on her?"

Rick looked at me, then at Adam.

"Better bring her a change of clothes, too," Adam said to Rick. "In case she needs to spend the night at the hospital."

"OK," Rick said, backing off. "I'll see you at the hospital." He gave me a quick kiss and dashed off.

I followed Adam blindly to the parking lot, feeling like the world had gone topsy-turvy. A group of students were lazily kicking a soccer ball around the quad, and someone was practicing the tuba in the music building. I stared at them.

How could they keep going on with their daily lives when my life had just been upended? In a haze, I got into Adam's car. The college radio station was on, but Adam quickly turned it off. "It'll be OK," Adam was saying as we sped through campus and onto the freeway. "Fairfax has a great hospital."

"He was complaining about his leg this morning," I said, struggling to hold back tears. "He said it felt strange. I should've listened."

"Shhhhhh," Adam said. "There's no way you could have known."

"I should've called a nurse. What the hell was I thinking? What if he was having a stroke right then and there? And I just *left?*"

"You don't know that."

"I'm the worst daughter ever," I said, dissolving into tears. "All I was supposed to do was keep an eye on him and I can't even do that. I live down the street and I've barely seen him the last month, I've been so busy working on my damn book!"

Adam reached over and took my hand. "Stop," he said. "You have to stop blaming yourself." I held onto his hand like an anchor, trying to steady myself and swallow my racking sobs.

We pulled up to the emergency room, and Adam escorted me into the building, flagging down an orderly to help me locate my father. I was passed from one person to another, told to wait in the waiting room, then brusquely

informed that my father was getting a CT scan and that I could wait for him in his hospital room.

"So he's alive?" I asked, breathless with relief.

The hospital staffer looked at me blankly. "I'm just telling you what our system says. The imaging department should know more." She handed me an ID badge, which I pinned to my shirt. "Is your partner coming, too?" she asked, looking at Adam. "If so, he also needs a badge."

"Um, no—he's just a friend," I said. "Or actually, more like my boss."

"I'm happy to stay," Adam said to me. "At least until Rick gets here. I don't feel comfortable leaving you here alone."

"Are you a family member?" the woman asked Adam. "If not, I'll have to ask you to wait in the lobby. Hospital policy."

"It's OK," I told Adam. "You have your donor meeting. You can't stand them up."

"That can wait. This is an emergency. I can stay in the waiting room if you want."

"No, you have to go. It's important. Please. Rick will be here soon."

"Have we made a decision?" the woman asked, looking at us impatiently.

"I'll let you know if I need anything," I said to Adam. "And thank you—for everything."

"Promise to call me, just so I know you're doing OK?"

"I promise."

Adam gathered me to him, and I pressed myself against his chest, feeling his arms holding me close.

"You'll be fine," he murmured. "I'll be waiting to hear from you." With a final squeeze, he let me go.

I turned to follow the employee to my father's room and was halfway down the hall before I realized I couldn't call Adam even if I wanted. I didn't have his phone number.

chapter sixteen

W HILE I WAITED FOR my father to return
from his CT scan, I sat in one of the
uncomfortable chairs in his hospital room and
talked to the nursing home's medical director
on the phone. I'd only spoken to the director
once before, when my father had fallen over the
holidays, and she sounded considerably more
somber this time around. She told me that soon
after I'd left that day, my father had complained
of fatigue and asked an aide to help him to his
bed so he could lie down. Even with the cane, my
father kept listing to one side, as if his left leg
could no longer support his weight. Alarmed, the
aide had called over a nurse, who arrived just as
my father crumpled to the floor. They'd called
an ambulance and gotten him to the hospital
quickly, where he was evaluated and given
drugs.

"Will he be all right?" I asked.

"The doctors will have to see what the scan
says," the director said. "They won't know the
full effects of the stroke until then."

"But he should recover eventually, shouldn't

he? I mean, he might need rehab but that's to be expected . . ."

"Ms. Corey, I can't give you a prognosis based on the very limited amount of information I have. You'll have to wait and see what the neurologist says. I'm sorry—I know you want answers, but that's the best I can do right now."

I hung up and immediately started reading up on strokes online. The information was confusing and discouraging. What kind of stroke had he had? What part of the brain? Was it big or small? As I was reading through a stroke recovery discussion board, my phone buzzed. It was Rick.

"I'm in the ER waiting room," he said when I picked up. "Where are you?"

"In my dad's room—I'll be down in a minute."

I retraced my steps through the rabbit's warren of hospital corridors, to a bank of elevators that chimed morosely every few seconds, depositing medical personnel, cleaning staff, and visiting family members. I took the elevator down several floors and stepped out into the main lobby, then crossed to the emergency wing of the hospital.

Rick was standing along one wall, a shopping bag full of clothes and toiletries in one hand and his motorcycle helmet in the other. It was a relief to see a familiar face in the anonymous and antiseptic surroundings, and I practically ran into his arms.

"Anne! Is your dad OK?" Rick asked, giving me a hug.

"I'm still waiting to find out," I said, pausing a moment just to breathe in the smell of cigarette smoke and diesel that clung to his clothes. "Thanks for bringing me my stuff."

As I took the bag from Rick, he looked around nervously. A woman with a bandaged head walked past, a child cried out in pain somewhere, and the automatic sliding doors kept admitting and expelling waves of hospital staff and paramedics. Rick fidgeted with his motorcycle helmet, transferring it from one hand to another.

"It's not the most uplifting place," I said, seeing him grimace as an old man gave a tubercular cough and spat into his handkerchief.

"I feel like I'm going to contract some disease just standing here," he said.

"Let's go upstairs," I said. "I can try to get you a visitor's pass."

"That's OK," Rick said, backing away slightly. "I don't want to impose."

"You're not imposing. You're keeping me company until my dad gets back."

Rick gulped, and I realized he'd gone gray. "You know, I think I should leave," he said, pushing his hair back. His forehead was covered with a thin sheen of sweat. "I'm sorry. These places make me nervous. I think I might still have some residual PTSD from the war."

"Of course," I said, taking his hand. It was clammy. "Do you need to sit down?"

"No, no—I should be OK," he said. He put his motorcycle helmet on. "I should go, though. Otherwise I'll be joining the ranks of the ill and infirm here in the ER."

"Yes—go home," I said, walking him out. "There's nothing to do here anyway."

"I'll call you," Rick said. He dipped into the parking lot, and I lost sight of him in the darkness.

I trudged back upstairs and unpacked the bag Rick had brought. I brushed my teeth, changed into pajamas, and curled up in a chair with a blanket, dimming the lights so I could get some rest. I'd just begun to doze off when the room was flooded in harsh light and my father was wheeled in on a rattling gurney. I sprang up from my chair, light-headed and disoriented as my father was transferred to the hospital bed and hooked up to several machines.

"Dad?" I asked, looking at his slack face. His eyes were closed, and his nose and mouth were covered by a ventilator. He didn't respond, and for a second I wondered if he was asleep.

"He's unconscious," a nurse said as she went through a checklist on a clipboard and then dropped it into a slot at the foot of the bed.

"Is he OK?" I asked her, trying not to hover while she yanked the safety rails in place.

"The doctor will be here shortly," she said, barely pausing in her routine. Seeing my face, she softened slightly. "Do you need some water? I can get you a cup."

I shook my head no and she left, closing the door behind her.

Sitting beside my father, holding his hand, I looked at his eerily still face and wondered whether he would ever wake up. The machines beeped monotonously beside me. I texted Lauren again.

"Dad's in his room. Still waiting to talk to doc," I wrote.

Lauren didn't respond. She was probably asleep or, hopefully, on a plane. My phone was almost out of battery, and I wondered if I could buy a charger in the gift shop but didn't want to risk leaving my father's side while I checked, so I laid my head on my father's bed and slept.

After what felt like hours, I was woken up by a brisk knock at the door and the gravelly voice of the neurologist on call. I leapt up, feeling my neck twinge painfully.

"Are you the patient's daughter?" he asked, reaching out to shake my hand. He was dressed in blue hospital scrubs and New Balance sneakers, and he had a black exercise band around his wrist. On his head was a bandana-style surgical cap that made him look like Hulk Hogan.

"Yes," I said, taking his hand. "I'm Anne. I've been waiting for you."

"It was a busy night," the doctor said. "Six-car pileup on the 10, plus a drive-by shooting in West Covina."

"Oh," I said.

The doctor pulled up some slides on the computer.

"What does it say?" I asked, staring at the illuminated slices of my father's brain, gleaming like the surface of the moon.

"It doesn't look good, I'm afraid," the doctor said gruffly, putting on his glasses. "This is the site of the most recent bleed." He pointed to a dark spot shaped like an ink spill. I blanched at its size. "But there are also several other areas that are cause for concern." Now he pointed to some faint smudges I could barely make out in comparison.

"What are those?" I asked, my mouth dry.

"Based on the image, it looks like your father has been having ministrokes for quite some time."

"He's had strokes before? Are you serious? How could we miss that?"

"They're easy to misdiagnose. Has your father been acting oddly? Any personality changes?"

"We were worried he might be suffering from dementia," I said. "That's why we moved him to an assisted-living facility this past fall."

"The symptoms are often similar," the doctor said. "Has he been falling?"

"He had a bad fall over Christmas, bruised his leg pretty badly. He told us he tripped. We've been trying to get him to use a cane ever since."

"Those might have been triggered by the mini-strokes. It's hard to know. Weakness, loss of balance, confusion and paranoia—those are all signs." He took off his glasses and put them in a chest pocket, then rubbed his eyes.

I took a shaky breath. "How long will he stay like this?" I asked, motioning to my father on the bed.

"It was a pretty severe bleed. We've got it under control now, but he's in a coma. There's no way of knowing when he'll come out of it or what complications he might face if and when he does. You have a sister, yes?"

"She's flying in now."

"When she gets here, we can discuss next steps. Does your father have a living will?"

"I have no idea."

"You should discuss with your sister what your father's wishes would be—if he doesn't improve."

I swallowed. "And in the meantime?" I asked. "What do we do?"

"In the meantime?" the doctor said, closing out the slides and standing up. "In the meantime, there's nothing to do but wait."

· · ·

THE NEXT DAY, LARRY came over with more clean clothes, my phone charger, and takeout Thai food.

"You're the best," I said as he handed me a bright orange Thai iced tea. "I've been eating crap out of the cafeteria vending machine."

"You have to keep up your strength," he said, dishing out some curry and pad see ew.

"You doing OK?" I asked. "Any news from Jack?"

"No," Larry said, scrunching his nose. "But forget about me. My problems are stupid compared to what you're going through."

"How are my students doing?" I asked. Larry, the godsend, had offered to cover my classes so I wouldn't have to leave my father's bedside.

"You should've seen their faces when I showed up today. I told them you had a family emergency and that I was the sub, and people actually groaned. Groaned!"

"They were probably hoping class would be canceled."

"Oh, no," Larry said. "Not on my watch. Spring break's not for another week. They *will* finish *Daniel Deronda*, even if it's really the same novel as James's *Portrait of a Lady*—just half as good and twice as long."

I rolled my eyes. "You know what? Maybe I *should* just cancel class."

My sister arrived at the hospital two days later, frazzled and unkempt, ranting about the bad weather that had caused her to miss her connection in Atlanta. Tossing her overnight bag onto the floor, she marched over to my father and stared at him for a moment as if waiting for him to greet her. She was looking at him so intently that I half expected him to open his eyes and comply. When he didn't respond, Lauren took a step back and her face contorted. But she didn't burst into tears, as I thought she would. She got angry.

"How could this happen?" she asked the doctor, berating him as if he were the one who'd caused the stroke. "I just talked to him the other day!"

"There's often no warning until it's too late," the doctor said, his voice preternaturally calm and clinical.

"Someone should've warned us this could happen," she cried. "We could have taken steps to prevent it. Aren't there medications he could have taken? Things he could have done?"

I tried to calm Lauren down, but she shook me off, firing off more questions at the doctor and listening bitterly to his responses. For the next few minutes, I stood silent as she cross-examined him, asking about his training, bringing up information she'd read online, mentioning ideas her doctor friends had shared. To each of her questions, the doctor gave cool, measured

responses, and Lauren's fury quickly spent itself. She suddenly looked lost and exhausted. I reached out to her again, and this time she didn't shake me off but sagged heavily against me.

"Now that you're both here," the doctor said, "we need to discuss whether you wish to put in a feeding tube."

"A feeding tube?" Lauren asked, blanching.

"Isn't that really invasive?" I asked.

"It's a medical intervention, yes. Your father's on a ventilator and can't chew or swallow. A feeding tube is the best way for him to receive nourishment, especially since we have no idea when or if he'll regain consciousness."

"Is the tube permanent?" I asked.

"In your father's case, it may be, since we don't know if he will ever regain the ability to eat."

"And what are the risks?"

"Some patients can aspirate or develop infections."

Lauren roughly cleared her throat. "What's the alternative?" she asked.

"We focus on making your father as comfortable as possible. Give him fluids, but that's all."

"You mean hospice?" she said, her voice wobbling.

"Yes. We move the patient to hospice care in such cases."

Lauren shook her head. "There has to be more

we could do. He's still so young—he's not even eighty!"

"Dad wouldn't want a feeding tube," I said, putting my hand on Lauren's arm. "You know him. He hates being forced to do anything he doesn't want to do."

"He doesn't know any better, though," Lauren said.

I shook my head. "He'd never want to be this way."

"He could still wake up—right?" Lauren asked, turning to the doctor.

"He could, but we'd have no idea when. It could be tomorrow, or it could be twenty years from now. And he'll likely have a substantially reduced quality of life."

" 'Substantially reduced'—what does that mean?"

"He may be paralyzed. He may have impaired cognition, memory loss, difficulty speaking."

My mouth felt heavy and dry. "If we forgo the feeding tube, how long until he . . . until he dies?" I asked. Even as I said the words, I couldn't believe they were coming out of my mouth.

"It could take a few days or he could linger for a few weeks."

A few days or a few weeks. Lauren and I sat there in stunned silence, contemplating my father's death sentence. He'd always been so vigorous, carrying us around easily when we

were kids, one under each arm. I remembered how he'd climb the roof after heavy rains to check for leaks, or how he'd mow the lawn under the hot sun, or how he'd moved us single-handedly from place to place, using only a hand dolly and his brute strength to move everything from our refrigerator to our sofa. When he talked, it always sounded like he was barking out commands, and Lauren and I learned to warn people that even when it sounded like he was yelling, he wasn't really yelling. Now, though, it was hard to believe that the silent, fragile figure under the white hospital sheet was really my father. When had he gotten so old? Until then, the thought of his death had always seemed strangely abstract, but this—this was final.

"How long do we have to decide?" Lauren finally asked, looking tearfully at the doctor.

"You have some time. It's a difficult decision, I know. We want to be here, not just for your father but also for you and your family."

"Lauren?" I asked tentatively. She was sitting with her hands clenched in her lap, her forehead furrowed.

"Do you need a few minutes?" the doctor said. "I can step out."

"It's OK," Lauren said, her voice distant and strained. "Anne's right. Dad wouldn't want this. He'd want to go on his own terms."

"Are you sure?" I asked her. "We don't have to make the decision right now."

"I'm sure," Lauren said. As I reached out to touch her, she crumpled into herself. I held her tightly, rocking her back and forth, my shirt turning damp with her tears.

For the next ten days, Lauren and I took turns sitting beside my father's bed, reading to him or playing music while he slept, leaving only to grab a shower and a change of clothes. I dabbed Vaseline on his dry lips and massaged his hands with lotion, little gestures of affection he never would have tolerated had he been conscious. Lauren brought her kids over for a final visit, the three boys standing solemnly over their grandfather's body, Tate trying to tickle my father's calloused feet and wondering why there was no response. "Stop it, buddy," Brett said, but his voice was halfhearted. He gathered his youngest son to his side and hugged him tightly. After they left, Lauren placed a picture of the boys by my father's bedside, along with Archer's Student of the Month certificate and a small vase of daisies. We spent the night at the hospice facility, sleeping on roll-away cots that had been placed beside my father's bed, waking every couple of hours when a nurse came in to take his vital signs and check to see that he wasn't in pain.

Lauren never lost hope that my father might revive, waving me over excitedly whenever he

grunted unexpectedly or spontaneously moved a limb. "What does it mean?" she kept asking. "Is it a sign?" When he made no further noise or movement, she'd inevitably looked disappointed and would sit with her hands folded across her chest, as if giving him the silent treatment for his recalcitrance. True to form, my father clung to life until the very end, even as his breath grew increasingly labored and drawn out. In those final hours, the waiting was both endless and terribly brief. When he finally slipped away early on a Sunday morning, Lauren and I were both seated beside him, each holding one of his hands. It reminded me of the Emily Dickinson poem—he seemed about to mention something, then forgot; consented, and was dead. We sat there stunned. Was he really gone?

A nurse came in to confirm, and only then did Lauren and I burst into tears.

chapter seventeen

I N THE DAYS AFTER his death, Lauren and I argued over whether to hold a service for my father. Other than his lady admirers at the retirement home, he had few friends and no living relatives beyond us. I argued that the most dignified option was to have no memorial at all. In the end, though, Lauren prevailed, and I went along, seeing how the process of planning seemed to help her cope with her grief. We decided on a small funeral service in Fairfax, inviting only close friends and family members. A few of Lauren's friends from Los Angeles made it down—Marni, Celeste, and an old business school friend I remembered meeting long ago. Larry was there, too, as were one or two members of my department. Rick was scheduled to be in Toronto for a book festival but offered to cancel his engagement to stay with me.

"Don't bother," I told him. "You never met my father anyway."

"But I want to be there with you."

"I know. I appreciate it. But really—it's not

327

worth it. Honestly, I didn't want to have a service at all."

"Are you sure?"

"Absolutely."

"I'd probably be no good anyway," Rick admitted. "Funerals aren't my thing—I've seen too many people die." He looked at me earnestly. "At least your father had a long life. He had the opportunity to grow old."

I smiled at him weakly. Part of me was secretly disappointed Rick hadn't insisted on staying. It bothered me a little that he traveled so much and that he was usually out of town when I needed him. Then again, I'd told him to go to his book festival, and part of me felt like I wanted to grieve alone.

During the service, I stood up to give a short eulogy about my father. Lauren hadn't wanted to do it, afraid she might break down. "You're a teacher—you're used to talking in front of people," she told me. I looked out at the sparse gathering of people, all of them looking at me with solemn expectation. I had no lecture notes for the situation, no lesson plan or learning outcome, nothing but a jumble of memories. Most of the people in the audience had never met my father, so I tried to describe him for them. I talked about how our mother had died when we were young and how he'd raised us himself, never remarrying and working, working, working

all the time. I described how he used to feed us hot dogs nuked in the microwave and Hormel chili straight from the can. I talked about how hard it must have been for him to raise two moody teenagers, and how he gave us a lot of responsibility at an early age.

"He wasn't talkative or particularly affectionate, and he had high expectations of us," I said. "But we knew he loved us, even though he didn't show it in the way other parents did." Even though my pet peeve was when people recited poems at weddings and funerals (how many times did I have to listen to the same damn Shakespeare sonnet?), I'd decided to end my own eulogy with a Robert Hayden poem I often taught in my classes. As I recited the lines, I could see Archer and Hayes getting fidgety, and Tate trying to wedge himself under the pew. Lauren was wiping her eyes and sniffling, while Brett tried to restrain them. Glancing to the back of the room, I saw a couple slip in late and take a seat. It was Adam and Bex.

Distracted, I blundered my way to the final, anguished lines of the poem—"What did I know, what did I know / of love's austere and lonely offices?"—and then sat down in silence, staring at my lap and waiting miserably for the service to be over. Lauren reached over and took my hand in hers. "That was nice," she said. Her hand was clammy, but I held it tightly in my own.

The service ended with a perfunctory blessing, and we were ushered into a waiting room where well-wishers lined up to offer their condolences. Standing in a makeshift receiving line, I shook hands briefly with Lauren's friends and then watched them flock to Lauren, enveloping her with hugs and cries of support. Steve had shown up with his wife, and I was suddenly grateful he believed in departmental esprit de corps after all.

"My profound condolences," Steve said, giving me an awkward pat on the back. "We're all so sorry for your loss." His wife, a doughy blonde whom I'd only met once before, impulsively gave me a hug. Larry, who was standing behind her, caught my eye and raised an eyebrow.

"Annie!" Larry said, giving me a tight hug when it was finally his turn. "Are you doing OK? What can I do? I'll do anything—I swear, I'll even grade your papers for you."

"Wow, you must really feel bad for me," I said, trying to smile. "Check with me in a few days—I may take you up on your offer." I peeked behind him in line. There were only two people left to greet, both of them friends of Lauren. "Hey— have you seen Adam and Bex? I thought I saw them come in."

"President Martinez? I didn't even realize he was here," Larry said, looking around.

"Adam's here?" Lauren asked. She'd detached

herself from her group of friends and now appeared beside me.

"Did you invite him?" she asked, pulling me aside.

"No!" I said. "I thought maybe you had. He was with Bex."

"Me? No way," Lauren snorted. "Remember how mean Dad was to him when he visited us in Florida that one time?" She gave a hollow laugh. "Maybe he came to make sure Dad was really dead."

I excused myself, telling Lauren I needed to use the bathroom. There was no one there, and I did a quick check of myself in the mirror. I looked sallow under the fluorescent lights, my eyes puffy and bloodshot, so I splashed some water on my face, straightened my dress, and left quickly. After doing a quick circuit of the building, I stepped out a side door and into an empty courtyard, a small and shaded oasis with overgrown ferns and a stone bench. As I stood there, breathing in the damp smell of moss and dead leaves, a couple entered the courtyard from the opposite side, the woman picking her way across the uneven brick path in high heels, the man steadying her with his arm. Even before they materialized from the darkness, I knew it was Bex and Adam.

"Anne!" Bex said, seeing me and coming over to give me a gentle hug. In her heels, she

was so much taller than me that she had to bend her knees *and* her waist to reach me. "We were just about to come inside. I hope we're not imposing—I heard about the service and wanted to come."

"Not at all," I said. "I'm glad you're here. Lauren will be really happy to see you."

"Is she inside still?" Bex asked, and I nodded, pointing to the side entrance.

"Are you coming?" she asked Adam, who wasn't making a move to follow her.

"I'll be there in a minute," Adam said. "Go on without me." Bex looked faintly surprised but then smiled amenably and disappeared inside.

As the door closed behind her, I turned to Adam.

"I'm sorry I haven't been in touch," I started to babble. "I didn't have your number, and things have been crazy. I'd been meaning to thank you for all of your help—driving me to the hospital and everything. You didn't have to do that—it was so thoughtful of you, and I didn't want you to think I didn't appreciate it or that I'd forgotten. I just—I just wanted to say thank you, thank you for being there, and I'm sorry. For not being in touch."

My throat was burning and I stopped, wondering if anything I'd said made sense. Adam was waiting, giving me the time and space to finish. When I finally petered out, he didn't respond

right away. Instead, he took my hand, guided me to the stone bench, and had me sit down beside him. I was wheezing a little, and he pulled a pack of tissue from his pocket and handed it to me, waiting as I dabbed my eyes and blew my nose.

"Thanks," I said from behind the wadded-up tissue.

"Take your time," he said, his hand on my back. Under its steadying pressure, I could feel my breathing become less jagged, evening out. After a few minutes, Adam finally spoke.

"I've been thinking about you a lot these last couple weeks," he murmured. "Wondering how you're holding up."

"It's been rough," I said, trying to clear my throat. My nose was now completely stuffed, and my voice sounded muffled and gluey. "Everything just happened so quickly. I think Lauren and I are still in shock."

"I'm sure you are," he said, shaking his head. "It was so sudden. But you've been incredibly strong."

"I'm not strong," I snorted. "I'm a mess."

"You're selling yourself short. You're stronger than you realize."

Adam shifted so he was looking at me. I felt myself melt slightly under his gaze.

"What you said in the car—about it being your fault—you know that's not true, right? You did nothing wrong."

"I'm not so sure of that," I said, looking down. "I keep wishing I could go back in time and change things . . . that maybe everything would have turned out differently if I'd just paid attention more, listened, understood the signs. Do you know what I mean?"

"I do," Adam said. He looked troubled.

"I don't know why I do this," I said, laughing bitterly. "I can't help myself. I must be a masochist."

Adam might have nodded in agreement, but I couldn't be sure. I reached for another tissue, blew my nose, added it to the snowball of used tissues on the bench beside me.

"You can't blame yourself," I heard him say. "I know that's easy for me to say, but it's true. You did the best you could."

"Maybe," I said, but my heart wasn't in it. What did Adam know about failure and guilt, anyway? I thought. He was the perfect son.

"I just feel like I was always a disappointment to him," I mumbled. "That I could have been a better daughter."

"Don't say that. I heard the last part of your speech, and it's clear your father really loved you."

"I'm not sure he knew how to show it. He was a pretty tough guy. But I don't need to tell you that." I laughed self-consciously.

"Anne," Adam said, and I looked up reluctantly.

"He was very protective of you," Adam said, speaking slowly and deliberately. "Fiercely so. I didn't understand it then. I thought he was hard to impress. Demanding. Stubborn. I was intimidated by him. But hearing your eulogy, learning of the sacrifices he made and realizing how much he cared for you . . . it made me see him in a new way. It made me realize I'd read him wrong."

He hesitated, grasping for the right words. "Your father loved you deeply. You have to know that. It's a real testament to him that he raised such an accomplished, independent daughter."

I felt my eyes starting to burn. *Don't cry,* I said to myself.

"I should go back inside," I said thickly, turning away so Adam couldn't see my tears. I stumbled to my feet and moved toward the chapel, dizzy with emotion and exhaustion. I felt Adam's arms around me, holding me steady as my body swayed with grief. I hadn't cried during the service, but now I felt something break inside. My father was gone, and I felt like I was spinning in a void. I was no longer Jerry Corey's daughter. I was no longer anyone's daughter. Lauren had her family still, but what did I have? I buried my face in Adam's chest and sobbed.

"WHO'S THIS FROM?" LAUREN asked, inspecting the large bouquet of flowers that was waiting for me on the front porch when we returned from

the service. Brett and the kids had left for Los Angeles already, but Lauren was planning to stay a few days longer so we could clean out my father's room and storage locker.

"I don't know," I said. "I thought we said no flowers."

"It's from someone named Rick," Lauren said, reading the card. " 'Dear Anne, Thinking of you during this difficult time. Affectionately, Rick.' " She looked at me, her eyes wide. " 'Affectionately'?" she asked.

"He's just a guy I'm dating," I said.

"A guy you're dating? Since when?"

"Since I don't know—October?" I said. "We work together."

"He's a professor?" Lauren asked. "Here at Fairfax?"

"Uh-huh," I said. I pulled off my dress and threw it onto my chair. Then I changed into my pajamas, even though it was still the middle of the afternoon.

"Why wasn't he there today?" Lauren asked, placing the flowers on my kitchen table and fussing with some of the blooms.

"He's out of town at a conference," I said, lying on the couch and shading my eyes. My head hurt from all the crying. "He wanted to come, but I told him not to cancel his trip."

Lauren came and sat next to me on the couch. She was still dressed in her black suit, but she'd

taken off her jacket and heels and her face looked drawn.

"Do you like him?" she asked.

I looked at her quizzically. "What kind of question is that?" I asked.

"I just want to know if you like him. Are you serious about him?"

"Yes, I like him," I said cagily. "And we're seeing how things go."

"OK," Lauren said. I waited for her to interrogate me further, ask me what kind of professor Rick was, what he looked like, how old he was, how much money he made, but she didn't. She sank back into the couch and put the back of her hand against her forehead.

"I'm glad you're seeing someone," she said, closing her eyes. "Maybe I can meet him sometime."

I looked at her in surprise, but her eyes were still closed. The torrent of sisterly advice I expected never came.

Early the next day, we went to the storage locker where we'd stashed most of my father's belongings before he moved into the assisted-living facility. I'd hired one of my students to help cart away the heavier things to Goodwill— my dad's old metal filing cabinet, an ancient ham radio transmitter, a wooden grandfather clock that only chimed at the half hour. Sifting through the detritus of our father's life, I wondered if it

was frugality or fear that compelled him to save so much stuff. Some of the stuff made sense (picture albums, passports), but others made me scratch my head (a broken plant stand, a puzzle missing half its pieces). Lauren and I worked steadily through the morning, stuffing his clothes and shoes into garbage bags, tossing everything else into the dumpster.

We took a break around lunchtime, sitting wearily among the remaining boxes. My arms were covered with dry pink welts and my fingers ached, and I drank greedily from the bottle of water Lauren handed over to me.

"Check this out," Lauren said, digging through a box that once held bottles of Gatorade. "I can't believe Dad saved all this stuff," she said, pulling out a stack of old report cards and notebooks tied together with a disintegrating rubber band. She loosened a Mead notebook from the pile. "What's this?" she asked, studying the faded purple cover dotted with stickers and doodles.

I tried to grab it from her. "That's mine!" I said.

"Whoa, wait a second," she said, pulling the notebook out of reach. She opened the notebook and began reading aloud.

" '*The Curse of Castle Montague*, by Anastasia Corey.' *Anastasia Corey?* Are you serious?"

"I was twelve!"

" 'Lavinia Montague had flaming Titian-hued tresses and sparkling emerald-green eyes. She

was the youngest daughter of the evil Count Manfred, tyrannical lord of the mysterious land of Vavasour.' " Lauren burst out laughing. "There must be ten notebooks filled with this stuff!" she said. "When did you find the time to write all this?"

"While you were on the phone talking to your friends and Dad was in his room avoiding us. I had this whole fantasy world mapped out where I was the spunky heroine with a mean father and an evil stepsister."

"No way. Was I the evil stepsister? What was my name?"

"Bertha Gorgonzola."

"I love it! I had no idea you had such a crazy imagination."

I sighed. "Dad was always telling me to stop making up stories and go *do* something. It's too bad he didn't live long enough to see my book come out. Maybe that would've changed his mind."

"I doubt it," Lauren said, grinning at me. She held up the rest of the notebooks. "So do you want to keep these or toss them?"

"Keep them!" I yelled. "Give those to me!"

I ended up keeping my notebooks, report cards, and a tarnished letter-opener that my father had used to tear open bills. Lauren kept an album of photographs, some old coins, and my father's wedding ring, which we found stuffed into a

Ziploc bag with some ancient aspirin pills. The rest we threw out or donated.

"I feel like an orphan," Lauren said.

"We *are* orphans," I said.

We'd asked that people make donations to the American Heart Association in lieu of flowers, and in the days following the funeral, Lauren and I sat at my kitchen table and wrote thank-you notes to everyone who had contributed. I was touched by some of the names on the list—a former student, an old neighbor, an acquaintance at the gym. The English department pitched in a sizable donation, as did many of Lauren's friends.

"Wow, Bex donated five thousand bucks," Lauren said, glancing down the list. "I can't believe she made it down to Fairfax for the service. That's so typical of her—she's so incredibly generous and sweet. And she's going through such a tough time herself."

"What do you mean?" I asked. I'd written so many thank-you cards, straining to be personal and original in each one, that my hand and my brain were cramping in unison.

"Oh, you know, all those stupid rumors about Jack. She can barely leave her house without being hounded."

"Oh, yeah," I said. I'd totally forgotten about the scandal.

"I'm glad she's got that library project to

340

distract her—from what everyone's told me, Adam's been a pillar of support." Lauren sighed. "She deserves to be with someone who realizes how amazing she is."

Lauren opened up a card and began to compose a note to Bex, writing smoothly and briskly. Unlike me, she didn't seem to have trouble finding the right words.

"Oh, look," I said in surprise, tracing my finger farther down the list. "I think Adam donated, too." His name appeared toward the bottom of the donor list.

"Must be a gift on behalf of the college," Lauren said without looking up. "Brett's firm also made a donation."

I looked more closely, but Adam's title and institutional affiliation weren't listed. "Adam Martinez," it read. "Gift in Memory of Jerome F. Corey."

"Can you write him a thank-you card?" Lauren asked. "I'll sign it when you're done."

I nodded. Opening up a fresh card, I hesitated, not knowing quite what to say.

Dear President Martinez,

Thank you very much for your donation to the American Heart Association in memory of our father, Jerome Corey. We have been overwhelmed by the generosity

and support of friends like you. Your gift will go toward heart disease and stroke research and education, patient care and outreach, and other life-saving efforts.

I paused. It was boilerplate. I wondered if I dared write something more personal, glancing at Lauren. She hadn't seen my breakdown at the funeral service. She hadn't seen Adam comforting me, or getting me another packet of tissues, or helping me stop my runaway hiccups so that I could return to the chapel and continue to accept condolences. Adam had walked me inside but quickly excused himself when the funeral director approached me with some questions. The last I saw him, he was standing next to Bex and one of her friends, listening to Lauren and nodding his head.

"Thank you for being there for me during this difficult time," I desperately wanted to write. "Thank you for listening to me, and for understanding my complicated relationship with my father, and for letting me cry on your shoulder. I will never forget your steadfast generosity and kindness." I felt the tears spring to my eyes again, feeling a roiling mix of grief, regret, and longing. Turning away from Lauren, I surreptitiously brushed my face with the sleeve of my sweater.

I'll write him a separate note later, I decided.

The last thing I wanted to do was invite more questions from Lauren.

"Thank you so much for attending the service," I wrote hastily, signing the card "Anne Corey" and passing it to Lauren, who barely looked up from what she was doing. She glanced at the card, announced that it "looked good," and signed. I slipped the card into an envelope and addressed it c/o The Office of the President, Fairfax College, Fairfax, CA, adding it to the stack of cards Lauren planned to deposit at the local post office.

Lauren left a short while later, promising to call me soon. "You should spend the summer in LA," she said as she hugged me good-bye. "You and Rick—is that his name? You and Rick could stay in our guesthouse. It would be good for you to get out of Fairfax."

I looked at Lauren in surprise. "Only if you want to," she added, seeing my hesitation.

"No—I really appreciate it," I said. "I'll definitely consider it."

"Now that dad's gone, we should really make more of an effort to, you know, hang out."

"I'd like that."

After Lauren left, I slowly climbed the stairs back to my apartment. With my sister gone, the apartment felt lifeless. I tried to tidy up, washing out some glasses and throwing a load of laundry into the washer. The bouquet of flowers Rick

had sent me on the day of the funeral had wilted and gone brown. I salvaged the least bedraggled flowers and placed them in a smaller vase. The rest of the arrangement I tossed in the trash, where they scattered bright yellow pollen all over the container and floor. I was cleaning up the mess when my phone started to vibrate. It was Larry.

"What's going on?" I asked. "My sister literally just left."

"Have you seen the news today?" he asked urgently.

"Not yet," I said. "Oh no—is it about Jack? Did they leak more secret footage? Lauren was telling me things are still bad—"

"No, no—it's not about that," Larry said. "It's about Rick."

"Rick??"

"Check the front page of the *New York Times*," he said. "And sit tight. I'm coming over right now."

I opened up my computer and went to the *Times* website. What I saw made my jaw drop open in shock.

chapter eighteen

FAMED AUTHOR ACCUSED OF PLAGIARISM
By Andrew Terasawa

The rumors began soon after the critically acclaimed author Richard Forbes Chasen received the Booker Prize for his sprawling and ambitious postmodern novel, *Subterranean City*. The book, people whispered, had been plagiarized.

Chasen, 35, known as much for his rugged good looks as his sinewy prose, has been the subject of envy for years. Ever since he burst onto the literary scene at the age of twenty-one, he has collected several major literary prizes and was recently named to the *New Yorker*'s vaunted "Forty Under Forty" list. The Booker was just the latest in a long string of professional accolades.

That is, until a commentator on an online discussion board posted an innocent question about Chasen's work.

"Has anyone noticed that Chasen totally rips off Dickens in Chapter 4 of *Subterranean City*?" a user named Bibliophyllis917 wrote. "Like not just parodies Dickens but actually copies his sentences word for word from *Bleak House*?"

"He's openly acknowledged his debt to Dickens," another member wrote back. "It's no big deal."

But the question posed by Bibliophyllis917 seemed to trigger a raft of similar observations. Discussion members pointed out sections of the novel in which pronouns or place names had been changed but in which the bulk of the language was otherwise identical to passages by contemporary writers, such as Salman Rushdie, Kurt Vonnegut, and Terry Eagleton. And Chasen didn't just borrow from the literary and scholarly elite. A member with the handle KirkDaedelus alleged that Chasen had plagiarized from Rotten Tomatoes movie reviews, contemporary romance novels, and even a corporate training handbook.

Chasen had already been accused of "self-plagiarism" by Rian Murphy, a journalist and critic who has repeatedly called him out for recycling previous work

on his *Paris Review* blog. Murphy has also expressed concern about Chasen's journalistic practices. "I've found numerous instances in Chasen's reportage where I couldn't locate or confirm his sources," Murphy says. "I started to suspect he might be fabricating quotations out of whole cloth. But when I confronted him about this, he always had some ready excuse. He claimed he had access to interviews that weren't publicly available, or that he was bound by journalistic ethics from revealing his sources. It was always something or other."

"It's sick," says one of Chasen's most vocal critics, the novelist Alice Duffy. "His utter inability to be forthright and truthful suggests something on the order of a mental illness."

Another writer, the legal scholar Lindell McKenzie, expressed shock when presented with evidence that Chasen had lifted several long passages from her 2007 nonfiction book, *On Justice and Inequality*. "When I saw how he'd taken my words without attribution, I felt— well, quite honestly, I felt like I'd been violated."

Chasen's supporters have bridled at these statements, calling them inflamma-

tory and hysterical. The *Guardian* book critic Angus Malcolm, a longtime friend and advocate for Chasen's work, says writers like Duffy and McKenzie are simply "jealous." "There's a long literary tradition of great artists borrowing from sources high and low," he said. "Look it up. It's called bricolage." Virginia Miller, a literary scholar at Cornell University, concurs: "Poets like Ezra Pound and T. S. Eliot often appropriated the works of other writers, and they were considered literary geniuses, not thieves."

Yet these latest accusations are giving pause to even longtime fans of Chasen's work. *The New York Times* has independently verified at least 67 instances of exact or near-exact plagiarism (see Table 1). Some instances are only a sentence or two long. Others go on for pages. Faced with such overwhelming evidence, Francesca Youngblood, a professor at Columbia who is writing a book on Chasen, said, "It's pretty damning. I mean, maybe it's a weird postmodern experiment or some kind of joke on the reader. I just hope he has some kind of explanation."

Efforts to reach Chasen for comment were unsuccessful, but his New York–

based literary agent, Timothy Brown, issued a statement in which he accused unnamed sources of mounting an "orchestrated vendetta" against Chasen. "Mr. Chasen is prepared to defend himself vigorously against these attacks," Brown wrote. "We are in the process of seeking legal counsel and will pursue all possible options. In the meantime, we ask the public to withhold judgment."

Whether Chasen's Booker Prize will be rescinded is unclear. When contacted, the Booker Prize committee confirmed that they were investigating the matter but declined additional comment. Chasen is currently listed as a "Writer-in-Residence" at Fairfax College in California. A spokesperson for the school confirmed his employment there but would not provide further information, citing confidentiality laws.

Currently, Chasen's publisher, Farrar, Straus and Giroux, has no plans to pull *Subterranean City* from the shelves. The novel has been a substantial hit for the press, selling nearly a million copies since it was awarded the Booker Prize in 2015. It was issued in paperback this past January.

Meanwhile, some are wondering why

it took people so long to raise concerns about Chasen's plagiarism.

The novelist Duffy has a couple theories. "First of all, I think a lot of people started the novel but didn't get very far," she said. "And then there's the incredible level of trust readers place in authors. Even if they notice fishy passages, they're inclined to give the author the benefit of the doubt."

Legal scholar McKenzie has another hypothesis. "I think that lots of people think plagiarism isn't that big of a deal," she says. "I mean, look at all these students who copy and paste from Wikipedia. They think it's a victimless crime."

She shakes her head. "I'm a writer," she says. "All I have are my words. If Richard Chasen steals them from me, he's taken the most important thing I have."

I felt like I'd had the wind knocked out of me. Rick—a plagiarist? My mind couldn't fathom it. There was nothing I held more sacred than words. It was what I studied, what I labored over, what I revered. To claim another person's words as one's own was unthinkable. It was *the* cardinal sin of writing.

I could still remember the first time I'd

encountered plagiarism and how deeply it had offended me. I was in the third grade, and the teacher held up a book report and announced that whoever had written it had forgotten to put his or her name on the report. Chris Manning had leapt up to claim it, and the teacher asked him to read it aloud to the class. As I listened to him stumble through descriptions of the various species of penguins, I felt a sudden, sickening jolt of recognition.

"That's *my* report," I blurted out, jumping from my seat.

The class was speechless.

"Is it true?" the teacher asked.

Chris looked at me blankly, shrugged, and handed me the report. I clutched it to my chest, incredulous that someone would dare take credit for *my* words.

"Next time, remember to put your name on your work, Anne," the teacher said.

More than twenty years later, I could still feel the anger I'd felt toward Chris. How *could* he? How could he claim my words as his own? And how could he be so cavalier about it when he was caught?

But Chris, I reminded myself, was a lazy and not-very-bright eight-year-old. Rick, on the other hand, was a highly acclaimed literary genius. There was no way he could pull something so egregious, and in such a clumsy, brazen

way. I was sure of it. It just didn't make sense.

By the time Larry appeared at my apartment a few minutes later, I'd almost convinced myself of Rick's innocence.

"It can't be true," I told him. "Rick wouldn't plagiarize."

"Did you *read* the article?" Larry asked. He'd arrived armed with a bottle of tequila and a box of tissues and couldn't seem to understand why I didn't need either. "You must be in shock. They put passages from Rick's novel next to their sources. It's pretty blatant."

"But there must be some reason he did this. Why would he risk it?"

"Maybe he can't help himself? Maybe he has a compulsive disorder?"

"Where he can't help but steal other people's words? What is that even? Graphokleptomania?"

"I don't know. You tell me. Did he ever let you read anything he was working on?"

"No," I said. "But I never really asked."

"Did you read his novel?"

"I only read about a hundred pages," I said guiltily. "I never noticed anything. What about you? Did you read his book?"

"Me? I told you. I don't read anything published after 1920."

"Should I call him?" I asked, reaching for my phone. Rick was supposed to be boarding a plane back from Toronto.

"Text him," Larry suggested. "He must have reporters hounding him like crazy."

I sent Rick a short text: "Saw the story in the NYT. Are you OK?"

He texted back almost immediately. "Don't believe all the BS. I'm being targeted. I'll explain everything when I see you."

"When will you be back?" I texted.

"Not sure. Postponed my flight until further notice. Trying to dodge reporters. Will call soon."

"See?" I said, showing Larry the messages. "He says he's being targeted. I bet he just forgot to cite his sources and the press is blowing things out of proportion."

"You sound like a freshman trying to explain why he accidentally on purpose stole his entire essay off of SparkNotes. This man is not an eighteen-year-old freshman, Anne. He knew better!"

I shut my computer. "I want to hear his side of the story first," I said. "I owe that to him."

Over the course of the day, though, the story seemed to metastasize. Larry forwarded me links to related stories on other websites, some with headlines like "The Con Artist" and "Pulped Fiction." The gossip blogs reported that a film version of *Subterranean City*, slated to begin shooting in the summer, was now up in the air. #ChasenQuotes started trending on Twitter, along

with memes of Rick claiming to have written everything from the Bible to Harry Potter.

I tried not to get sucked into the media frenzy, but the more I read, the less I could explain away Rick's transgressions. If it was true, Rick was a cheat and a liar. He'd duped countless people— his readers, his fellow writers, and, worst of all, *me*. If it wasn't true, then Rick was the victim of some byzantine conspiracy perpetrated by some unknown enemy. In my gut, I knew which scenario was more likely.

When I next reached Rick over the phone, he was still defiant. "It's a witch hunt," he said. "I bet no one's work would stand up to such scrutiny!"

"So you *did* plagiarize?" I asked.

"Absolutely not! Anne, how could you even think that? I had a numbskull research assistant— this girl could barely string two words together! I'm sure she did a sloppy job on sourcing, and now *I'm* getting blamed for her incompetence!"

"Why don't you issue a statement?"

"It's not that simple," Rick said. "The publisher's to blame, if you really get down to it. They placed an absolutely inhumane amount of pressure on me to meet my deadline. I had no choice but to rely on research assistants—they gave me no choice. But of course they want to place the blame squarely on my shoulders, blame me for not supervising my assistants adequately."

Rick snorted angrily. "I'm being pilloried for something that's not my fault! It's not such a big deal, really. All the publisher has to do is reissue a new edition with citations. Problem solved."

I heard Rick chastising someone in the background. "Tell them to piss off!" I heard him grumble.

"Are you still in Toronto?" I asked.

"Ugh, I miraculously made it out, but now I'm stuck on a layover in San Francisco. I think I should lie low here for a few more days until things die down. I've got some friends I can crash with."

"Want me to fly up?"

"No, no—you stay put. Don't worry—once the next scandal du jour hits the news cycle this will all blow over. Just promise me that if anyone calls you for a comment, you'll hang up."

"OK," I said, feeling uncertain and confused.

"Listen, I've got to go—I'll call you later."

The next day, though, the *Times* published a slew of follow-up articles, uncovering problems with Rick's first novel, and then with nearly every essay or article he'd ever written. The Booker committee announced soon after that they were revoking Rick's prize. Lindell McKenzie and several other writers announced they were filing lawsuits. Rick's publisher announced it was pulping all remaining copies of the book and issuing refunds to anyone who felt they had been

defrauded. While running errands at the campus bookstore, I noticed that all of Rick's books had been pulled from the shelves.

"Can you tell me what's going on?" I asked Rick the next time he called. "I'm trying to be supportive, but this is getting out of control."

"I don't know what to say," Rick cried. "You have to believe me."

"You did it, didn't you? I've looked at all the evidence—it's damning. What were you thinking?" My voice was taut with anger.

"I *wasn't* thinking, truth be told," Rick said, his voice breaking. "I'm in a very dark place right now."

"But how could you do this?"

"I didn't mean to hurt anyone. I never deliberately stole from people. I'm seeing a psychiatrist now to figure out why I'm so damaged. He says I was betrayed by my early success. I didn't want to disappoint anyone, so this was my way of coping." He sighed heavily.

"What a mess," I groaned. "I don't know what to do."

"Annie, just knowing you're by my side—"

"Hold on—I . . ."

"You can't leave me now! Are you breaking up with me?"

"I just—" I felt myself grasping for words. The truth was, I *did* want to break up with Rick. I just didn't know how to do it.

"Haven't you ever made a terrible mistake and regretted it deeply? I'm not a bad person. I want to change, make things right. Please—you have to have faith in me."

"But—"

"I honestly don't trust anyone else. I need you more than ever right now. I—I don't know what I'd do if you left." Rick's voice shook with emotion. "I wouldn't be able to survive—I'd do something terrible, I know it."

"Don't say that!" Rick sounded like he was coming unhinged. What if he did something drastic? What if he hurt someone? What if he hurt himself?

"It's true. I have nothing to live for. Please—give me a chance. I've lost everything—my career, my prizes, everything. Don't make me lose you, too."

"OK," I said, trying to calm him down. "Just promise me you won't do anything to hurt yourself. I'm here. When do you come back?"

"Early tomorrow morning. I'm planning to head straight to campus from the airport. I'll meet you at my office first thing—just knock."

"OK," I said. "Don't worry. I'll be there."

After I hung up, I frantically called Larry, who whistled incredulously when I gave him the latest update.

"I can't believe he's actually going to show his

face at school," Larry said. "I'd want to crawl into a hole and die."

"At least he's not bailing on his students," I pointed out, desperate to find something—anything—redeeming about Rick's behavior.

"But think of the humiliation!"

"Come on, Larry," I pleaded. "We shouldn't all pile on. He screwed up and he's sorry. Give the guy a break. Please? For me?"

I spent the evening worrying that I'd been too hard on Rick. Had I pushed him over the edge? He'd made a huge mistake, but now he sounded truly sorry and truly despondent. I slept poorly that night and headed to campus early, even though my first class didn't meet until later in the afternoon. As I walked into the department, I stopped in surprise. Pam was standing in front of Rick's office, pinning a notice to the door. Some empty file boxes were on the floor next to her. I quietly walked up and read the notice over her shoulder.

NOTICE: PROFESSOR CHASEN IS ON MEDICAL LEAVE. HIS WORKSHOP HAS BEEN CANCELED. PLEASE REFER ANY QUESTIONS TO DR. CULPEPPER, CHAIR.

"What's going on?" I asked, startling Pam.

"Oh!" she cried, fishing a thumbtack from her mouth. "Anne! You're here early!" Her eyes lit

up. "I've been dying to talk to you. I thought *you* of all people would know what was going on."

When I looked at her blankly, she gasped. "Or wait—did you guys break up?"

"Is Rick not coming back?" I asked.

"All I've been told is to put up this sign and to pack up his books." Pam looked at me with pity. "So you don't know anything either? He didn't tell you where he was going?"

"He's in San Francisco," I said. "He's supposed to be back soon."

"Really? Not according to Dr. Culpepper, he isn't," Pam said knowingly. She looked around quickly and then lowered her voice. "So do you think it's all true?"

"What's true?"

"The plagiarism? The stealing other people's work? I read somewhere that he paid a ghost-writer to write all his books!"

"I don't know," I said. "You'll have to ask him yourself."

"Poor baby," Pam said, clucking maternally. "So you're as much in the dark as the rest of us, aren't you? No wonder you look so terrible. This must have completely ruined your spring break."

"Actually, not really, Pam," I said, my voice icy. "My break sucked, but not because of Rick. It sucked because my dad died." I walked away before Pam could respond.

Once I was safely in my office, I tried to call

Rick's phone, but his voicemail box was full.

"where are you??" I texted. "call me!"

I waited but there was no response.

"are you coming back?" I wrote.

Still no response.

"PLEASE CALL ME ASAP," I finally texted.

I called Larry, feeling panic building in my chest. In my mind, I saw Rick climbing over the railing at Golden Gate Bridge, or stepping into rush hour traffic, or—God forbid—loading a gun.

"Rick's vanished," I said. "He's not answering his phone. His class has been canceled. He's apparently on 'medical leave.' Do you think—do you think he might have hurt himself?"

"Wait—you don't think he was suicidal, do you?" Larry asked.

"He was saying some crazy things on the phone to me yesterday—"

"Like what?"

"Like how he has nothing to live for any-more—"

"You're kidding."

"I made him promise not to do anything, and he seemed to calm down by the time I hung up. But maybe—oh God, do you think?"

"Did you talk to Steve? He should know something, right?"

"He's not in his office."

"What about Pam? She seems to know every-thing."

"She was trying to pump *me* for information!"

"OK, stay calm. We don't know anything yet. Just don't panic."

"Should I call the police?"

"No! Don't do anything yet. I'll be in as soon as I can."

On a whim, I checked online to see if any new stories about Rick had been posted since the previous day. On the *Times* website, I noticed an update on the sidebar and clicked. The Associated Press had a new report, just two sentences in total:

> Discredited novelist Richard Forbes Chasen has checked into a rehabilitation center for undisclosed personal reasons. His representative has no further comment at this time.

EMILY YOUNG HADN'T BEEN by my office much that spring, busy training for the upcoming NCAA championships. I'd kept up with her mostly through the school newspaper, reading up on her latest games and the team's steady rise in the rankings. Her next tournament was scheduled to be in Oregon, so I was surprised when I saw her waiting outside my office, dressed not in her tennis gear but in a brown sweater and jeans, her hair hanging loose instead of in its usual ponytail. I realized I'd almost never seen her wearing street clothes.

"Do you have a minute?" she asked.

"Of course!" I said, motioning her to come in.

"I have some news about grad school," she said. "I found out I got into Berkeley and Columbia with full funding."

"That's fantastic news!" I said. "You must be thrilled!"

But Emily didn't look thrilled. In fact, she looked like she was about to cry.

"What's wrong?" I asked. "Tell me."

"It's about a guy," she said.

Oh no, I thought. All this time, I'd assumed Emily was still single. I never saw her on campus with anyone, and she never volunteered any information. She must have met someone in the last few months and was having relationship panic now that graduation was fast approaching.

"Let me guess—is it about whether or not to break up with your boyfriend before grad school?"

"Yes!" Emily said. "How did you know?"

"I was your age once," I said, smiling. "Tell me about him."

"Well, um, you actually know him."

"I do?" I ran through my male students in my head, trying to figure out who could possibly be dating Emily.

"Yes." She hesitated, biting her lip, her hands nervously clenched in her lap. "I haven't told anyone because it's sort of a secret." Lowering her voice, she whispered, "It's Rick Chasen."

I felt myself go numb. Emily must have seen

the shock on my face because she reddened and started stammering, "I know he's my professor and all, but I'm twenty-one, and he's not that much older than me, really."

"But he's your professor," I said, my voice hollow.

"He's not really my professor anymore. I dropped his class after we started dating."

I didn't say anything at first, and Emily looked like she might burst into tears again.

"You're upset," she said. "I shouldn't have said anything."

"No, no—I'm just surprised. Go on."

"He's the most amazing professor I've ever had," she said tearfully. "He really cared about what I had to say. It's so hard to find college guys like that. They're all so immature and superficial. But Rick *listened* to me. He told me I was the best writer in the class and that I shouldn't let my talent go to waste. Did you know he was nearly killed by a roadside bomb in Iraq? And that he lost his best friend in the attack? I nearly cried when he told me. He's way stronger and braver than I could ever be. I just—I have so much respect for him. He stands up for what he believes is right, even if his life's at risk!"

I handed Emily a tissue and she blew her nose. "How did you two start . . . dating?" I asked.

Emily blushed. "We started hanging out a lot in his office so he could help me revise my stories.

He would ask me to close the door so we could talk without being bothered, and we just got to chatting about other stuff. He mentioned that he'd been dating someone but that she made him feel really inadequate. He called her a frigid bitch. I let him vent to me, and one day, he said, 'Em, I have something to confess. I really want to kiss you. If you weren't my student . . .' I—I told him I didn't have to be his student anymore, and . . . well . . . it sort of went on from there. He told me I was beautiful. No one's ever said that to me before."

I cleared my throat. "And why are you telling me now?" I asked.

"I don't know who else to talk to," she cried. "I was with him in San Francisco last week when this whole scandal broke. He was so upset. He said he was being set up and that no one believed him. I told him *I* believed him. I know what it's like to be under a lot of pressure to succeed. Before I left, he told me I was the only person he could really trust and that we were soul mates. I love him, Professor Corey. He's my first real boyfriend. I swear he's the best thing that's ever happened to me."

She choked back a sob. "He checked into rehab, and now his phone doesn't work and I have no way to get in touch with him. But I need to talk to him! He loves me—I know he does. I'll go wherever he wants me to go, as long as we're together." She looked at me beseechingly.

"I know you're friends with him. Do you have his contact information? Can you pass a message along to him?"

I shook my head. "I don't know how to reach him," I said. "He didn't give me any information, either."

"Has he been fired?" she squeaked. "They say his class has been canceled. Is he ever coming back?"

"The administration won't tell us. And we're under strict orders not to talk to the press." Steve had sent out an e-mail just that morning asking us to stay mum and refer any snooping reporters to him directly.

Emily looked devastated. "Please don't tell anyone about this," she begged. "I don't want to get him in any more trouble. I'd kill myself if the administration found out."

I looked at Emily, weighing what I should do next. Should I say anything to her? Or should I keep my mouth shut? She looked at me pleadingly, and I felt a twinge of responsibility and guilt.

"Emily," I said. "I need to tell you something. Rick is not who you think he is. He's not . . . dependable."

Emily looked at me quizzically.

"I don't know what he's told you," I continued. "But you can't trust everything he says. He's— How do I say this? He's an opportunist." I winced

to myself, realizing I was saying the exact same thing to Emily that Adam had said to me six months earlier.

"What do you mean?" Emily asked. "He's always been super upfront with me."

"I know more about him than you do. You might as well know—we weren't just friends. We were dating each other."

A look of horror crossed Emily's face, then disgust.

"*You're* the girlfriend?" she asked.

"I guess you could say that," I said.

I wasn't prepared for what happened next. Instead of recognizing Rick as the two-timing prick that he was, Emily turned on *me*.

"So you're the one that made him so miserable," she said quietly. "You're the one who was pushing him away."

"I didn't push him away, Emily. He's been feeding you lies. He's been using you, don't you see? He was using you the way he used me."

"No," Emily said, shaking her head. "I don't believe it. He'd never do that. He knew how much I respected you, so he was trying to protect me."

"Protect you from what?" I asked.

"From *this*," Emily said, standing up. "From retaliation. I shouldn't have said anything. He knew you'd try to get back at me if you found out."

"Emily!" I said. "Stop! Don't do this. I only said something because I care about you. I don't want you to get hurt!" I tried to keep her from leaving, but she recoiled from me, grabbing her bags and storming to the door.

"You know," she said. "I used to look up to you so much. You were my role model. What was I thinking? I don't want to be like you *at all*."

After she left, I sank to the floor. She'd responded just the same way I'd responded when Adam tried to warn me about Rick—with rage and disbelief. I wanted to kill Rick. He'd seduced me and he'd seduced Emily, and he'd told us both the same lies. How stupid could I be? Emily had an excuse. She was twenty-one and hopelessly naive. But what was *my* excuse? I was a grown-up, yet he'd known exactly the right things to say to me, told me exactly what I wanted to hear.

You're a fucking idiot, Anne, I told myself.

But the worst part wasn't that Rick had lied to me or led me on. It wasn't that he'd stolen other people's work and passed it off as his own. It wasn't even that he'd preyed on an innocent undergrad girl. It was that *I* was partly responsible for all this. Emily had been my favorite student, the younger, better, more hopeful version of myself. I was supposed to protect her. Instead, I'd delivered her right up to Rick's doorstep. And I would never forgive myself for that.

From: nesahc_drahcir@gmail.com
To: Anne Corey <A.Corey@Fairfax.edu>
Subject: salutations from Rick
Date: April 3

Dearest Anne,

I'm so sorry I didn't have a chance to speak to you before checking into treatment. My doctor placed me under a 5150 involuntary psychiatric hold and wouldn't let me contact anyone until I was safely here in Arizona. It's been a tremendous relief to escape from the immense stress of recent events. I've been practicing transcendental meditation, doing individual and group therapy, and adhering to a strictly organic, gluten-free, raw-food diet.

I've realized I need to focus on myself and work on healing my mind and body. I'm sorry I couldn't finish off the semester at Fairfax, but I'm sure the department understands my situation. Thank you for always being there for me. If you could collect my mail and forward any bills to me here, I would appreciate it.

Love,
Rick
PS This is my new e-mail address. I've shut down my author website.

From: nesahc_drahcir@gmail.com
To: Anne Corey <A.Corey@Fairfax.edu>
Subject: It's Rick—DO NOT DELETE
Date: April 4

Anne,

I'm not sure if you received my e-mail from yesterday. I'm worried it might have ended up in your spam folder or that you deleted it because you didn't recognize the e-mail address. It's me and I'm in a treatment center in Arizona, doing the hard work of putting myself back together. Please drop me a line just so I know you are doing ok. I miss you dearly.

Love,
Rick

From: Lawrence Ettinger <L.Ettinger@Fairfax.edu>
To: Anne Corey <A.Corey@Fairfax.edu>
Subject: Ruh-roh
Date: April 6

Just got this e-mail from Rick. Is he stalking you??? BLOCK HIM.
I just did.

---------- Forwarded message ----------
From: nesahc_drahcir@gmail.com
To: Lawrence Ettinger <L.Ettinger@Fairfax.edu>
Subject: Salutations from Rick Chasen
Date: April 6

My dear Larry,

How are you doing?

As you've probably heard, I've entered inpatient treatment for anxiety and depression and am focused on getting my mental machinery sorted out. I'm writing to see if you might pass a message along to Anne. I've been trying to reach her for the last several days, but she's either not receiving my e-mails or has decided to ignore them. If the former, could you please give her my new e-mail address and ask her to contact me? If the latter, perhaps you could apprise me of the reason for her sudden aloofness.

I confess my feelings are hurt. I didn't expect her to be so inconstant in my time of need.

Sincerely,
Rick

From: RF_Chasen722@yahoo.com
To: Anne Corey <A.Corey@Fairfax.edu>
Subject: Please respond
Date: April 15

Dear Anne,

I see that my last few e-mails have bounced back as "undeliverable," so I'm writing to you from a different account in the hopes this message will make safe passage to your inbox.

It has come to my attention that you might be under the misapprehension that I had a "thing" with Emily Young. Emily is a young, impressionable young girl who, like many of my students, developed "feelings" for me. Unlike my other students, however, Emily avidly pursued me—indeed, entrapped me. She would dress provocatively and flirt outrageously with me. She frequented my office hours. She enrolled in my workshop a second time. In sum, she seduced me.

Emily is a silly girl who has never meant anything to me.

Rick

From: Pamela Mitchie <P.Mitchie@Fairfax.edu>
To: Anne Corey <A.Corey@Fairfax.edu>
Subject: Flowers in the lobby?
Date: April 20

Dear Anne,

I believe you've left for the day, but a huge bouquet of flowers was delivered to you just now. I took the liberty of peeking at the card and it looks to be from Rick!!!!!!!!! Are you guys back together???????
    I'll leave the arrangement on my desk for now, and you can pick them up whenever you're in next.

Big hugs,

Pam

"How do you spell love?"—Piglet
"You don't spell it, you feel it." —Pooh

R. Chasen
Miraval Treatment Center
Sedona, Arizona

Dr. Anne Corey c/o
Department of English
Murphy Hall 217
Fairfax College
Fairfax, CA

April 25

Dear Anne,

By the time you receive this letter, I will have left treatment. I beg you to give me a chance to speak to you face-to-face. I understand you've blocked my phone number and various e-mail addresses, so please forgive me for employing traditional US Postal Service to reach you.

I have thought long and hard about my life during this past month, and I've come to the realization that I have hurt and betrayed many of the people I love most deeply through my own selfishness and fear. As part of the process of taking moral inventory, I am making amends to each person I have wronged. Please forgive me, Anne.

I'm planning to spend the summer at the American Academy in Rome, where I've secured a Writers in Exile fellowship. I would be honored

if you joined me. You have been my muse for the past year, and without you, I am rudderless. Think of it—an entire summer spent in an ancient villa, like a modern-day version of the Brownings!

With all my love and respect,
Rick

chapter nineteen

I TOSSED RICK'S LETTER INTO the paper shredder and listened to its satisfying munching. I'd already tossed Rick's novels into the garbage, along with his yoga mat and an old concert T-shirt he'd left at my place. I'd purged my inbox of all his e-mails, blocked his number on my phone, deleted the messages he left on my office voicemail. The bouquet of flowers I told Pam to keep, much to her ill-concealed delight.

"Are you sure?" she asked, sniffing one of the blooms. "They're gorgeous. He clearly spent a pretty penny on them."

"Take them," I said, making a face. The arrangement was identical to the one he'd sent me after my father's death, down to the "Thinking of You" card stuck to a plastic prong. I felt nauseated even looking at it.

"If you insist," Pam said, taking the bouquet and placing it more prominently on the reception desk. "You know, maybe you should give him a second chance—you two were a cute couple."

I shot her a death stare, and she laughed

nervously. "Or maybe you need more time?" she ventured.

As I walked away, I could see her picking up her phone.

I tried to be on campus as little as possible, going in only to teach my classes and hold office hours. I strictly avoided department meetings or any school-related events, finding them intolerable. In the beginning there were the pitying looks and the well-meaning greetings—"How *are* you?"—that I didn't know how to answer. Were they talking about my father? About Rick? Both? After the initial show of concern, people didn't know how to act around me. My colleagues began skirting by me in the hallways, avoiding my eyes, smiling at me wanly. I felt like a campus ghost, a harbinger of bad luck. I began to keep my office door closed, both to detract visitors and to contain my bad mojo.

The only person I really saw was Larry, who came by regularly to keep me company in the evenings. He would mop up my tears and urge me to eat something besides Nutella out of the jar, and then the two of us would lie on the couch and get drunk, having competitions to see who was more pathetic.

"I'm a middle-aged follicularly challenged loser," he'd begin.

"I'm a frigid bitch."

"I'm a flaming douche nugget."

"I'm an orphan."

"My boyfriend dumped me for his career."

"Mine cheated on me with a student."

"Hey, Anne?"

"Yes, Larry."

"What does 'flaming douche nugget' mean anyway?"

One night, Larry pulled up a picture of himself on his computer and, using Paintbrush, started drawing in hair.

"What are you *doing?*" I asked.

"It's called poor man's art therapy," he said. "I'm trying to work through my issues."

"I think you're going to be in therapy for a long time," I said, getting up to head to the kitchen. "Hey, do you want more wine?" I asked, checking the empty bottles that now covered my kitchen counter.

"I think we just finished the last bottle," Larry called out from the living room.

"No—I think there's a little left in one of these," I said, inspecting some red wine I'd left out, uncorked. "Oh, wait," I said, raising it to my eye and squinting inside. "It looks like some fruit flies drowned in it overnight."

"Retch," Larry said, gagging.

"Maybe I could just sieve the flies out."

"OK, stop," Larry said. "We're pathetic, but let's not stoop to new lows."

• • •

I WAS IN MY office one afternoon, getting ready to leave for the day, when I heard a knock on the door. The only person who ever knocked now was Larry. Even Pam had started to avoid me after she suggested I join her church singles group and I told her I'd rather date Satan.

"Come in!" I called out.

The door opened and a man in sunglasses and fedora slipped inside, shutting the door behind him quickly. He pulled off his hat, revealing a full beard and a man bun.

"What the—" I said.

It was Rick, incognito in his new facial hair and disguise.

"Are you kidding me?" I said, snorting. "You look like an idiot."

Rick looked stunned, then hurt.

"I'm a broken man," he said. "I'm nothing without you."

"God, you really are a one-trick pony," I said. "Did you steal that line from a book? You're pathetic."

Rick put his hand to his heart, like I'd wounded him physically.

"I know you're mad," he said. "I know I betrayed your trust. I'll never forgive myself."

"Ugh," I said, getting up from my desk. "You're shameless. Get the hell out."

"I'm still in love with you."

"You're in love with yourself! Look at you with that . . . that *lame* man bun and beard! Who do you think you are? Jared Leto?"

"Let's run away to Rome and start over. We'll find a romantic little pensione and hide from the world."

"Are you high?" I asked. "Is this what you told your other girlfriends? That you'd whisk them away to *Rome?* No, thank you. I'm perfectly happy where I am."

"I can take care of you, Anne—help you with your writing, be your editor and first reader, build your confidence. You look tired, Anne. I'm so sorry—I'm sorry I've made you suffer."

"I can take care of myself! God, you really are a raging narcissist, aren't you? Get out of here or I'm calling campus police."

"You wouldn't do that, would you?" Rick said, coming closer to me, his voice suddenly threatening.

I stepped back and reached for my phone. Most people had left for the day, but I knew Larry was still in his office.

"🖊✂ " I typed.

"What are you doing?" Rick asked. "Who are you calling?"

I ignored him, mashing my fingers against the screen.

"🖊✂✂✂✂✂✂✂✂✂✂✂"

"Give that to me," Rick said, reaching over

379

to grab my phone. I pulled it out of his reach.

"Don't you dare touch me," I said. "I'll scream, I swear I will."

Rick moved toward me, and I dodged from his grasp, my heart pounding in my chest. Where the hell was Larry?

"Don't you dare say anything," Rick hissed. "That would be a huge mistake."

"Get the hell away from me!" I said, my voice rising.

The door suddenly burst open and there was Larry, phone in hand, panting from his mad dash down the hall.

"Hey, Anne, so sorry to interrupt! Uh, FERPA, I mean, uh, there's a student I need to talk abou—"

He suddenly recognized Rick. "OMG," he gasped.

"Larry," Rick said, moving toward him, his voice oozing charm. "It's good to see you."

"Slow your roll," Larry said, entering a kung fu crouch. I looked at him in shock. Larry had never taken martial arts in his entire life. I suddenly realized he was imitating Keanu from *The Matrix*.

Rick laughed outright in Larry's face.

"Are you serious?" he said. "What is this? *Kung Fu Panda?*"

"At least I'm not a fraud and a coward like you are," Larry said.

"You really want to do this?" Rick said, advancing toward Larry. "I saw hand-to-hand combat in Fallujah, you know."

"I'm not scared of you," Larry said, rocking back and forth on his legs. He crooked his finger at Rick.

"Get out," I told Rick, my voice sounding eerily quiet and composed. While Rick had been laughing at Larry, I'd grabbed my office scissors from my desk drawer. They were the only thing I had in my office that remotely looked like a weapon.

"Oh shit," Larry said. "Watch out. She's gonna Bobbitt you."

I pointed the scissors at Rick. "Don't test me," I said. "I *will* cut you."

Rick looked flabbergasted. Between me and my scissors and Larry in his kung fu crouch, he couldn't tell which of us was crazier.

"Get out," I spat at him, menacingly opening and closing the shears.

Rick moved toward me, and I sliced the air between us, coming uncomfortably close to his belt buckle. He jumped back, his eyes wide. Without waiting for me to say anything else, he spun around and scurried out, clapping his fedora on his head like some cartoon criminal.

Larry slammed the door after him and locked it, then turned to me, breathing heavily. "That was

awesome, Anne," he said. "That was so *Edward Scissorhands!*"

In the days following the incident, I filed a restraining order against Rick, and the Department of Campus Security posted a couple of officers outside the building as a precautionary measure. Larry insisted on walking me to my classes and standing sentry while I taught, and for a week, he slept over at my apartment, armed with a badminton racket in case Rick was lurking in the bushes or hiding in my closet. I threw myself into my teaching, distracting myself from my father's death and Rick's betrayal by filling my days with student conferences and writing workshops. I told myself that while I'd failed Emily, maybe I could redeem myself with my other students, and I spent many late nights fine-tuning my lectures and grading essays.

As the days passed with no further sign of Rick, I began to relax. I knew, deep down, that he would never bother me again. He was a coward, through and through.

THE SEMESTER WAS FINALLY coming to an end. I'd been left alone for the most part, allowed to hide out in my office, so I was surprised when Steve poked his head in and cleared his throat.

"Do you have a minute?" he asked.

"Sure," I said. "Come in."

"I haven't seen you around much," Steve said,

settling into my chair. "What are you working on?"

"Just finishing up some copyedits," I said wearily. "The press wants them by Friday."

"Still on track with your publication date?"

"Yes—so far so good."

"Well, congratulations," Steve said. "That's excellent news. And now I have even more good tidings to deliver."

I looked at Steve, puzzled. I'd already signed my employment contract for the following year, and everyone already knew my book was coming out.

"I'm pleased to let you know that you've won this year's Distinguished Teaching Award," Steve said.

"I have?" I said, incredulous. People like Larry won the college Distinguished Teaching Award. They were considered legends. I couldn't imagine myself in the same category as them.

"Your students nominated you last fall, and we found out the results today. I heard you were the unanimous choice."

"Wow," I said. "I'm speechless."

"It's a tremendous honor. You'll be receiving a special medal and certificate at graduation, plus a tidy little sum of money to purchase books. We're all very proud of you, Anne. It's rather nice to have a bit of good cheer to spread around after the, ahem, events of the last month. The

college will make an announcement in the next few days, and you'll receive an invitation to an honorary luncheon afterwards."

Steve was beaming at me, his face pink with pride. "Felicitations!" he cried, shaking my hand exuberantly. I let myself smile for the first time in what felt like months.

MY COPY EDITOR HAD asked me to double-check a citation, so I dutifully headed to the library to track down the book I needed. Construction on the new addition to the building was slated to start in the summer, and library staffers were already moving items into storage and rearranging bookshelves in anticipation. Luckily, the book I needed was still in the library stacks on the second floor, and though the area had been cordoned off to students, the research librarian gave me permission to access the area.

Before heading upstairs, I took a minute to look at the architectural mock-up that was on display in the lobby. There, under a glass-enclosed dome, was a miniature replica of the renovated library, dotted with miniature trees and people. Bex's gift would update the infrastructure and also add a modern annex with a student café and a state-of-the-art space for Manuscripts and Special Collections. A small placard noted that the complete structure would be renamed the Chandler-Beckington Library when it reopened.

I walked up the stairs to the second floor, my hand on the worn wooden banister, feeling a little sad that this would be my last time in the stacks for a while. No more leisurely browsing through the dark aisles. No more sampling interesting books, buffet-style, from the shelves. No more quiet afternoons tucked into a window seat, reading through my selections.

I stepped over a velvet rope barring access to the bookshelves and headed straight for the PR-PS section. The air was cool and dry, and I breathed in the familiar, comforting smell of paper and ink. Natural light came in through the glass windows but was soon swallowed up as I walked farther into the stacks. Squinting, I tried to make out call numbers—I was looking for PR865 and found myself in the PR600s, then 700s, then the 800s. The row ended, and I quickly slipped to the other side to continue my hunt.

Someone was standing at the other end of the row, quietly looking out the window at the court-yard below, his back silhouetted by the light.

"Oh!" I exclaimed. "Sorry—I didn't realize there was anyone else up here."

The person turned around, and for a second I couldn't make out who it was.

But then the person said "Anne," and my chest tightened at the familiar sound. Adam.

I blinked, my eyes adjusting, and saw him

standing there, a folder tucked under his arm. My hands suddenly felt damp.

"Hi," I said, walking tentatively toward him. "I was just here looking for a book. The librarian gave me permission to come up." My voice sounded shrill in the empty stacks.

Adam nodded, turning back to the window. "There's a great view from up here," he said, pointing to the quad littered with students sunbathing on the grass, or playing Frisbee, or studying. A banner was stretched across two trees with the message "GOOD LUCK ON FINALS!!!!!" painted in large black letters with a bunch of red and white balloons bouncing gaily in the breeze.

"I like to come up here every once in a while to get away from the craziness," he said. "It's always nice and quiet up here."

I stood next to him, watching the activity below. Through the windows, I could hear muffled laughter and the sound of hip-hop playing on a distant boom box. For several seconds we stood in uncomfortable silence, staring out the window and avoiding each other's eyes.

"How are you doing?" Adam asked. "It's been a hard semester for you."

Ugh, I thought. Even Adam felt sorry for me. Poor, pathetic Anne, whose dad had passed away and whose boyfriend then disappeared in a cloud of scandal.

"I've had better semesters," I said. "I'll be glad for summer to get here."

"I'm sure," Adam said, nodding. "Listen—I'm sorry about everything with Rick. I had no idea he'd stolen from so many people's work."

"You didn't?" I asked, surprised. "I thought maybe you suspected it. When you warned me he wasn't trustworthy, isn't that what you were talking about?"

Adam shook his head. "No, not at all. I was actually thinking of something else entirely."

"Was it about his political activism? Rick told me that you two clashed over his union work."

"Is that what he told you?" Adam laughed. "Wow, he really is a true fabulist."

"It isn't true? You didn't fire him from his job at Houston?"

"Me? Fire him? Absolutely not. He agreed to leave after he was discovered having an affair with one of his students. The parents found out and wanted to press charges, but in the end the girl wouldn't cooperate. And technically, Rick hadn't done anything wrong, at least according to the school's fraternization policy. The girl was over the age of eighteen and she was no longer his student."

"That's awful."

"After he left, we found out he'd actually been involved with several undergraduate women at the same time. It was a real mess. You can

imagine my surprise when I saw they'd hired him at Fairfax."

"Ugh, I'm such an idiot," I said, flinching. "I can't believe I went to bat for him. He should be barred from ever teaching again." I looked at him curiously. "So why did you still help him out, knowing all of this?"

"I didn't do it for Rick," Adam said, his voice husky. "I did it for you."

I felt my face get warm. Adam was standing so close to me that I could practically touch him. If I took just a half step forward, I would be in his arms.

"I should've listened when you warned me about him," I said.

Adam shook his head. "No, I should never have said anything. You were right. It was none of my business." He cleared his throat slightly. "I care for you, Anne. I didn't want you to get hurt. I— He didn't deserve you."

Adam was looking at me now, his brown eyes holding mine. My heart caught in my throat. *This is it,* I thought. He wanted a sign from me, a hint of encouragement—I was sure of it. I could feel the dam of pent-up emotion about to break.

I started to say something, but there was a sudden slap of flip-flops from the stairwell.

"Dr. Corey!" I heard someone say. "Yo, are you up here?"

I saw Chad Vickers's curly head peek out from behind a bookcase.

"Chad?" I said.

"There you are, Dr. C!" he exclaimed. He loped over, one earbud dangling from his ear, his skateboard under his arm. "The librarian told me I could find you here."

"Is this one of your students?" Adam asked me, looking amused.

"Yo—you're the president, aren't you?" Chad said, his eyes widening. "What're you doing up here?"

"Just checking out a book," Adam said, pulling a random book off the shelf. I tried not to laugh.

"Cool, cool," Chad said, his head bobbing up and down. "That's tight. Our president reads. I'm down with that."

"What do you need, Chad?" I asked.

"Oh, yeah. Right. I need your signature, Dr. Corey. So I can graduate." He began rummaging through his backpack.

"You're a senior?" Adam asked. "Congratulations!"

"I know, finally," Chad said. "It only took me six years. I've been on academic probation forever, but Dr. C—she helped me out. Let me take her class three times so I could finally pass." He found a crumpled sheet of paper and tried to smooth it out on his knee.

"You must have learned a lot in her class," Adam said.

"Oh, yeah, for sure. Like Tennyson's legit GOAT. His poetry's dope."

"I agree," Adam said, nodding and laughing.

"Here's the form from my academic adviser," Chad said, handing me the crumpled piece of paper. "Sorry it's so mangled."

"Anne—I'll catch up with you later," Adam said, making a move for the stairwell.

"Wait—" I said, scrambling to find a pen in my bag. "This will only take a minute."

"Oh, man," Chad said, realization belatedly dawning on him. "Am I interrupting something?"

"No!" Adam and I said in unison.

"Sorry—I do have to run," Adam said. "But Chad—good luck, and I'll see you at graduation." I felt my heart sink as he disappeared down the stairwell.

"He seems like a cool cat," Chad said to me after Adam had left. "You guys know each other well?"

"Sort of," I said. I finished signing the sheet of paper, and Chad tucked it back into his backpack.

"If it's OK with you, I'm gonna run this back to my adviser before he leaves for the day," he said. He popped in his earbuds, dropped his skateboard, and coasted the twenty feet to the stairwell. I half expected him to ride his

skateboard down the stairs, but soon I heard the descending beat of his flip-flops.

Turning back to the shelves, I closed my eyes and rested my head against the book spines, feeling a swelling of disappointment and despair. Had I misread the situation? Why had Adam left so abruptly? I shoved my hands in my pockets and felt the slip of paper with the call number for the book I needed. Pulling it out, I saw that the number had been so badly smudged by my perspiration that it was almost impossible to read. Was it PR865 I wanted? Or was it PR866? I steadied myself against the walls of books, suddenly feeling claustrophobic.

When I finally got to the correct spot, I scanned the call numbers for a match. I double-checked and then triple-checked, but the book I needed wasn't there. I left the library empty-handed.

chapter twenty

T HE MORNING OF GRADUATION dawned overcast and humid. Usually, the ceremony was held outside in a grassy amphitheater, a picturesque venue with concentric stone steps and towering trees that made commencement look like an ancient Druid ritual. The threat of rain, however, threw the plans in doubt, and up until the last minute, we weren't sure if the ceremony would be relocated indoors. In the end, the college decided to go ahead with the outdoor ceremony but issued everyone a plastic poncho in case. I was wearing my rental regalia, feeling damp and uncomfortably hot, my shoes squishing in the moist grass and my poncho tucked under my arm. Since I was receiving an award, I would be seated on the dais with the board of trustees, student speakers, and other award recipients. Larry waved at me as I processed in, holding up his own teaching medal and giving me a thumbs-up.

Graduation was considerably less entertaining without Larry seated beside me cracking jokes and offering assorted beverages and snacks. I

paged through my program as the rest of the faculty processed in and then the undergraduates, beaming and waving at their parents in the audience. Around me, I could hear my more jaded colleagues grumble about wasting their morning at the ceremony. The pomp and circumstance weren't for us or even for the students, they complained—it was for the parents, who ogled us in our robes like we were a circus menagerie and then misted up seeing their own children in Fairfax's red-and-black regalia. I couldn't help it, though—I had a soft spot for graduation. Every time I heard the familiar Elgar melody, I felt myself getting sentimental. From the corner of my eye, I thought I saw Emily Young dressed in her regalia, her mortarboard covered in rhinestones and photographs, and I felt a bittersweet mix of emotion. I'd heard from Pam that she'd accepted her Columbia offer but deferred it for a year, under the pretext that she wanted to work for a year and travel. In truth, I suspected she was planning to follow Rick wherever he was. Part of me didn't blame her. She was in love.

From where I sat in the third row, I could make out the back of Adam's head. His hair looked as if it had been freshly cut, and he was seated next to the white-haired chairman of the board of trustees. Every once in a while, I could see him lean over to whisper something into

the trustee's ear. With a pang, I thought of our Princeton graduation more than ten years earlier. I'd slumped in my seat, hungover on peach schnapps, fighting off waves of nausea and self-pity. I never did see Adam on graduation day.

Adam made his opening remarks, and a series of student speeches followed. The salutatorian, a classics major, gave a Latin address that no one but Steve understood. The valedictorian, a former student of mine, gave a dull but unimpeachable speech about hard work and big dreams. A local judge who was receiving an honorary doctorate pontificated on civic responsibilities. I shifted nervously in my seat. The awards were coming up next.

Three of us were getting the Distinguished Teaching Award—a guy from political science, a woman from chemistry, and me. I watched as the two other recipients were called up and introduced by their deans, congratulated, and applauded. When my turn came, I stood up and walked to the front of the dais as the dean of humanities introduced me.

"Professor Anne Corey is a scholar of nineteenth-century British literature, specializing in the work of women writers. Although she has only been at Fairfax for a few years, she has already made her mark on the college. One faculty member notes, 'She is a brilliant scholar, a devoted teacher, and a generous colleague—a

true humanist, in all senses of the word.' Another colleague writes, 'Professor Corey makes the text come alive for her students. Suddenly, these supposedly boring nineteenth-century novels become interesting and relevant to their twenty-first-century lives.'

"Her students concur, praising her ability to present difficult material in a clear and engaging way. 'She uses real-world examples, and she has a great sense of humor,' one student said. Several said, 'She made me fall in love with literature.' One student, who has taken every class Professor Corey has offered, wrote, 'Professor Corey is my hero. She taught me that books are powerful and that language can make and remake entire worlds. I want to be her when I grow up.'

"For her record of excellence in teaching, I am pleased to award the President's Distinguished Teaching Award to Professor Anne Corey."

I was blushing as I moved to shake the dean's hand. I turned to face Adam, who placed the teaching medal around my neck and handed me a certificate, sealed in a large envelope. "Congrat-ulations," he said, formally shaking my hand. In the audience, I could hear Larry whooping, "Go Annie!"

It was the quickest graduation ceremony I'd ever attended, cut short after Adam conferred the degrees and it began to rain. Instead of processing out, everyone disbanded in a helter-skelter kind

of way, pulling on their ponchos and running for cover. I found Larry huddled under a tree waiting for me, his fluorescent-orange poncho wrapped around his almost-hot-pink regalia.

"I want to be just like Professor Corey when I grow up," he said, pretending to pray to the sky. "She's my *hero*."

"Shut up, Larry," I said. "I was dying of embarrassment up there."

"Oh, don't be so modest," he said. "Isn't it wonderful to be worshipped?" He reached over to inspect my medal, pulling his own medal out from under his poncho to compare. "Wait a second," he cried. "I think your medal's bigger than mine. No fair!"

I'd invited Larry to be my guest for the luncheon, so we dropped off our damp regalia in our offices and headed to the President's House, Larry keeping me dry under his enormous black umbrella. Because of the rain, the luncheon had been moved from the garden into the main house, with several round tables covered in white tablecloths and scattered with red and black confetti. Larry and I were seated at Adam's table, along with the other teaching award recipients. Adam hadn't yet arrived, leaving two empty seats diagonally across from us. I peeked at the name cards. "President Adam Martinez," read one. "Guest," read the other. I felt my heart constrict with jealousy, wondering

who Adam had invited to be his plus-one.

"I'm done with him," Larry said, complaining about Jack. After weeks of no contact, Jack had finally resurfaced with a new phone number and new plans for the future. Larry allowed himself to start hoping again. "He kept telling me, 'Just hold on a little bit longer. We'll be together soon.' But then the next thing I know, I'm reading in *People* that he and Bex are in Paris renewing their vows. Paris! And just to twist the knife further, they're apparently trying to have another kid."

"I saw that," I said. "I'm sorry. I thought maybe he'd changed."

"No kidding! He's back to playing the Happy Family Man, just because of this stupid vampire sequel. He cares more about his image than about me."

Our salads were served, and Larry picked listlessly at the leaves. "I can't eat," he said. "I can't sleep, I think I'm losing the rest of my hair." He sighed heavily. "They shouldn't call it a breakup. They should call it a breakdown."

Adam seated himself at the table, apologizing for being late. He greeted Larry and me from across the table, but our conversation was almost immediately interrupted by an elderly alum who came over to introduce herself. The seat beside Adam stayed empty. As soon as the alum left, one of Adam's aides appeared with something for him to sign, and he scanned the page quickly.

"Did you not like your salad?" a server asked, leaning over Larry to take his untouched plate.

"Oh, no, the salad was delightful," he said. "I'm just not hungry. I got dumped the other day."

The server, a young woman, looked embarrassed. "I'm sorry," she said before hurrying away.

"See?" Larry said. "It's like I have the cooties. No one wants to hear about a breakup. No one wants to hear about my tawdry personal life."

"The woman just asked about your salad, Larry. She didn't expect you to spill your guts."

"You're right," Larry said. "I'll just be mute now." He pretended to zip his lips.

I glanced at Adam. His salad lay untouched, and he was jotting something down on a small pad of paper. I wondered where his guest was and then hated myself for caring.

I turned back to Larry. "You'll feel better in a few weeks," I said, lowering my voice.

"A few weeks? I'll be lucky if I ever get over this. My heart doesn't heal so easily."

"Give it time. I read someplace that it takes half the length of the relationship in order to get over a breakup. You dated Jack for six months, right? So it should take you about three months to get over him. You'll be fine by September." I tried to sound as clinical as possible.

"Are you really telling me that my feelings can be reduced to a *math equation?*" Larry asked.

"Everyone's different, of course," I said. "I mean, it definitely takes women longer to get over breakups than men."

Larry sighed. "I do think Jack's already over me. He's surrounded by so many beautiful people. I'm sure he's already found someone else."

" 'Men are only as faithful as their options,' " I quoted.

"Oscar Wilde?"

"No, Chris Rock."

I heard a slight noise and turned, but it was only Adam retrieving a pen that he'd dropped under the table. He was closer to us than I'd realized, and for a second, I wondered if he could actually overhear what we were saying, though it seemed unlikely given the various other conversations going on around him.

I turned back to Larry. "I think you should just learn to hate Jack. That'll make it easier for you to get over him. Trust me."

"But how do you hate someone you once loved?" Larry asked. "I hate *myself,* not Jack. I'm not like you, Anne. I can't just stop loving someone and cut them off!"

"It's self-preservation. I don't just suddenly stop loving the person. I just convince myself that what I thought was love was really just temporary insanity. A brief lapse of judgment. It makes things easier. I have to protect myself."

"But how do you *do* it? You're *merciless*. When someone crosses you, it's like they might as well be dead to you. I can't do that . . . I always come crawling back."

"Oh, Larry!" I cried, my voice welling up with emotion, desperately trying to avoid looking in Adam's direction. "I might seem heartless, but I'm not. If you knew how agonizing it can be . . . You're not the only one that's ever kept loving someone, even when you know there's no hope."

I tried to compose myself, blinking back tears of exhaustion and self-pity. Larry reached over and squeezed my arm.

"I know, Annie," he said. "I've always known you had a huge heart."

We got up to leave, Larry complaining of a headache and me longing to crawl into my bed. The rest of our lunch companions were still eating dessert and ordering coffee, so we made a quick circuit around the table, apologizing for our early exit and wishing everyone a good summer.

"Congratulations again," Adam said, rising to shake my hand. "Our students are lucky to have you." He held my hand for a beat longer than I expected and then reached over to grab something from the table. "Don't forget your certificate," he said, handing me the envelope and looking at me meaningfully. I looked at the envelope and then at Adam, puzzled, but he'd already turned away and hastily left the table.

I tucked the envelope carefully under my jacket and ducked with Larry into the rain, the two of us jogging the few blocks to my apartment. He promised to call me the next day, and I watched him head out into the storm, the bottom of his trousers wet with rain and his black umbrella bobbing in the wind.

My apartment was dark and humid, and I could hear raindrops beating forlornly against my kitchen window. Jellyby hopped onto the couch behind me, purring and butting her head against my hand.

"Oh, Jelly," I sighed, kicking my shoes off and putting my feet up on the couch. "What a year." I opened up the envelope holding my certificate and check. The certificate was on thick parchment, with my name written in calligraphy and a large gilt college seal at the top.

The President and Trustees of Fairfax College
hereby award
ANNE COREY
the President's Distinguished Teaching Award
in recognition of demonstrated leadership
and commitment to teaching
conferred on this second day of June.

It was signed by the chair of the board of trustees and by Adam.

But there was something else in the envelope.

I pulled out a small slip of paper that had been folded in half, my name written hastily on top, the writing barely legible.

What's this? I thought, unfolding the paper. It was a handwritten note, dashed off in black pen. Before I could even read the words, I recognized the handwriting. Many years ago, I'd spent hours studying those narrow, slanted letters, seeing them as a kind of code, trying to figure out what the words meant. Adam had finally written to me again.

Dear Anne,

I've been struggling to figure out what to say to you. It feels silly even to write this note, but then I remember how writing all those letters to you so many years ago helped me express myself. I've always felt like I could say things to you that I couldn't say to anyone else.

I know it's been thirteen years since we broke up: thirteen years since I made the biggest mistake of my life. There hasn't been a day that's passed that I haven't beaten myself up for letting you go. I know you've probably moved on and that I'm thirteen years too late, but I need you to know that my feelings for you have never changed. As I'm writing

this, I can hear you telling Larry that it just takes time to get over a relationship and that women take breakups harder than men. You're wrong. I've never gotten over you.

For a long time, I tried to forget you and date other people. I avoided reading anything about you. I even half convinced myself I hated you. But I was lying to myself. I wouldn't admit it then, but the reason I came to Fairfax was for you.

You probably suspected all of this. After all, you've always been good at figuring me out. I'm sure you noticed how I looked for any excuse to bump into you this past year. I never said anything, though, because I couldn't tell what your feelings were, and when I did open my mouth, I just seemed to put my foot in it.

At the risk of making a fool of myself once again, let me tell you this: I've loved none but you.

Besos,
Adam

I stared at Adam's note, shaking. I read it again and then again. Adam still had feelings for me, even after all this time. I thought of how he'd driven me to the hospital after my father had his stroke, how he'd held me at the funeral, how he'd

told me in the library that Rick didn't deserve me. He'd been trying to tell me all along that he still loved me, but I was too stupid to realize. I jumped up from the couch, my heart thudding painfully in my chest. Impulsively, I ran out the door.

It was still raining heavily outside, and I'd dashed out without grabbing an umbrella or even a jacket. All I knew was that I had to see Adam as quickly as possible. I ran down the empty streets to his house, ignoring the driving rain, hoping he was still there. The front door to the mansion was open, the guests were gone, and the caterers were rolling the last of the round folding tables from the reception area.

"Do you know where President Martinez is?" I asked. "I need to speak to him."

"Check the library," one of the caterers said. "I saw him go in there a little while ago."

The library door was open a crack, and I could see the warm glow of a lamp inside. I pushed the door open.

Adam was sitting on the leather couch, reading. He looked up, surprised, and jumped to his feet.

"Anne!" he said. "Come in. Please—sit down."

I sat across from Adam, not quite sure how to begin. "I got your note," I said, feeling agonized and inarticulate. "I—"

Adam was looking at me intently, his face drained of color. When I paused, his gaze

flickered and he dropped his eyes. I realized he thought I was going to reject him.

"I love you," I said, my voice choking with emotion. "I've always loved you. I've never gotten over you, either."

I was crying now, openly and shamelessly. The look of pain on Adam's face quickly melted into one of relief and joy. He pulled me to him, and I found myself sobbing.

"I'm sorry," I cried. "I— It was my fault. I couldn't swallow my pride. I pushed you away and then I was too stubborn to apologize."

"Anne," Adam said. He leaned over to kiss me, and I felt a surge of recognition and joy and relief. "I love you, I've been in love with you from the moment I saw you," he said, burying his fingers in my damp hair and wiping the tears from my face.

I touched Adam's face, remembering it, memorizing it. To be so close to him again after being so far away was indescribable. Could this really be him? Was I really holding him? Was this real? Adam was usually so hard to read in public, always with his professional face on, revealing nothing. Now, though, I was so close that I could see every line of his face, every movement. I pressed my lips against his eyes, his cheeks, his mouth. He held onto me tightly, as if he never wanted to let go of me again.

The words came tumbling out of each of us, bursts of confession mixed with explanation and self-recrimination.

"I wasn't sure how I'd react when I saw you again," he told me. "And honestly, I wasn't even sure if you wanted to see me. But then you came to the reception, and I was so glad you were there."

"Really?" I said. "You didn't seem glad. I actually thought you were still mad at me after all these years."

Adam shook his head. "I was overwhelmed. I couldn't believe I still had such strong feelings for you."

"But Larry told me you didn't even recognize me!"

"Oh, I recognized you. I just—I couldn't believe how beautiful you looked. And how out of reach. You looked so confident and pulled together. I was sure you were married or something and that I had no chance."

"But I wasn't!"

"I didn't know that," Adam said. "I tried to talk to you after convocation, but then Rick showed up, and it was pretty clear there was something going on between the two of you."

"Don't remind me," I groaned. "God, I wish I'd never met Rick. Why didn't I listen to you when you warned me?"

"I shouldn't have said anything," Adam said. "I

was jealous, and I guess I was hoping you two would break up."

I leaned my head against Adam's chest for a moment, thinking. "But what about Tiffany?" I finally asked. "Weren't the two of you seriously dating? I heard you two were getting engaged."

Adam gave a short laugh. "Tiffany was very welcoming when I first arrived at Fairfax. She showed me around town and introduced me to a lot of different people. I thought I'd made it clear we were just colleagues, but I guess she had other ideas. I feel bad about that. I didn't mean to lead her on."

"And Bex—what about her? It seemed like the two of you were getting close, too."

"Bex?" Adam said, sounding surprised. "No—there was nothing there. We worked closely together on the library renovation project, that's all. Why do you ask?"

I blushed. "I was jealous," I admitted. "Couldn't you tell? It must have crossed your mind at some point that I might still have feelings for you."

"I didn't want to get my hopes up," he said. "After New Year's, I thought maybe there was a chance we could rekindle things, but then you came into my office and asked for my help with Rick's job and I realized you two were really serious. I knew I had to step back."

"I can't believe how stupid I was," I said. "And Rick was totally MIA when my father had his

stroke. Did you know he barely even came to the hospital to visit me? And he didn't come to the funeral either."

"I was wondering about that."

"I mean, I gave him permission not to come, but still, you would think he would have made more of an effort. *You* saw what a wreck I was . . ." I cringed at the memory. "I never got a chance to thank you for comforting me after the funeral—"

Adam gave a rueful laugh. "I worried about that . . . about whether I'd overstepped again. I knew you were in a bad place, and I wanted to be there for you. But when I got that very formal letter thanking me for my donation—I assumed you were asking me to back off."

"I'm sorry," I cried. "That wasn't it at all—I was planning to send you a more personal note, but then this whole Rick debacle happened and . . ." I gave an exasperated sigh. "I really had no idea Rick was such an ass."

"I thought I'd completely misread you," Adam said. "That I'd butted into your life yet again. So when we saw each other in the library, I'd convinced myself that we were going to remain professional colleagues—that that's what you wanted. But when you opened up about Rick, I found myself getting hopeful again. It was hearing you talk to Larry at the luncheon that finally pushed me to say something. I couldn't let you go on thinking that I didn't care and that I

was over you. Men have hearts, too, you know." He smiled and kissed me again.

"This library," I said, looking around the room. "It's beautiful. When I first saw it, I wanted to kill you. This was supposed to be *my* dream library."

"It *is* your dream library," Adam said. "Remember how we used to go on those walks in college and point out the houses we liked? And you saw that home with a beautiful library, and I promised I'd give it to you one day?"

"Of course I remember."

Adam laughed. "We weren't together, but I still designed this library with you in mind. I kept thinking to myself, *What would Anne want?* and *How would she want her ideal library to look?*"

"It's perfect," I said.

Adam hesitated. "Do you see those books over there?" he asked, pointing to a set of books with faded leather spines and marbleized boards. I reached over to look at them more closely. All of the spines read *Persuasion.*

"My favorite!" I exclaimed, pulling one out to look at it more closely. "I still have the copy you gave me in college, you know."

"Open it," Adam said.

I opened to the frontispiece, mottled with age. "Is this a first edition?" I gasped.

An envelope slipped out of the pages of the book and fell to the floor.

"What's this?" I asked, reaching down to pick it up. The envelope had been torn open roughly. I flipped it over and stared at the writing on the front. It was my own handwriting. I stared at it for a moment, confused. The postmark read "Princeton, NJ. PM. 3 JUN 2003."

Shaking, I reached into the envelope and pulled out a cameo ring. The ring I'd mailed back to Adam in a fit of rage thirteen years earlier. The ring I might as well have thrown into the trash, I was so certain I would never see it again.

"You kept it," I said, running my fingers over the familiar pink-and-gold face.

"I've been holding onto it all these years," he said. "Just in case you came back. Just in case you'd give me a second chance."

He reached over and took the ring from me.

"Annie," he said, dropping to one knee. "I've known you were the one from the moment I met you. Will you marry me?"

"Yes," I said, my heart in my throat. Adam slipped the ring on my finger. It still fit. He stood up and brought my hand to his mouth. "I thought I'd never be happier than the first time you agreed to marry me, but this—this is even better." He wrapped me in his arms, and I felt myself dissolve in his embrace. Suddenly, he pulled away and shut the library door.

"Remember what happened last time I proposed?" he asked, smiling.

"Yes, I remember," I said, blushing. "How could I forget?"

"It would be scandalous for the college president to be discovered making love to his fiancée in the campus library. But you know, this is my own personal library in my own private home."

"What if someone comes in?"

"No one will—I told the caterers to lock up when they left."

Adam pulled me to the window seat, where the rain was still beating against the windowpanes.

"I've been waiting for this moment for a long time," Adam whispered. "It's like something out of a dream."

"No," I said, smiling into his eyes. "It's like something out of a book."

chapter twenty-one

R EADER, I MARRIED HIM.
　　Just kidding. I can practically hear Larry groaning, "That's such a cliché!"

As much as we both wanted to, we couldn't just run off to the courthouse—not this time. Larry would never forgive me. Neither would Adam's mother. Adam needed to notify the board of trustees and let them know there'd be a new resident moving into the president's mansion. An official engagement announcement would have to go out in the fall. And besides, Larry scolded me, who got married after a quick engagement anymore? This wasn't a shotgun wedding. There were venues to book and vendors to hire and dresses to buy—at least a year of preparation before the big day. I let myself imagine having the kind of wedding that ended all my favorite novels, with flowers and cake and a wedding breakfast for all my friends.

Adam and I spent the summer in Fairfax, taking long walks around the campus, supervising the campus library renovation, and sitting together quietly in Adam's private library, reading and

writing. With the campus once again deserted for the summer, we enjoyed a degree of privacy that would never have been possible during the school year. We took advantage of it to the fullest, knowing that once classes began again in the fall, we'd be the objects of increased curiosity and scrutiny. Even Pam didn't yet know about us, having left for a family cruise the minute the semester was over. I could only imagine her shock when she finally heard the news. She would probably scream—and then pick up the phone.

In July, Larry forwarded me an article he'd come across about Rick. It turned out Rick had also fabricated parts of his biography, from his time in Iraq to his undercover research missions. The closest he'd been to Fallujah was Dubai, where he'd filed his stories from poolside at a luxury resort. His stories of harrowing under-cover missions and near-beheadings were taken from episodes of *Homeland*.

"Wow," I said. "And I thought *I* suffered from imposter syndrome."

"He brings new meaning to the phrase 'Fake it 'til you make it,'" Larry said drily. "I bet he's not even British."

Rick had eventually resurfaced in Brooklyn and was shopping around a new book, a memoir of redemption called *All for Love*. A reporter had located the original proposal and uncovered more

instances of plagiarism—including, I realized with a shock of recognition, a passage taken from my own book. I'd written, "Charlotte Brontë took solace in the written word, channeling her unrequited affections into her literary masterwork, *Jane Eyre.*" In his proposal, Rick had written, "I took solace in the written word, channeling my unrequited affections into this literary memoir of love, loss, and second chances." I tried not to gag out loud. A little while later, I heard Rick had sold his proposed memoir for a reported six-figure advance.

My own book was already in press when I remembered, with horror, that I'd thanked Rick in the acknowledgments. In a panic, I called up my editor, Ursula Burton. We'd never met and only corresponded by e-mail, so when I first heard her clipped English accent on the line, I quailed. She told me it was "far too late" to edit the acknowledgments and that "any change at this point would cost the press a pretty penny."

"Listen," I blurted out. "I know you're friends with Rick Chasen, but we had a really messy breakup and it's a long story, but I'll pay for any changes—"

"What are you talking about?" Ursula said. "Who is Rick Chasen?"

"Richard Forbes Chasen? The novelist? He told me you were good friends from university."

"The plagiarist? I've never met the man before in my life."

"I thought— He told me— Didn't he tell you to publish my book?"

"My goodness, no. How absurd! I make my own editorial decisions." She paused for a moment and said, "Richard Forbes Chasen, you say? Well, we can't have someone like that receive more undeserved credit, can we?"

She immediately cut his name from the book. Snip-snip. I felt a flood of relief that I owed Rick nothing—that this accomplishment was mine alone.

Months later, I was letting myself into the President's House when Adam called down from upstairs. "A box came for you," he said. "I brought it into the library."

I found a heavy cardboard box sitting on one of the tables, "OXFORD UNIVERSITY PRESS" printed on both sides.

"Adam!" I called. "Come down!"

I began to slice through the tape with anticipation. Adam came in and stood a little behind me, resting a hand lightly on my hip. "I think it's from my editor," I said, pulling the box open. "They're my author copies."

There was a handwritten note inside.

Welcome to the ranks of women writers.
—Ursula.

I pulled a hardcover volume from the box. The book jacket showed a nineteenth-century woman's profile in silhouette, set like a cameo into an oval frame. The title *Ivory Tower: Nineteenth-Century Women Writers and the Literary Imagination* ran along the top of the frame, and below was my name, Anne Corey.

I touched the cover silently, running my fingers over my name and blinking back tears.

"You did it," Adam said, reaching over to squeeze my hand.

"Open it," I said, handing the book to him. Adam looked at me quizzically, then took the book from me. He studied the cover for a moment, then let the book fall open to its dedication page.

"To Adam Martinez," it read. "*Besos.*"

"How did you—?" he said, looking incredulously at his name on the page.

"Ursula let me add a dedication at the last minute," I said.

Adam looked overcome. He let the book close and pulled me in for a kiss. Then he placed my book on a shelf in our dream library.

acknowledgments

This novel is a love letter to books, but it is also a love letter to book lovers. The biggest one I know is Lisa Sternlieb, who always said "you don't want to be like me" and whose advice I continue, happily, to ignore. Lisa—thank you for your unabashed love of literature and for being a model of integrity and authenticity in an imperfect profession. I also want to thank Chris Corey, who read countless drafts of this novel and refused to let me quit, even when I wanted to slap this thing on Amazon for 99 cents. I want to thank my high school friends—Lizzy Castruccio, Lydia Cho, Riva Kim, Sharon Gi, Tarry Payton, and Janna Conner—who knew me when I was at my most bookish and idealistic. In college, I found friends like Miki Terasawa, Sandhya Gupta, and Maria Wich-Vila, models of empathy and grace. All of you have inspired elements of this book.

English professors are "my people," and I want to thank Jane Hafen, Laura Murphy,

Anne Stevens, Megan Becker, Maile Chapman, Kelly Mays, Denise Tillery, Jessica Teague, Emily Setina, and Miriam Melton-Villanueva for talking books (including romance novels!) with me. I am embarrassed at the thought of Deborah Nord or Maria DiBattista reading this book, but I want them to know that I love and admire them deeply and that Dr. Russell is definitely not based on them! I also want to thank all my students, past and present, for making me laugh and sometimes cry. My love goes to my parents, David and Sonia Lee, who cultivated my love of reading and writing, and to my in-laws, Bonnie and Rob Sonneborn, avid readers and lenders of books. I want to thank my husband, Brad Sonneborn, who kept asking if this book was about him (of course!) and my kids, Lucy and Bobby, whose favorite thing to do is to pore over the Scholastic book catalogue.

Finally, I want to thank those who helped usher my book into the world. My agent, Jennifer Johnson-Blalock, picked this book out of the slush pile and heroically helped me fix the pacing and plot. Not only did she give me a crash MFA, she showed me that the querying and publishing process could be humane. My editor at Gallery Books, Kate Dresser, "got" this book from the beginning, and I thank her and her assistant, Molly Gregory, for

being such wonderful stewards of this work. Thanks as well to Mary Beth Constant, whose copyediting skills and sense of humor are A+. I am proud to have worked with such smart, funny women.

Books are produced in the United States using U.S.-based materials

Books are printed using a revolutionary new process called THINKtech™ that lowers energy usage by 70% and increases overall quality

Books are durable and flexible because of smythe-sewing

Paper is sourced using environmentally responsible foresting methods and the paper is acid-free

Center Point Large Print

600 Brooks Road / PO Box 1
Thorndike, ME 04986-0001 USA

(207) 568-3717

US & Canada:
1 800 929-9108
www.centerpointlargeprint.com

BC

E
z

U83.1